MW00878238

Tim Curious

Written and illustrated by

Roddy Thorleifson

ISBN-13: 978-1492714927

ISBN-10: 1492714925

Illustrations by Roddy Thorleifson

2

For: Sue, Rachael, Thora, and also for: Adéle, Al, Aline, Anne, Anne-Marie, Audrey, Barb, Barry, Bob, Christine, Chuck, Dave, Deb, Debarati, Dorothy, Ed, Eric, Georgine, Gerry, Grace, Harold, James, Jennifer, Jim, Joy, Katherine, Kevin, Linda, Liz, Lois, Maggie, Mary-Louise, Mullein, Murray, Nancy, Pat, Paul, Ralph, Riel, Rose, Roy, Simon, Shelley, Suzanne, Susie, Tony, Thor, Tracy.

4

Characters

Tim Euston (16) Apprentice to local carpenter.

Sadie Euston (14, May 20) Tim's sister.

Thomas Pellis (56) Trader in Yonkers.

Nat Pellis (22) Storekeeper, Thomas's nephew.

Luke Lauper (15) Tim's friend.

Jack Lauper (33) Luke's father, laborer.

Frederick Philipse. (51) Justice of the Peace.

Amos Short (28) Laborer, former sailor.

Dan Eliot (18) Sailor, met Tim in jail.

John Gainer (40) Tim's master (employer), carpenter.

Josh Gainer (18) John Gainer's son.

Matilda (Pellis) Walker (46) Nat's sister, Sadie's employer.

Abby Euston (36) Tim's mother, Matilda's kitchen maid.

Bessie (22) Nat's part-time servant.

Abe Balding (60) Man Tim delivers to in the city.

Zeke Felix (50) Farmer north of Yonkers.

Moses Walker (52) Matilda's husband.

Abner Wall (45) Trader in New York City.

Eustace Gainer (36) John's wife.

Sam Baker (45) Major in the Continental Army.

Chapter 1

January 30, 1777.
Yonkers, New York.

Tim heard a girl scream. It sounded like his sister, Sadie. They had been playing tag with the children. She had just been with them.

"No! Don't!" came her shout, from around the corner of the street. Tim turned and ran back. There she was! A man had hold of her. It looked like he was pulling her through a door.

"Stop it!" yelled Tim, grabbing her arm. Sadie shrieked in pain as he pulled her back. "Let her be!" Tim demanded and the man turned. It was Thomas Pellis. His eyes flashed with anger as he raised his walking stick. Still holding onto Sadie's hand, he swung at Tim, hitting his shoulder. But the man had shifted his weight, allowing Tim to pull the two of them back out the door. Boys attacked from all sides. Thomas stumbled and then they were all down in the dirt fighting.

"Help me!" Thomas begged. "Someone help me!" He struck one boy and then another. One of the boys had hold of Thomas's free arm. Tim managed to pull the stick from the old man's hand and he struck him hard across his forehead. Thomas fell back stunned.

"Cease this!" shouted a young man as he came out from a shop door. It was Nat Pellis, the man's nephew. He grabbed the stick, wrenched it from Tim's hand and grabbed hold of his shaggy straw-colored hair. "Stand off!" Nat demanded in a voice worthy of a drill sergeant. "Let him up!"

"He tried to rob me!" sobbed the old man who was crouched on his knees, holding up his hands and looking pathetic as a trickle of bright red blood ran down his forehead. "The wicked boy! He tried to rob me, he did!"

"No! He didn't!" cried several children, and they all started to shout out their own versions of the fight.

"Quiet!" Nat demanded as he threatened them with the stick, "or you'll all be clapped in irons! Now you!" he said to Tim who was struggling to get loose. "You're coming along with me!"

"Good fellow, Nat," said his uncle. "You take him in! To jail with the scoundrel!"

"He had hold of Sadie!" Tim pleaded as Nat held him bent half over. "She's only fourteen! He meant to have her inside!" he said as he stumbled along with both hands gripped around Nat's wrist to ease the pull on his hair.

"He lies!" said Thomas. "A thief is what he is. A robber! Attacked and robbed, I was! And in front of my own home!"

Thomas lived alone in a one room hut next door to the store. He had been living there for a year and he hated the children who played in the street. They were always shouting and shrieking.

The children did not think much of Thomas either. He liked to swat them on the backside with his stick when they were in his way. They were afraid of him, too – afraid of the look he had in his small pig-like eyes. He was a fright just to look at, with his pale leathery skin and gray whiskers poking out in every direction. At one time, he had been handsome, but now his skin had yellowed and wrinkles had formed around his smug, squinting expression. Since the arrival of Thomas Pellis, a new threat had descended upon the children of Yonkers. It was not just because of his playful cruelty and nasty sense of humor. Sadie had recognized it right from the start, just by the look in his eyes.

"Stand aside! What's the matter here?" asked the town's watchman when he met with Nat and the small mob that had assembled on the main street. He was a carpenter and one of a group of volunteers who took turns at keeping order. When on duty, he carried a five-foot-long staff with a polished brass tip, just like a constable would in a larger town.

"Well sir, we have two stories," said Nat in his clear, mature voice. "Mister Pellis says this little scoundrel tried to rob him. And then there's the children here," he said with a smile, "friends of the boy they are, who claim the old fellow tried to nab a girl."

"He did!" called out three boys at the same time, but the watchman silenced them by raising his hand.

"The boy's a scoundrel!" said Thomas, whose face was still streaked with blood. "He tried to rob me, he did. And then he beat me with a stick! Always been a bad one, he has."

"Indeed 'tis true," agreed Nat. "Quite a reputation, this one."

"You're apprenticed to John Gainer?" asked the watchman as he took hold of Tim's collar.

"Yes, and my name is Tim Euston."

"Well then Tim Euston, by the authority vested in me, I place you under arrest. You shall come along with me and you'd best come along quietly or you'll make it worse for yourself."

The watchman began to lead him along, but Tim started to argue and then to resist, for he knew the crime of robbery would likely mean a long sentence at hard labor. The watchman shook him harshly and turned to the boys who followed. They were shouting in defense of their friend.

"Stand off! All of you!" the watchman commanded. "Or I'll have the lot of you carted off to the jailhouse!"

The boys fell silent. They watched poor Tim stumble as he was led away. Thomas marched along side, on his way to swear out a formal complaint to the Justice of the Peace.

Nat was arguing with Luke Lauper, one of the boys who had fought with Tim to save Sadie.

"He'd never do such a thing," Luke insisted. "Tim's never stole nothing! And Thomas had hold of Sadie! He was dragging her in through his door!" Luke could speak out loud and clear now. His father had just arrived and Luke now had courage enough. Jack Lauper looked like his son – black haired and wiry.

"I know what I saw," said Nat as he started to turn away. "It was robbery."

"No no no, he's a good boy!" said Jack, with one hand on his son's shoulder and the other held palm up, as if holding back Nat's words. "Surely, you're mistaken."

"It is now a matter for judge and jury to decide," drawled Nat. "I know what I saw with my own eyes. The boy had hold of the stick that struck down Mister Pellis. They were all beating him and it was Tim Euston who led the pack."

While this went on, another man had his hand on Jack's sleeve, tugging on it and trying to talk while coughing, hacking and gasping for air. He had a peg leg and leaned on a crutch, and looked half crazed as he tried to make himself heard. He wanted to tell them he had seen it all. He had seen Thomas Pellis with his hands on Tim's little sister, but he could not get enough words out to gain anyone's attention.

Finally, Nat threw up his arms in exasperation. "Well then, I suppose we should all go to the hearing. We'll give our testimonies together and let the Justice of the Peace decide. All of you!" he called to the crowd with a dismissive wave of his arm, "back to your business!" He turned and strode off, leaving them to their gossip and speculation.

"It's that old Thomas who's the bad one," said a woman holding a crying baby.

"Yea, I've suspected him of sinful desires," agreed her friend. "You can see it in him, can't you? In his eyes. Wickedness, it is!"

. . . . .

Tim was at the back door of the mansion that belonged to the local Justice of the Peace. A servant told them Colonel Philipse had guests and could not hear their complaint now. The Steward asked what it concerned. He was in charge of both the Philipse mill and the family's other operations and he was entertained by some vivid testimony from Nat and Thomas Pellis. Both were clever with words.

The Steward turned to the accused and gave Tim a long look, from the freckles on his nose down to the mud on his shoes. Tim was small for his sixteen years, but he stood like a soldier with his shoulders square and his lower lip thrust out in defiance. "Well well well, my boy," the Steward said, "and what have you got to say for yourself?"

"I am innocent!" insisted Tim. "He had his hand upon my little sister and he had the Devil in his eyes. And he was pulling her towards his door. For sure, he was!"

"He lies," snorted Thomas. "He's a known thief."

"Is he?" asked the Steward with a look to the watchman.

"That's not been brought to my attention."

"And," said Nat, "he's the son of a woman of ill repute."

"She ain't neither!" shouted Tim.

"Quiet!" growled the watchman as he yanked Tim back by his collar and slapped him hard on the ear.

The Steward had heard enough. "I will take your complaint to the master and he will try to find time for a hearing."

Apologies were made for the demand on the Steward's valuable time and they turned to leave.

"One more thing," said the Steward to the watchman. "You take the boy for a moment," he said to another man. "Over here," he said, and led the watchman through the stable door. "What sort of a boy is he?" he asked in a low voice.

"Tim Euston? He's been in town for three years only, bound to John Gainer. I've not heard he's a problem – never been brought to me. But they say he's kept company with some of the boys who went and joined with the rebels – fallen under a bad influence, perhaps. I could ask around."

"That'd be good. Find out what you can before the hearing," said the Steward with a nod. They came back to where Tim was waiting. The men wished each other a good evening and Tim was taken in the direction of the town's little jailhouse. It was not really a jail, but just a storehouse. In the fall, when space was needed, it would be filled with sacks of grain, but for the rest of the year it could be used to house drunkards, lunatics and other troublemakers.

The watchman stopped at his home to get a lantern. His hired hand went to the fireplace and shoveled a small iron cauldron half full of burning embers. They went back out. There was just a hint of red left in the western sky. In the lantern, a yellow flame flickered behind thick glass.

At the jailhouse, they climbed an outer stairway to a small loft. On the floor was a trapdoor secured with a very large padlock. The watchman unlocked it and pulled back a heavy bolt. Hinges creaked as he opened it wide. Nothing but blackness could be seen down the hole. It looked like it might be a hundred feet deep. The hired man knew the procedure. First he lowered the pot of embers down to the floor twelve feet below. Next, he took hold of a rope that hung from a pulley above. At the end of this was a short stick.

"Climb on," he said. Tim put the rope and stick through his legs so he could sit on the stick while gripping the rope with his hands. The watchman turned a large crank to draw the rope onto a winch. The wooden axle creaked loudly. Tim was raised up and swung in place over the hole. The crank was reversed to lower him into the darkness.

"You'll find firewood in the corner," said the watchman. "Don't build it up too high or you'll run out of wood before I bring you more."

"I won't," said Tim just before he heard the trapdoor slam above. He felt around. The fire pit was a shallow box filled with sand in the middle of the room. He found some wood, poured the embers out of the iron pot and laid a few sticks on top. He sat cross-legged and blew on the embers, making them glow bright orange, to start the wood burning. He would have to be careful to keep it going. It was the end of January, a cold time of year to go without a fire. *But will it make a difference in the long run?* he wondered as his memory went back to the last time he'd been up to White Plains for the County Court of Sessions. There had been a hanging. It had been a young man the crowd had watched – a boy practically – and he had been convicted for the crime of robbery.

In recent decades, children have been growing up sooner, maybe because of better nutrition. When you try to picture a teenager in colonial times, think of someone who looks two years younger.

Chapter 2

We know what they're thinking.

As a ray of sun struggled to break through gray winter clouds, a rough looking man limped back and forth on his crutch and peg leg – his free hand moving fast and an excited look on his face. His name was Amos Short. He was the one who could not talk for coughing when Nat Pellis and Jack Lauper had been arguing. But today, Amos was up to form and he was coaching the witnesses for the defense.

"We're all here, yea?" said Amos, waving to the last of the boys to come close. "Good then. Now... now remember all, we've only to tell the truth plainly," he said with a finger raised. "We've only to say what we saw and heard, and then to put our trust in God Almighty, and surely our dear Tim shall be delivered! Now let us all join hands together and lift up our hearts with hope and hold ourselves firm in readiness for our struggle for justice!"

"And we'll tell 'em he had his hand upon her," said Luke Lauper, "and that he was dragging her through his door and that he had evil in his eyes."

"And that he held a knife to her throat!" said the youngest of the boys.

"No no no," said Amos, "we don't have to be making up anything. When you've nothing to hide, then you've nothing to gain by the inventing of a story. And besides, they've only to ask the watchman or Nat whether they saw a knife, don't they? They'll both answer with a 'no' and so will any other witness that was there. And then the Justice of the Peace will wonder whether every word you've said is a lie and then they'll wonder about the rest of us, too. All just making up stories, they'll say. No no, boy, a lie is the last resort of a man who knows he's guilty."

"Well..."

"You tell a lie, boy," said Luke "and you'll send Tim to a hangman's noose and then his death will be your doing and all will know you for a liar and a scoundrel and you'll not have a friend left in this town or any."

The boy stared back at Luke in shock.

"Ah... ah...well said," said Amos with a nod. He had not expected so strong a statement from a boy of sixteen. Luke was like his father. Both carried themselves in a half crouch, as if ready to pounce.

"We've right on our side, we have," said Luke, "and they'll know it's the truth by the easy way that we'll tell it. Won't they? They can bring us in one at a time and we'll all tell the same story, for it'll be the truth and there's only one version of it."

"Ah... well... ah," stammered Amos, but then their attention was distracted by a young man who walked up, as if looking for someone.

"Amos Short?" the stranger asked when he noticed the crutch and peg leg.

"I am, himself."

"The hearing's been called off. The Justice of the Peace has unexpected visitors."

"Called off?"

"So I'm told."

"Well! What are they to do with Tim?"

"Don't know."

"Well then!" said Amos, turning back to the boys, "ain't that an odd thing? You'd think such an event as this would be important enough. Why... it'd even offer something for the man's unexpected visitors to watch, wouldn't it? Something to talk about afterward."

"What're they going to do with Tim?" asked one of the boys.

"I don't know," said Amos. "Normally, the trial would be up at White Plains, held there when the circuit judge came around for the County Sessions. But what with war and disruption, that's all off now, ain't it? Down on the Isle of Manhattan, it be martial law, now that Major General Billy Howe and his redcoats have hold of it. And up north of the Croton River, it's George Washington that rules. But as for hereabouts – betwixt and between – well, who knows? They're a-calling this the neutral ground, ain't they?"

"It ain't very neutral," said Luke, "when our local gentry has raised up a militia and is going out on patrol."

"No it ain't!" said Amos. "And they're under the command of Billy Howe, ain't they? But no one quite knows for sure who has the true right to lay down the law here in Yonkers town. They're saying it'll be our own justice of the peace here in Yonkers who'll make the decision on whether Tim's to go to trial. And if he does, it'll likely be down in the city."

"But he doesn't have to send him down there, does he?" asked Luke.

"Yea yea, no he don't. So they're a-saying. And that's why we're all here to give our sworn testimony in Tim's defense, so he'll turn Tim free."

"And if we don't, they'll send him to New York City to be tried before a military court, won't they?"

"That's what they're saying," said Amos with a shrug, "for neutral ground or not, 'tis Billy Howe that's the power that be hereabouts, ain't it? And he must be wanting them sent down too, for he could tell Colonel Philipse to handle it himself, couldn't he? Even to order a hanging, maybe. If the Major General says so, it's so. But... but still, what I'd like to know is..." he asked, turning back to the young man who had brought the news. But he was gone.

· · · · ·

"And what in blazes are you doing in here?" asked John Gainer when he finally found Amos in the tavern. John was Tim's master. He was an ordinary looking man and he dressed like most tradesmen with a hat cocked on three sides.

"Well John, I'm having me a sit down and I'm enjoying my pot of beer," Amos replied. "Have yourself a seat too, why don't you? It's been a long day."

"Where... where are the boys?"

"Sent home, home to their mothers. Not much use for them now, is there?"

"What about the hearing?"

"Who knows?" Amos said with a sigh as he lifted his mug for a sip. "Maybe tomorrow, maybe next week. It's out of our hands now, ain't it?"

"Are you daft? It's tonight, up at the mansion! You knew that!"

"Ah, but you haven't heard. Called off, it was. And for what? The arrival of a surprise visitor, I'm told. And ain't it almost predictable, too. A poor boy like your Tim, when he's in need, he's forsaken by him who could see justice done and set him free. Left to the..."

"It's on!" insisted John. "The hearing's on! The Justice of the Peace is waiting for you and the boys!"

"Nay nay, it's been called off. It was not a half hour ago that I was brought the news. Sent the boys home, I did, for there was nothing left…"

"It's not called off, you blockhead! The Justice and Nat and Thomas are all there a-waiting for you!"

"But I was told…"

"I don't care what you were told. I've just come from there and they're waiting. Where are the boys?"

"Sent home, like I says. We were told it was called off."

"Who told you?"

"A young man! A stranger he was!"

"You were misinformed then! We've got to get the boys back and get down there."

"They've gone home!"

"Listen to me! You go up the east half of town and I'll take the west. We'll find as many as we can and go straight up to the mansion!"

John chose the larger part of town as he could run faster. They were able to round up all but one of them, but with delays and questions from the boys' parents, it took time. John was up to the mansion first with three boys. He met the Steward coming out.

"Is there still time?" asked John, but he knew the answer from the look on the man's face. The hearing had gone ahead with no one to speak other than Nat and his Uncle Thomas.

"It's over," said the man. "Your boy will stand trial. The Justice had little choice. Where were you?"

"A stranger – a young man – he came and told Amos Short the hearing had been called off. He sent the boys home. I tracked down Amos in the tavern and we had to go out after the boys who had all gone home."

"It's too late?" asked Amos, as he came up with three more boys.

"What's this about a stranger?" asked the Steward.

"Indeed, a young man, he was," said Amos. "Came to tell me it's called off. I'd no reason to doubt him. He looked respectable enough. An ordinary sort."

"Well well."

"And I'll wager you had Thomas and his nephew there," huffed Amos, "telling a fine pair of stories. And who do you suppose might have been behind the mysterious young messenger?"

"It'll be best if we not make accusations in public," said John quietly.

"Where's Tim now?"

"Back in the lockup," replied the Steward. "He'll be on his way down to the city tomorrow."

"In chains?" asked John.

"Of course. But he'll go up for trial in a couple of days only, so if you can make it there, then there's still hope."

"If I'm not stopped by a young man," muttered Amos. "And you know who would be a-hiring him, don't you?"

"Now now," cautioned John as he glanced to the side. "Don't make any accusations that you can't prove. You'll have a hard time defending yourself against a charge of slander. They'll outtalk you, for sure."

Amos looked in the same direction as John. By the side of the road stood Thomas and Nat Pellis. Nat gave them a dark look and turned away. Thomas followed along, looking like he was laughing at a joke.

"We know what they're thinking, don't we?" said Amos.

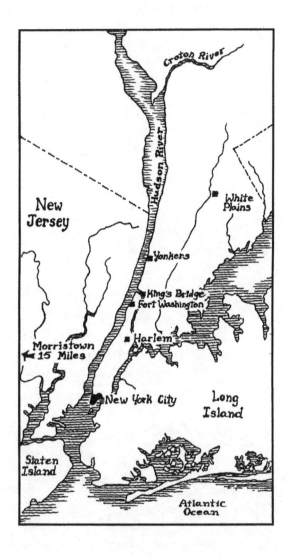

Chapter 3

The alternative is death.

Moonlight shone through a barred window in the town's jail, lighting up the smoke as it drifted up and out into the crisp night sky. The window at the top of the wall served as a chimney. Tim sat bored and angry, as he kept his toes warm by the fire. He was trying to decide whether to throw on another log when he heard footsteps.

"Ooo, a fine little jailhouse you've got here, captain," said a young man. The good humor of a prisoner always rang false.

Leather-soled shoes stamped up the stairway, the trapdoor opened and in the light of the lantern, Tim saw the tired face of the watchman on duty.

"Climb on!" he said impatiently.

"Ooo, a swing! What fun!" The creaking started and the stranger was lowered down. "Do I climb off now?" he asked.

"Do you want to eat before tomorrow night?" was the reply. The rope creaked back up and the trap door slammed.

"Good evening," said Tim, trying to sound older and braver than he was. The idea of being locked in a room with a drunken stranger did not please him.

"And good evening to you," said the man as he bent forward and squinted to get a look at Tim in the dim light offered by moonlight and glowing embers. "And I'm pleased to find you here. I was hoping I'd have some company."

"What brings you here?" asked Tim. He was trying to sound calm, but his voice shook. The man did not sound much older than Tim, but there was enough light to tell he was bigger.

"Battery, they call it," the man sighed as he felt around to select a good place to sit. The floor was covered with straw. Tim had heard mice crawling through it. "The name's Dan Eliot. And what's yours?"

"Tim Euston."

"'Tis a pleasure, Tim Euston," Dan said as he sat down. "Euston, eh? The watchman said your name's Tim Useless. You must be tired of hearing that one. The boys always called me Dan Idiot. Eh? Dan Eliot? It's too tempting not to."

"I'm Tim Useless because I'm useless for carpentry."

"Why's that?"

"I keep making mistakes with counts and measurements."

"It'll come to you, by and by."

"So I've been told, but I've been apprenticed three years now and it ain't come yet. I just keep on making stupid mistakes."

"That's no good for carpentry," said Dan quietly.

"No good for much else either."

"You could be a sawyer."

"Until I get a sore arm." Tim knew a sawyer whose family half starved while waiting for a sore arm to get better.

"It does happen."

"Who'd you batter?" asked Tim.

"Oh, it was just brawling. Acting like a 'Dan Idiot', you might say. Just two days ago, I came to town looking for work. I know a fellow who lived here until recently. You know Theodore Andres?"

"He took his family and moved north last December. There's a few who have moved out."

"So I've been told."

"How'd you end up getting arrested for brawling?"

"I'd looked up a friend of mine by the name of Thomas Pellis. You know him?"

"I do," said Tim after a pause.

"A comical fellow he is, eh?" chuckled Dan. He waited a moment, got no response from Tim and went on. "Well, we went down to the tavern and we drank ourselves a couple of pots. And then in comes some young fellows who start to poke fun at the poor old fellow. Some clever jests, they were, that implied he had improper desires for young girls. Old Thomas had his own clever jests to offer in response and that led to fighting words. At the keeper's suggestion, we took it outside and then push led to shove. I took on the worst of them in a good boxing match – all fair and square – good to amuse ourselves with. Well, to no one's surprise, it was Dan Eliot who emerged as the undisputed victor. I even bought them drinks to celebrate – the ones who stayed. But word got back to my opponent's mother, who then went to her husband, who happened to be a man of some rank around these parts. The Justice was ready to act at a moment's notice and Papa saw to it that I was arrested and charged with the battery of his little boy."

"Battery?"

"A rather harsh interpretation of events, I'd say."

"I'd have thought," said Tim after a pause, "that he'd just convict you for a common nuisance and let you work off your fine, filling ruts or sawing firewood."

"You'd think so! What do they gain by sending me down to the city to stand trial?"

"Perhaps they're in need of cheap labor down there."

"Perhaps," chuckled Dan. "Not enough forced labor to be had in New York City, it seems. Only four thousand of them! Prisoners of war!" After a pause he asked, "What are you in for?"

"Battery."

"We've something in common then."

"And robbery."

"Ooo, and that too, eh? Well well! You might swing from a rope for a crime like that."

"I ain't guilty though," insisted Tim.

"Ha! And neither am I."

"No, truly I'm not! I never stole nothing from him and I never meant to! He lies, he does, that fine old friend of yours!"

"Who?"

"Your friend! Thomas Pellis!"

"Old Thomas? You battered him?"

"He had it coming, too."

"When did this happen?"

"Day before yesterday."

"Did it?"

"It did indeed!"

"It was you who gave him that bruise upon his forehead?"

"I did that much. And he had it coming! I did it only in defense of my sister!"

"Your sister?"

"He had his hands upon my little sister, he did. And he meant her harm! I saw the look in his eyes."

"Did he? I would not have thought that of old Thomas."

"And he's got his nephew out a-telling lies for him, too. And I had witnesses, I did! I had my friends! But somehow they never showed up for the hearing. So here I am awaiting trial."

"I heard the watchman talking to someone about that, when he escorted me over here. Something about a stranger having gone and told someone that the hearing was called off due to an unexpected visitor."

"Is that what happened?" asked Tim, after a pause.

"That's what I overheard."

"Well well."

"How old's your sister?"

"Fourteen only."

"No!" responded Dan, sounding disappointed. "So that's what was behind the clever jests in the tavern. I'd not have thought that old Thomas would... would stoop to that sort of devilry."

"He had the Devil in his eye – indeed he did."

"And here it was I who fought to defend him. We had been a-drinking and talking about all we'd been up to. And he didn't mention a word about it. And now here I am in jail for defending the likes of him."

"He told you nothing about it?"

"I'd asked him about the cut and bruise on his forehead. A good lump he's got. I'd asked him and he said he'd been coming up to a door when someone was coming out."

"Not the first lie he's told in the past couple of days."

"How do you like that! I defend a friend from public abuse and for my reward I'm criminally charged. And worse yet I'm associated with the sort of blackguard who preys upon the weak and innocent."

They sat in silence, listening to the crackle of the fire and the rustle of a mouse.

"They need cheap labor to repair the roads," said Tim. "I should thank you on behalf of the county for the work you'll be doing."

"The city, not the county. I'm being sent to be tried in the city."

"Well then, I thank thee on behalf of the City of New York. Perhaps you'll be helping to improve the fortifications, too."

"And I'll thank thee, Tim Euston, for the work that you'll do on them. We'll likely be on the same chain gang together. Yea, toiling elbow to elbow and working for good King George and the common weal."

"A fine pair of public spirited fellows we are," agreed Tim, as he contemplated working long hours in winter weather with poor food and a cold shackle upon his leg.

"And it's always that way, isn't it?" said Dan, half to himself as he scratched his head of curly blonde hair. "'Tis the 'better sort', and the 'middling sort', too. They're the ones who have control of the courts. And with them, they hold dominion over the 'lesser sorts' like ourselves. And here we'll be wrongly convicted and enslaved. That's what it is, ain't it? Enslavement! That... that Thomas Pellis. Why should beating him get you in here? He shouldn't be above us."

"No, but he has family who are merchants and landowners."

"And that is all it takes. That gets him preferential treatment. Them that has, gets. Had your father been a landowner and a merchant with more money than the Pellises, then who'd be in jail now? It'd be old Thomas, wouldn't it?"

"Likely," said Tim with a shrug.

"What's your father do?"

"My father is off in Boston. He's a merchant with a sickly old crow for a wife. My mother was his 'kept woman' and me and Sadie are his bastard son and daughter. Had his wife died like she was supposed to then he might have married my mother. That's what he'd promised. I might have been well off, but the old crow lives on forever so he never did marry my mother. Then when Mom's teeth all started to rot away, she got to be less pleasant for company. So he had her put away. Paid off and sent away, she was – all three of us. We lived down in the city and he kept sending her money until he went bankrupt and after that, Mom found work up here in Yonkers, work for all three of us."

"A sad story," said Dan, quietly.

"My sister serves the same master as my mother. Their mistress is Matilda Walker. She was a Pellis – a niece of old Thomas and she's the sister of his nephew Nat. And it's my sister, Sadie, that old Thomas has an eye for."

"All in the family, is it?"

"Nearly," huffed Tim.

"You a servant too?"

"Mom had money enough for me to be bound as an apprentice to a carpenter – John Gainer."

"You could do worse than that."

"Indeed, it could be worse."

"Not tonight though," laughed Dan. "Not for Tim Useless."

"Is it much better for Dan Idiot?"

"No! Well… though, we could be lying on our deathbed with a heart so hardened by hatred that we've no hope of salvation."

"Indeed we could be."

"Count our blessings, we should."

"Accept with humility what hath been accorded unto us."

"Humility has never been one of my gifts," said Dan with a half smile, after taking a moment to think it over.

"No! I can't imagine that!" laughed Tim.

"But who would stand to gain, were I as humble as I ought to be?" asked Dan, sounding like he was about to deliver a speech. "It be King and gentlemen who want us lesser sorts to humbly obey – pay the King's taxes and plough the gentleman's fields. Ain't that the fact? And what sort of a preacher is it who preaches the wisdom of obedience? It's the preacher who has a gentleman landowner for a brother. And can we blame them – any of them? Don't we feather their nests with our humble labor? Isn't it the sweat of our brow that puts the butter on their bread and the meat on their plates and the logs on their fires and the lace on their sleeves?"

"Indeed it is," said Tim with a nod, "though, I suppose, more so over in old England. But there's many who want it to be that way here too, isn't there?"

"Do you think so?" said Dan with a smile. "Sounds like you're a patriot then. And for the cause of freedom." There was just enough light for Tim to see his expression.

"I wouldn't admit to that, not to a stranger. Not in the town of Yonkers – not these days. They call patriots 'rebels' hereabouts."

"They're all tories here?"

"Half-and-half it was, but most of the patriots have gone north. What's left behind have either declared for the King or they've kept quiet."

"You're for the cause of freedom, though?"

"Why should I admit it to you?" asked Tim, with suspicion in his voice.

"Smart boy," chuckled Dan. "You never know, these days. But I'm idiot enough to admit that I would have gladly fought under Washington and the Continental Congress. I would have, but I missed out on the chance. I was at sea. I didn't even hear the news of it until the battles of last fall were all fought and lost. Maybe this spring, I'll go sign up, if there's still battles to be fought."

"And I will too," said Tim quietly, "if they'll take me."

"Well, bless you, my brother!" declared Dan. "Let me shake your hand!" and he waved his hand in the darkness, trying to find Tim's. "Bound by our word, we are! But… what do you mean, 'if they'll take you'?"

"They wouldn't last summer. I was fifteen and short. The sergeant said I'd be needed on the home front."

"Oh."

"They laughed at me when I walked away."

"Did they?"

"Six of us walked down to the city to sign up and… and they took five out of the six."

"And you went home alone?" asked Dan, with sympathy in his voice.

"There were others who weren't taken."

"Nobody can say you didn't try."

"I've grown an inch, since then."

"There was just talk of war," sighed Dan, "when I signed onto a merchant ship and sailed away. Now they can say I suspected it was coming and that I ran off in fear."

"You couldn't have known it would all come so fast."

"Yea, indeed," said Dan quietly, after a pause. "Well, at least the two of us are alive and able to fight again, aren't we?"

"If we ever have a chance. Everybody's talking about peace talks coming soon."

"Around here they may be talking about peace talks, but up north, they say they're in it to the end. No compromise. That's what I'm told."

"We can only hope," said Tim.

"At least one more battle, eh? For those of us who missed out – a chance to take a stand and show 'em what we've got to offer."

"Just one!" moaned Tim quietly, sounding almost desperate.

"How'd the war go for your five friends?"

"One died of camp fever, and one was wounded up at the battle of White Plains and now he lays about his mother's house mending. Two are prisoners down in the city and the other one is over in Jersey with the Army."

"Only one out of the five still able to fight on?"

"Two. The other one's getting better."

"And the others might get out. They're saying there'll be another prisoner exchange."

"I hope so," said Tim. "We'll need them once fighting season comes."

"I'd hate to spend the summer marching up and down a parade ground while peace talks are going on. There are some who say a young man could serve the cause better by hiring onto a privateer and helping in the capture of English shipping. And not working for a tory shipper, like I did last year! But what do you think about privateering? Get onto a good American privateer and fight the enemy and get a share in the booty? What do you think? They say that it'll be the capturing of their ships that will injure the interests of the ruling class in old England – more than fighting battles. And if we were on with a privateer we'd stand a chance for riches, wouldn't we? I've heard tell of boys no older than yourself who came back with more than he could earn in ten years of working – enough to get themself started in life."

"Make up for the misfortune of their birth," said Tim.

"Maybe the two of us should bust out of this shack and aim our feet for Boston. Come spring, there'll be many a privateer who will sail from that port and they'll be looking for boys like us, won't they? And too short and too skinny ain't no problem for a sailor, is it? They'll want you as long as you've courage enough to climb the spars in any weather. Could you do that?"

"I've climbed to the top of the tallest trees hereabouts."

"Didn't go stiff and start to whimper when you looked down?"

"Nope."

"Well, there you go. You ever been to sea?"

"No."

"Doesn't matter. They'll be taking all comers, so long as you're young and strong. Yea, there's riches to be had on the sea. Though I must say, I did promise myself I'd never ship out again. You know what some sailors do for three hours out of four, out at sea? They knit! Knitting needles a-clicking away! Some did carving or leatherwork. They'd pay me to help, sometimes. Yea, we're all needed when the sails need to be trimmed, but the rest of the time we're idle. And a few balls of yarn or a few pieces of leather don't take up much space. There's some who earn themselves a few pence ever day, doing their handiwork. And that's on top of their pay. And there was one fellow! He could argue politics or lay bets or tell stories or sing songs and keep on a-knitting all the while and never drop a stitch! One stocking after another! Click, click, click went them needles! It can drive you daft! But still, there's money to be made at sea these days at privateering. Legalized piracy, it is! How hard do you suppose it would it be to break out of a wooden jailhouse like this?"

"I looked it over during daylight. Without a hammer and chisel, it'd take a while."

"How long?"

"You got a knife?"

"They took it from me."

"Days then. Weeks," sighed Tim. "We'd have to break a rock and use it to scratch through oak. We may as well gnaw through it with our teeth."

"Well then, wouldn't you think we'd best start gnawing? The alternative is likely to be death by hanging, ain't it?"

This story is set in February and March of 1777, in the second year of the American War for Independence. It had started with battles in Massachusetts when the Royal Governor had sent red coated regulars to seize military equipment stockpiled by a rebellious colonial assembly. Local militias drove them back and surrounded Boston. The militia was an "irregular" military force made up of the larger part of the colony's adult males. Most owned their weapons and had been training more frequently than the traditional one day a month. As news spread through New England, revolutionary committees took control of local government. In June, a force of 2500 British redcoats drove 1500 patriot militia from a hill that overlooked Boston harbor, but almost half the British were killed or wounded, far more than expected. From New Hampshire to Georgia the uprising spread and by May of 1776 not one British soldier remained in arms in the thirteen colonies. The Americans hoped they had achieved the military credibility needed to persuade their mother country to return things to the way they had been before it had started to try to impose new taxes. At this point only a small minority wanted full independence.

Twelve years earlier, the capture of Canada by the English had ended the threat posed by the French. King George III decided the Americans should pay more taxes to cover the cost of their own defense. Until then, the only taxes paid to England had been customs duties and these were often evaded. The Americans felt they should pay no new taxes without the right to vote in their own Members of Parliament. This tax protest was a part of a movement favoring political and legal reform, with rebellion in Corsica and riots in Madrid, Ireland and London.

An assembly of colonial representatives calling itself the Continental Congress met in Philadelphia. Delegates insisted they were loyal and issued their demands in the King's name. During the early months of 1776, the mood changed and in July they voted in the highly controversial Declaration of Independence. America had a regular army with George Washington as commander. The American Army, often called the

Continental Army, grew to 23,000 men. King George replied with a force of 32,000, commanded by Major General William Howe, and it landed on an island at the mouth of the wide Hudson River. The British were better trained and equipped and in a series of battles they captured the islands around New York City and all of New Jersey. 3,600 Americans were killed, 4,000 taken prisoner and thousands more were sick or had deserted. This represented about one in forty of the thirteen colony's white, adult males. Starting in December, after the British had gone into winter quarters, Washington revived confidence in the patriot cause with victories at Trenton and Princeton, and in many other small actions in New Jersey. By spring they were able to be hopeful again.

Chapter 4

'Tis a risky business.

"I just want to go and tell him to think about making himself presentable," said Sadie Euston to her mother when halfway out the back door.

"Just don't be long then," said Abby over her shoulder. "We've work to do and I can't do it all myself."

"I will be back shortly!"

"Make sure of that," Abby grumbled, turning away and holding her hand to her cheek. It was swollen from a toothache and the damp air that blew in through the doorway felt very cold.

Sadie looked back to see if her mother was watching from the door. She almost always had a toothache. It was frustrating because she did not have to suffer the way she did. Matilda had said more than once that she was willing to pay to have them pulled. *What twisted desire*, Sadie wondered, *possesses the heart of my mother to make her want to cling onto rotten teeth?*

Everyone spoke well of the local surgeon and said he was excellent at pulling teeth. Abby's teeth were so far gone, they'd "pop out like corks," as the surgeon claimed. *But instead,* thought Sadie, *the foolish woman chooses to suffer day after day with her face swollen and red! And spending good money on medicines that hardly work at all. And she likes to praise the soldiers for their courage in battle. Why can't she show some courage herself?*

Snow lay on the fields and rain was starting to fall. The weather had been miserable for weeks. Sadie's mother was just as miserable and her brother was in jail and his one adult witness would likely get drunk today and still be drunk tomorrow when he testified in court. *A stinking, dirty drunkard!* Sadie told herself as she walked along. *All we've got is him and boys. How will their testimony stand up to Nat and Thomas Pellis, who will be dressed up in fine clothes and looking like a pair of gentlemen?*

A big wagon loaded with barrels passed by, the horses at a trot. Their hooves splashed in the ruts, splattering Sadie's white apron. The rain was now a steady drizzle and she slouched along, holding onto the ends of her hood and the ties of her cloak, trying to keep the rain from going down her neck. Amos Short lived at the edge of town, down a trail and into the woods in a one room shack. She would give him a good scolding, turn around and leave. *What more can I do?* she told herself. *I can't force him to stay sober, can I?*

Sadie was almost there when she saw him – Jack Lauper, Luke's father. He was creeping out the door of Amos's shack and looking around, like he was afraid someone was watching. He always walked in a half creep. So did Luke, but this time Jack was creepier than ever. He did not see Sadie because she was peeking around the edge of a thicket of brush at a bend in the trail. The look of him frightened her. She ducked down further behind the branches and then behind the trunk of a large tree. The dead leaves that covered the ground were wet and made little sound. As he passed by, on the same trail she had come up, Sadie kept hidden behind the tree. She did not know why she felt a need to do this. She knew him well and had no reason to fear him. But the look of him today, it warned of something sinister.

After a few more steps, he broke into a run – a smooth cat-like run that he could keep up for miles. *What's he running from?* Sadie wondered as she came out from the trees. She looked up and down the trail and shook her head. Now she was crouched down and creeping along, like he had been. The door of the shack was open. *Why would Jack leave the door open?* Something felt wrong and Sadie was tempted to turn back and forget about it all. "Let Amos take care of himself," she muttered, but then hesitated. *What's happened?* she wondered and forced herself to go on. She took another step towards the door and another look back. *What if someone sees me? But... but why should that matter? I've done nothing wrong!*

Inside the door, she saw his foot. He lay face down, just beyond the table.

"Amos?" she asked. She looked back again and could see no one. The only sound was dripping and the distant caw of a crow. Inside the shack she stepped slowly.

"What are you doing there?" she called out in case someone was hiding. No one answered. She felt her whole body going stiff with fear.

"Amos! Wake up!" she ordered. It took all her courage to go closer. There was something red in his hair. Blood? She could hear him breathing. His chest rose and fell. There was definitely a smell of rum.

"Amos," she whispered. No answer. "Amos!" she shouted. Still no response. She reached out and prodded his shoulder. He did not move. She struck his shoulder with her fist. "Wake up!" she called, but still he did not move.

"Oh dear!" she whispered. All was still quiet. She went out the door, took three steps and broke into a run, just like Jack had – looking side to side as if in fear of getting caught.

It was hard work running through muck, but Sadie found the strength to run all the way home. Matilda was in the kitchen.

"Sadie, where…"

"Amos is on the ground and he won't wake up! There's blood in his hair!"

"Oh! What were you doing there?" scolded Matilda. She was not an uncaring woman, but she felt this would mean an extra burden that was not rightly hers to bear.

"I just went to tell him to stay sober and make himself presentable looking for court tomorrow."

"Oh! Is it still raining?"

"No, it's stopped."

"Come on then." Matilda tied on her hood, an oblong shaped piece of cloth with the ends twisted and tied under the chin. Sadie got her cloak and draped it over Matilda's shoulders. She tied it as they were going out the back door. Nothing more was said. They walked quickly towards the home of the surgeon, but he was not in.

"I don't know," said the cook. "Someone came and he went with him."

They went to find the watchman on duty. When the women told him the news, he shook his head and grunted. His wife brought his cloak and hat and gave Sadie a sour look, as if it was all her fault. He led the way to the shack, going at an easy pace. When they arrived, the door was still open. Inside, they found Jack Lauper and the surgeon. Sadie could tell by the looks on their faces that Amos was dead.

"Someone broke his head with a club of some sort," said the surgeon. He was a tall man with a narrow nose. "Attacked from behind, he was. No signs of a struggle. Likely he did not know what was coming... and I think it likely he suffered no pain."

"He was breathing when I found him," said Jack.

"And when I found him too," said Sadie. "Just after..."

"Just after what?" asked the surgeon.

"Just after Jack left. I was coming up the path when he was coming down."

"Were you?" asked Jack. "I didn't see you."

"I ducked into the bushes," she replied, feeling self-conscious. They were all staring at her. She pushed a strand of her straw-colored hair back under her white cap and brushed her fingers across her nose, as if to wipe off the freckles.

"When he was coming back?" asked the surgeon. "When he was leaving here and heading back towards town?"

"Yes," replied Sadie. "Then I went in and saw Amos and tried to wake him up, but he wouldn't."

"What do you mean, you 'ducked into the bushes'?"

"When Jack came out he looked so... so... Like he was scared of something! I just ducked in behind a bush – behind a tree – and let him run past."

"Jack was running?" asked the watchman.

"Well," said Jack. "I'd just found a friend of mine knocked out. Out cold and with blood on his head! I feared for my own safety, I did!"

"From whom?"

"What do you think?" said Jack, with wide eyes, along with a stupid half grin.

"A witness?"

"From the man who knocked him down!"

"What brought you here this morning?" asked the surgeon.

"To see how he's doing – if he's going to be ready for the trial tomorrow. I came to advise him to lay off the rum, to make a good impression before the judges."

"That's why I came, too," said Sadie.

"We both know him well!" laughed Jack.

"Knew him well," corrected the surgeon. "And how long were you here before you came to blows?"

"Came to blows?" asked Jack. "With who?"

"With Amos."

"I resent that very much!" said Jack, straightening up and frowning. "I laid not a finger upon him. I came here and found him lying where he lays now."

"No fighting words? No punches thrown?"

"No!"

"I see you've got a cut on your knuckle," said the surgeon, pointing to Jack's hand. One knuckle had a cut with dried blood.

"I… I punched the wall of my own house," said Jack. "Just this morning."

"Why?"

"I was a-thinking of Thomas Pellis, I was! Him and his lying nephew!"

"And you didn't strike Amos a blow this morning?"

"You said yourself there was no sign of a struggle," said Jack, with a "Hah! I caught you!" tone in his voice.

"I said that, 'tis true, but I spoke not the truth," said the surgeon as he went to Amos's body and knelt down. "Look here," he said, turning the body over to show the face. The eyes were half open. "Now, as you see, his lip's been cracked and he has a loose tooth." The surgeon poked his finger into the half open mouth and wiggled a tooth.

"I did not kill Amos Short! I can tell you that right now – in the sight of God, I can! I did not lay a finger upon him!"

"You've been in many a brawl, haven't you?" asked the watchman.

"Yes, many a brawl. But I don't go and club and kill my friends!"

"You and Amos brawled out in front of the tavern, just this past Christmastime."

"I was drunk and he was drunk! It was a good boxing match. There was no hard feelings neither! We were friends again the next day! I've no reason to kill Amos! But you and I know who does! Is not Amos Short the prime witness for the trial of young Tim Euston? And wasn't Tim saying to everybody that Thomas had his hand upon young Sadie here and the Devil in his eye?"

"Indeed he was," replied the surgeon.

"Yes, but nonetheless," said the watchman, "we've Sadie here saying you ran from the shack looking scared. And we've a bloody knuckle that matches a bloody tooth."

"You are not going to pin this crime on me! Were I to kill a man I would plan it out better than this."

"It was just on impulse then?" asked the surgeon.

"Yes!"

"You agree then?"

"I do!"

"That you punched him without forethought?"

"Ah… no! Not that I punched him. That whoever punched him – whoever cracked him over the head! It… it was not me! Thomas or Nat or whoever was the young man who went and told Amos that the hearing was called off – likely it was one of them! You will not pin this on me! I am innocent! I swear that before God Almighty, I do!"

"Your faith is an inspiration," said the watchman. "But I fear this is now a question for a court of law. By the authority vested in me I do place you, Jack Lauper, under arrest and I'd advise you to come along peacefully or face an additional charge for resisting lawful arrest. Do you understand?"

"Of course I understand. I will come along peaceful as a lamb, I will. And I'll swear my innocence before any court of law and may God strike me dead and cast me into hellfire if I speak one word of a lie."

"Good for you. I'm taking my other two prisoners down to the city today and tomorrow the court sits. If the judges believe your story, you could be a free man again by tomorrow evening."

. . . . .

"A man who can afford a big lawyer," said Dan Eliot, "will be tried according to law and precedent, but if he can't it'll be trial by whim and convenience." He was sitting on the floor of one of New York City's many new jailhouses. Until recently, it had been a church, but with four thousand prisoners of war to house, the generals had commandeered a few buildings for use as temporary prisons. This particular church had promoted a brand of dissident religion favored by people who supported the rebellion. After the British had invaded Manhattan Island the October before, at least half the city had fled, including most of the congregation. The prisoners from Yonkers were put in a small room. The jailers felt that if they were put in with the rebels up in the nave, they would fall under a bad influence.

"I don't know," said Jack with a shrug. "Would a gentleman get a proper jury trial either? Not these days, I don't think. Not with war and martial law."

"Perhaps not," said Dan, "but likely a rich man could improve his position by the right coin into the right hand – bribe his way out of almost any charge, I'd think. I've been hearing stories. There are captains and colonels and generals who seem to think there's more than one way to plunder an enemy. Let the lesser soldiers strip the corpses and loot the houses, but the higher-ups will gain even more by the demanding of bribes. And from who? Not just the criminals. From any merchant who hopes to sell provisions to the Army, that's who. And that's not the limit either. There are red coated soldiers selling stolen arms and supplies. And who are they going to? To their own enemy – the American Army – the King's own weapons going to the rebels. But not directly, though. They're employing middlemen. A crooked redcoat will steal weapons – outright stealing it is! And then he'll trade them to a middleman who smuggles them out and sells to the rebels. Then they're trading the gunpowder for firewood and the muskets for beef – and for high prices. And sometimes these are the same merchants who have paid bribes so they can sell provisions to the British."

"They say there's a lot who are getting rich these days."

"Oh indeed yes. Almost thirty-two thousand soldiers they still have hereabouts – here and down on Staten Island and across in Jersey – and there's thousands more civilians too, now that the city's filling up with tory refugees. It'll take a lot to keep them all fed and warm and they can't bring it all across the sea, can they? And they can't bring it in from enemy territory – the enemy territory that surrounds them. Upstate and most all of New England and down the coast – it's almost all firmly in patriot hands now, isn't it? The prices in the city are sky-high."

"Everybody's out to get what they can get," agreed Tim.

"They are. And just you wait and see if someone doesn't come here and take you out to be 'questioned' and then ask how much you'd be able to offer for a good word directed to the gentlemen who will stand in judgment of you."

"Yes, that may come, I suppose," said Jack. "But I suspect our watchman has already told them a few things about us. Me and Tim don't have no relatives willing to buy us out of a scrape – and the watchman would know that, too. And how about you, Dan Eliot? How are you set for the paying of bribes to crooked officers?"

"Not at all," replied Dan, shaking his head. "No, there's no rich grandmother in my family. I got relatives upcountry and over in Massachusetts, but none of them are any wealthier than I am – not any more. And I don't know that they'd help if they could. I was the black sheep, you might say."

"The black sheep?" laughed Jack. "No! I can't see that!"

"We are all in need of witnesses," sighed Dan. "Or at least you are. I suspect my goose is already cooked. He was a rich boy and I got in a few good punches before he conceded defeat. A bit of a mess, he was."

"Well, your goose in no better cooked than mine," said Jack. "I've no witness, except for your sister," he said with a smile to Tim. "And she only saw me running from the scene of the crime so she's a witness against me, though it's no fault of her own."

"But surely, it was Thomas or Nat," said Tim. "They're the ones that got the motive."

"I don't know," said Jack. "I was into the store that same morning and Nat was there and I heard him say that his father was feeling poorly again. Sick in bed, he said he was. That means Nat would have been in the store right through the whole day with no time to nip out and kill somebody."

"And Thomas?"

"He was in the store too, but I don't know where he was earlier. He has a motive, for sure, but do you think he would ever have nerve enough to be so bold? It is not anyone at all who can go out and kill a man."

"The watchman knows Thomas had a motive. Surely, he'll ask around."

"He ought to," said Jack, "but he might just decide the town's better off without my type. A sailor that don't want to go to sea no more. I have no tradesman's skills to offer and I have a reputation for drunken brawling. When an extra hand is needed for harvest or haying I'm a sought after man, but this time of year my type is not too attractive in the eyes of the better sort."

"And ain't that just the heart of the matter right there," said Dan as he shook his head. "A man's only worth what he's worth to the higher-ups – to those with power and position – to those with land to rent and those who know the law and know how to use it to their own benefit. The rest of us have no property so we can't vote. We've no money to pay for lawyers so our legal rights are beyond our reach. Without a trade a man's little better off than slaves. Indeed, if we were slaves we would at least have a master who would be looking to protect his interest in us. We'd have ourselves a market value – what our master could fetch for us at auction. Then we'd have someone able and willing to buy us out of a scrape. Indeed we neither of us might never have been in this jail now, had we been slave to a man of substance. The watchman would have let us go, out of consideration for our master's financial interests."

"But I'm a bound apprentice to a carpenter and I'm still in jail," said Tim.

"You are, but didn't you tell me that you're Tim Useless," Dan said, smiling, "who can't be relied upon for accurate counts and measurements? Sure, you're bound to a master, but word is going around that you've been a poor choice and the watchman likely knows that."

"Well… what are we to do then?" asked Jack, who did not like to hear poor Tim called down like this.

"I say we ought to break our way out of here," said Dan quietly. "Break out, 'borrow' a boat, cross over to the Connecticut shore and make our way up to Boston. There we find ourselves a privateer who's looking for a crew. Then, once we've won prize money at sea, we'll be able to get ourselves a good start in life. Buy a farm or pay someone to train us in a valuable trade."

"We could hardly walk that distance before spring," said Tim.

"We could end up back in a New York City jail," said Jack, "just as easy as we could end up rich."

"But what's the alternative? If we stay here and wait for justice, then we might end up at the end of a rope. Jack, you'll almost surely hang. And if you don't, then as an alternative you'll starve in jail or freeze your toes off doing forced labor under the eyes of a red coated soldier who's waiting for an excuse to shoot somebody. Think about it a while. There's some things worse than death, ain't there?"

At this time a surgeon was a skilled tradesman whose status and training was comparable to a carpenter or blacksmith. He would provide hands-on care: setting bones, draining abscesses and bloodletting. There were physicians as well, a small number of gentlemen with university educations. Usually the physician would interview his middle or upper class patient and make a diagnosis. The patient would then go to an apothecary who would suggest a medicine.

Chapter 5

I do thank thee most humbly.

While Tim was sitting in jail, weighing in his mind the potential benefits and costs of employment aboard a privateer, his master, John Gainer, was on his way south. The rented wagon he drove bounced and swayed along the wet, rutted post road. It was loaded with firewood, potatoes and boys. The eighteen miles down to New York City would usually take four or five hours. These days it took longer with red coated soldiers at checkpoints. If their superiors had heard rumors of rebel saboteurs on the way, or of arms being smuggled out, they would be asking more questions and searching more wagons. The trip could take all day.

"Now listen! I want all you boys to be staying close by when we get to the bridge," said John for the second time. "You start looking around and they'll think you're paid to look around."

"I want to be a spy," said one boy.

"No, you don't want to be a spy," said John. "You want to be a scout."

"What's the difference?"

"There ain't always a difference, but if you're in uniform and you just ride out to take a look around, then you're definitely a scout. If you're a sneaky little scoundrel who will buy information from whoever and sell it to either side, then you're definitely a spy. But either way, you won't be liking it much when somebody decides to beat the truth out of you."

"I wouldn't talk!"

"You'd squeal like a pig," said Luke Lauper as he reached over to yank his pigtail. The boy squealed.

"Were you to be recruited as a spy," said John, "you'd likely start out by meeting with an army officer, be he one of the regulars from down here, or a rebel from up north or over in Jersey. He might be in uniform and he might not. He'd tell you what sort of information they wanted. How many enemy soldiers did you see coming through, or what sort of ships came upstream or down, or what sort of rumors were going around. Then he'd tell you that from time to time a man would come to you and give you a password. It might be, 'So how's old Widow Dunrea a-doing? I'd heard her leg was trouble.' "

"Why'd he ask that?"

"Because you don't know any Widow Dunrea. And that's how you'd know it was your 'contact', as they call them. You might say that she was much better since the doctor was brought in. And then you'd tell him all that you figured was worth telling in the way of military intelligence. That means useful information – something a general would like to hear to help plot his strategy – and strategy means his plans for ambushes and battles. And that'd be it."

"Would he pay you?"

"If you'd demanded something. And maybe he'd give you a new password for the next time somebody else came to see you. And that'd be all he'd say. You likely wouldn't get to know anybody else either. That's the way it ought to be, too. That way, if you were caught and tortured, you'd have nothing to tell. No names. No secret plans. Nothing except the name of a well-known officer – the one you'd seen at the start – if you'd seen one at the start. That way you'd be a benefit without being too much of a cost. And that's the way they'd want it. It's hard not to tell all if they go to work on you. If you're picked up and you're kept awake for three days, you'll likely be too daft to remember why you're not supposed to talk."

"How'd they keep you awake for three days?"

"When you nod off, a couple of big men hoist you up by the elbows and walk you around the room. And if you fall asleep on your feet they leave you to fall. You'll surely wake up by the time your nose hits the floorboards."

"That's how they torture you?"

"Usually."

"I thought they cut your fingers off."

"No no no. Not if they mean to turn you loose. They don't want you to go home and show everybody your stubs and tell them heartrending tales of outrageous cruelty. That way you'd just fire up the hot heads and have them all angry and swearing revenge and then going out to join the enemy's army. They'd not want that, would they? What they'd want is for his friends to be saying. 'Tortured? You don't look too bad to me, boy. You sure you were tortured?'"

"That's smart," said Luke.

"And don't you think it won't happen to you – whether you offer to spy or not. That's the treatment my cousin got, just last fall. He wanted to mind his own business and not fight for either side. He was out walking down the road one day, off to visit his mother. And some horsemen rode up – loyalist militia. One of them had been suspicious of him and he got questioned. Four days later when he got home, he looked five years older and he was useless for work for a week after. He still has nightmares of falling and hitting the floorboards. His dad makes him sleep out in the hayloft so his hollering doesn't wake up the whole house."

"And he didn't do nothing?"

"Just minding his own business," said John with a shrug. "Mistaken identity, it was."

By this time they had made it to the bridge that led across the Harlem River that separated Manhattan Island from the mainland. There was a row of wagons and packhorses waiting for their turn to cross over. After John's story the boys were all scared of being taken in for questioning and they stayed close by the wagon.

· · · · ·

It was almost dark when they made it into the city. New York was big, covering an entire square mile – the whole south end of the island. They had been told there would be little chance of finding a room in any hotel. It had a population of twenty-two thousand before the war, making it the second largest city after Philadelphia. Half of the population had fled, but others had come to take their place. But a third of the city's houses had been burnt to the ground the previous September and space was at a premium.

John was lucky. Before dark, he found the house he was looking for. It belonged to the brother of a Yonkers man. Like a lot of property owners in the city, he was willing to take them in for a few pence worth of firewood. John and the boys were given a bowl of soup in exchange for the potatoes they had brought with them.

After supper, everyone gathered around the fireplace. They sang songs, told stories and listened to a skinny boy who read from a book of poetry. Finally, the master of the house announced it was bedtime. He and his wife had the curtained four-posted bed in the corner of the front room. Everybody else either squeezed onto two bedframes or simply had to find a patch of floor big enough for their bedrolls. Thirty-three men, women and children were already crammed into this three-room house. None were resentful about an additional seven being added in for the night. Even the little ones knew they needed all the firewood and potatoes they could get.

. . . . .

John and the boys were up before dawn and over to the courthouse by nine o'clock. The opening ceremony was impressive with so many military men in uniforms, and with lace and brightly polished buttons and swords. Finally, the presiding officers of the court took their places upon the bench. They were elegant in rich fabric, but they were also scary to look at with expressions of cold command on aristocratic faces. The oldest of the three started by delivering a short sermon about justice and duty to one's anointed highness. Next, a gray haired man off to the side shouted out something in Latin and called the first case. The lesser charges were dealt with first. Clerks sat at a table below the judges and seemed to know ahead of time which of the accused was guilty – and that was nearly all of them. A man in fashionable attire did the talking and he performed like a master. Charges, testimony and judgment slid past with the efficiency of hands of cards played at a high-stakes poker table.

Eventually, Tim was led in with chains on his hands and feet. He was placed upon a raised platform behind the prisoner's bar, with an enormous guard just behind him, ready to give him a cuff to the back of his head if he spoke out of turn. Everyone in the large and crowded room turned to look at Tim and he glanced fearfully back and forth. It felt so strange to him – so nerve-racking – to be the center of such interest.

Some of the witnesses had been interviewed earlier in the day by a clerk and, during the luncheon break, the judges had heard a summary of conflicting claims. With the threatened abduction of a maiden in distress and a hoard of villainous young bandits, this case would be the highlight of the day. The judges were sure to please the crowd by allowing plenty of time for testimony.

The first to have his say was Nat Pellis. He stepped up to the witness bar in a fine looking suit of dark blue linen edged with a modest amount of lace – just enough for a member of a family of small merchants. In his strong, clear voice, he told of running to his uncle's calls, to find him besieged by young rascals – beaten and terrorized – his face streaked with blood.

Next came the old man himself, looking elegant in a new suit of pale brown. With too much rented lace on his cuffs and collar and a powdered wig on his head, he looked to be the equal of any of the judges. They might consider him overdressed for a man of limited wealth and education, but Thomas offset this risk by speaking in a humble, apologetic tone.

"I must confess I had been drinking a bit too much that day and…and when I found the children all at play – playing a game of tag they were and… well… well, just on an impulse, I crept up behind the girl and… and just to be playful, I suppose, I snuck up and I poked my fingers in her ribs and I shouted 'You're it!' Well! She shrieked so loud… I jumped a foot off the ground, I did. And then I felt I had to beg apology so, without thinking, I grabbed hold of her arm before she could run away, not wanting her to get away before I could explain and… and fearing the reaction of others, were she to claim she had been rudely assaulted. And then… and then, while I pleaded for her to understand, well… well, she just kept on a-hollering 'Let go! Let go!' I didn't even realize I still had hold of her arm and first thing I knew, the boys were attacking from all sides. It was only then that I realized that I had been deceived! I was victim of an attempted robbery – a planned and deliberate robbery!"

Next was the testimony of the boys. The judges heard the oldest two who told similar accounts of hearing Sadie's cries

– of running back to see her being pulled towards the door and of the look of anger and guilt in Thomas's eyes.

Finally came the decision of the court. The evidence was insufficient to convict Tim of robbery and he was free to go. Though the question was not before the court, the judge also expressed his opinion on the evidence against Thomas. There was clearly not enough to consider a charge against him for an attack on the girl. There was no way of telling whether he intended anything more than an ill-considered prank, or had attempted anything more than an awkward effort to beg apology.

The next prisoner to be brought to the bar was Dan Eliot. The surgeon described the victim's cuts and bruises in vivid detail. Another witness agreed that Dan had beaten the boy severely. After this, Dan begged forgiveness and insisted he had lost his temper in the heat of the moment, no doubt due to his foolish decision to drink too many mugs of beer.

A stern but brief lecture from the judge was followed by a solemn pronouncement of guilt. Foolish Dan Eliot found himself sentenced to one year at hard labor.

By now, it was well past suppertime and the judges were in a rush to finish the day's business. Jack Lauper came out, looking guilty in his usual slouch, with his shifty eyes and his hands clasped under his chin, as if to deliberately show off the iron cuffs and chains. First the surgeon was questioned, then the watchman. The final witness was Sadie, who could only tell the truth, no matter how harmful it might be for poor Jack. She finished by turning a shamed face to the prisoner, who offered his forgiveness with a kind smile and a shrug. The judge scolded Jack for his wickedness, found him guilty of involuntary manslaughter and sentenced him to fourteen years at hard labor. The relief on poor Jack's face was visible to everyone. He, and almost everyone else, had expected the death sentence.

Before the court adjourned for the day, Dan was called back into the room and brought to stand before the judges' bench, next to Jack. The judge said some consideration ought to be offered to Dan because of his youth, and to Jack because he had no prior convictions for a major crime. "I am willing," said the judge, "to reduce your sentences by half if you are willing to serve out your time upon a vessel of His Majesty's Royal Navy."

"Surely, I would m'lord, if you feel me worthy," said Dan, without hesitation.

"Indeed yes, your grace," said Jack, almost at the same time as Dan. "And I do thank thee most humbly."

The guilty were led back into the prison below and the innocent were unchained. Tim got smiles and hugs from his crying mother and sister, and all his friends were grinning and teasing him about his good luck. Even Luke managed to smile at him, though he was still thinking of the look his father had given him just before he was led through the door. It might be seven years before Luke saw him again. It might be never. Many sailors died on a voyage, especially during time of war.

As everyone was turning to make their way out, Tim gave Luke a look and they both knew what the other was thinking. "The innocent are to be punished and the real killer will walk free in the town of Yonkers.

Chapter 6

Just a daydreamer and a dullard.

Life went back to normal for Tim Euston. Two days after the trial, he was at work with the crew of woodcutters led by John Gainer's seventeen-year-old son, Josh. Since the arrival of General William Howe and his enormous army, there had been few calls for carpentry on the neutral ground. John had even considered moving down to the city, expecting a rush of work on barracks and prisons. He went there, asked around and changed his mind. The invaders had brought carpenters and more were included among the refugees. The high prices offered for firewood and lumber meant John could do better at the harvesting of wood than he could at his skilled trade. The invaders held only a small region around New York City and local producers had themselves a captive market. Since December, John had gone from five employees to fifteen and he would have hired more if he had access to more woodland. Everybody was into the game and local landowners who had not gotten around to burning and breaking their land for crops had found themselves with a wealth of wood.

Halfway through the day, Tim was sent to the Pellis store to get an axe handle. He took off running, but once around a bend in the trail, he slowed to a walk to enjoy a break from the swinging of an axe and the pushing of a saw. When he got to town, things were quiet. They had been for months. Many of the whigs – the patriots – who stood for liberty and supported the Continental Congress, had left for safer ground to the north. Few of those who supported the King had come to take their places. These royalists, who called themselves loyalists, were going all the way down to the city. Having already been chased out of their homes, these refugees could not feel safe enough on the neutral ground.

When Tim went into the door, he saw Nat at the counter having a hushed conversation with a stranger. Both turned to give him a look. The stranger stepped back and made a gesture with his hand to tell Tim to go ahead.

"Just a handle for a felling axe," said Tim as he looked down to the floor to show he was sorry for disturbing them.

"I've a nice one – fine quality," said Nat as he strode down the aisle, behind a counter which ran around three sides of the store. "A good strong piece of hickory, it is. Thy master will be well pleased."

"I thank ye," muttered Tim as he reached out to take it. Nat would mark down the cost on a ledger. John would likely pay with firewood. "And good day to ye," added Tim as he went out the door, just as Thomas Pellis was coming in.

"Timothy Euston!" he said with a yellow-toothed smile and a pat on the boy's shoulder. "Back at work, eh? Good to have you back in town." This was his usual way of talking. He had been a trader all his life and was charming by force of habit.

"And it's good to see you out of jail, Thomas," said the stranger with a smile. Tim heard this just before he closed the door. It was good to hear someone teasing him. Usually it was Thomas Pellis who did the teasing.

Tim went around the back of the store. On his way into town he had stopped in to see his sister and mother and had found them both out. "Sadie's likely over at the Pellis store," a neighbor had said when he left. The store belonged to Nat's father. He was old and sickly though, so Nat was the one almost always seen behind the counter. Most days, they had a hired woman working in the kitchen and when she fell behind, Nat would get Sadie to come help. She did not get paid anything extra for this. It was seen as part of her labor for her own master and mistress. And the mistress, of course, was Nat's sister.

Tim went through the back door of the store without knocking. This would save the cook from getting up from her work to answer the door. "Good day?" he said quietly as he peeked around. No answer. Likely they were all together somewhere, doing laundry. Women often made a social event out of washday. *Misery loves company,* thought Tim with a smile. Sadie hated washday.

Tim went back around the outside, eyeing the clapboard siding of the building. Like any woodworker, he was always looking at wood. The subtle variations in quality and variety held so much meaning after three years of working with it. He then saw the stranger, the man who had been talking to Nat. He was looking right at Tim and he seemed angry about something. Tim lowered his eyes and hurried along, muttering "good day" as he passed by.

. . . . .

"All went well enough," said Thomas with a shrug. He and Nat were alone in the store.

"As well as could be hoped," snorted Nat. "The whole town's been talking of little else."

"Let them talk."

"It's a stain upon the name of Pellis. A stain upon the whole family when one's suspected of that sort of thing."

"What sort of thing? All I did was have myself a bit of harmless merriment by teasing a girl. It's her and others who jumped to conclusions and the wise judge as much as said so before the court."

"Lack of evidence isn't proof of innocence," drawled Nat.

"What made it all into a scandal was when someone went and secretly hired a stranger to deliver a false message saying the hearing's being called off. That's what got the whole town a-talking, eh? And who was behind that little prank?"

"I could hardly sit by and do nothing," said Nat as his ears began to redden.

"But don't let it grieve you, boy," said Thomas with a smile. "What's done is done. We've all just got to look ahead to all the opportunities that are opening up to us, eh? Time of war is time of profiteering, it is. But it'll be only the clever few who will answer the call, eh? Those clever traders who will provide what's needed to those in need. Think of the fortunes that were made in the last war and here we are set to see it all happen again."

"Yes, that is all true, but I don't think we should be getting drunk on expectations."

"And here comes our new best friend back again," said Thomas, looking the other way. "I'd best leave the two of you to plot strategy. No need to make a spectacle of ourselves here, all huddled together, eh?"

"Indeed, we should not," replied Nat, as he leaned his elbows on the counter and watched his uncle leave while the other came in.

"That kid who just came in for an axe handle?" the stranger asked as he stepped up to the counter.

"Tim Euston?"

"He's your dreamy apprentice?"

"He's Tim Useless," said Nat with a nod.

"Well well well, so he's the pretty boy behind the prisoner's bar."

"Ah yes, all those freckles and dimples. So pretty, he should have been a girl, as they say."

"So that's him. Now tell me, does he have himself a lovely set of ears as well? I saw him putting them to use just now, just below that hole in the wall," the stranger said with a nod towards an open window at the side of the store.

"Was he?"

"Just for a moment, before he saw me watching him."

"He would have heard nothing important," said Nat as he went to close the window.

"A nosey boy is what he looked like. And a nosey boy who does too much sniffing might have to have his nose clipped – especially when it's a boy who surely bears a grudge."

"No no, he's more of a dull-witted boy. That's what they say about him – a dreamy boy who isn't always listening when he should be. And mistake prone too, they say, or at least Josh says so. He's as harmless a boy as we could hope for."

"Well, what was he doing nosing around here?"

"He was probably going around back to visit his sister. She helps out when Bessie can't keep up."

"The damsel in distress is here, too?"

"Not right now," said Nat, sounding defensive. "She's a good little worker. But you do have to tell her things twice, just like her brother – tell her what to do and then ask her what she's to do. If you tell her you need the old dog fed and the horse watered, she'll miss hearing about the horse because she's still thinking about the poor old dog."

"Ha! A little scatterbrain, is she?"

"But she makes up for it by looking pretty and rushing about. And Bessie likes to have someone to talk to."

"To listen and sometimes to hear?" asked the stranger.

"Yes, listening – an important task that always needs doing."

"And do you still think our Tim Useless is a good boy for the job?"

"He's as good as any," replied Nat.

"Not a curious bone in his body? Not a grudge against you and Uncle Promise? No suspicions? You know that suspicions can do damage enough if they're talked about. He ain't both a listener and a talker, is he?"

"No, just a daydreamer and a dullard," chuckled Nat.

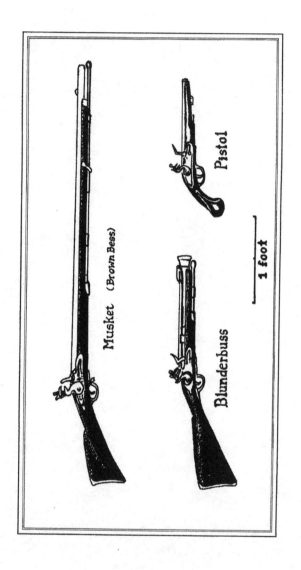

Musket (Brown Bess)

Pistol

Blunderbuss

1 foot

Chapter 7

Useless you are and will always be.

"Tim!" called John Gainer as he rode up. He had come to where the crew was cutting, sawing, splitting, stacking and bundling.

"Yes sir," said Tim while running over, hoping to be sent into town on another errand. He had been cutting wood. It was better than sawing planks, but not much.

"I've a task for you. Tomorrow, first thing, you'll go for a wagon and team." He did not have to say where. The local blacksmith rented horses and wagons. This was where John always rented. "You'll come back here, load it with bundles and haul them down to the city."

"To the city?"

"Why him?" asked Josh as he rose from where he was tying a bundle. Driving a wagon would properly go to an older boy who had earned a better job. And it usually went to a man who owned his own horses and wagon.

"Isn't he the right boy for the job?" asked John, not sounding like he wanted an answer.

"Well... I'd say not," replied Josh. "I'd say that..."

"That's enough, son..."

"He's not ready for a task that..."

"That's enough!" snapped John in the tone he used when he would take no more. Josh went quiet and took a step back with an expression of sincere indignation. He said nothing more, though. A boy who defied his father could expect to be caned and then shunned for a day or two. He could not even expect sympathy from his best friends. Were a boy of

Josh's age to lose his temper and beat his father, his punishment would be severe. He might as well beat the constable. He could hang for such a crime, though more likely he would get off with a severe whipping and a few months at hard labor.

. . . . .

Next morning, Tim was awake and out of bed before anyone else. He moved slowly, though. He had a few sore muscles. The news of his new status as teamster had got him excited. That had made him go at his work with too much energy. By the time the winter sunset had signaled quitting time, he had been exhausted.

Tim crept over to the fireplace and lit a candle on a thick piece of oak that had kept on smoldering right through the night. He put it in a lantern and went out to the storage room to pass some time sharpening a saw. Once he heard the others getting up, he went back to help Mrs. Gainer with breakfast. As always, each of them got a big bowl of oatmeal with milk and a spoonful of molasses.

Tim could have left for the blacksmith's, but he waited for Josh and the other workers to get moving. That way, he could leave with them, wish them a good day, and let them watch when he headed the other direction towards the blacksmith's shop at the north end of town.

Tim whistled a Scottish jig and said "Good morning" to everyone he passed. As he approached the blacksmith's, he saw a wagon hitched to a team of horses.

Likely mine, he thought, but then he noticed Nat Pellis talking to the blacksmith. They turned to look at him. Nat made a comment and both laughed. Tim was not sure, but it almost seemed like they were laughing at him.

But then Nat said, "Good day to thee, Tim Euston. Can it be true? I am told you're to be riding down to New York City today, but that can't be true!"

"It is. My master…"

"That must seem like easy work after sawing planks and chopping firewood."

"It does. I thought…"

"Now there's something that I have to say to you, Tim," Nat said, as he pointed his finger and spoke in a tone that had hardened and with a face turned angry. Tim crouched down, expecting to be slapped.

"I owe you an apology," said Nat, breaking into a smile. "To think I testified against you before a court of law – a military tribunal – when there you were, innocent as a lamb. What a thing to do, eh?"

"Ah… well… I don't…"

"I believed my Uncle Thomas when I should have been listening to your little friends. But I suppose family has to hold together, don't they? And the Old Goat is my uncle, eh? But still, once I heard all the testimony in court, I knew I'd been wrong. And old Thomas as much as admitted it, himself. Telling about how he'd only meant to give her a little scare and how the poor girl had jumped to conclusions and then he had jumped to his own conclusions. What a pair, eh? And we can't blame her though, for she's just a girl. But he can't claim tender youth for an excuse, can he? Silly old fellow, eh? Imagining that he's being robbed? What a thing to think! Well, justice was done and you're out of jail now, and all's well. And here you've got a new job! Unlucky one day and lucky the next, aren't you?"

"I am that," said Tim.

"Well then, I'd best let you be getting to your task, hadn't I? While there's still daylight, eh?"

"Oh, well... ah..."

"Watch out for robbers," said Nat as he turned to head back to the store.

"Let's get you going," said the blacksmith from behind. He had a stable and a few horses attached to his shop. Until Yonkers grew big enough for both a blacksmith and a livery stable, he would provide both services. He gave Tim a short lecture on the proper treatment of horses and how to avoid injuring them by driving them too hard. There was not much he had to say that Tim did not already know. People were always talking about horse problems. Still, Tim nodded his head and said "ah-ha" or "indeed" after every comment. Next, the blacksmith handed Tim his traveling papers. A passport had been written in fancy script by the Justice of the Peace and it stated that Tim Euston, age sixteen, had lawful permission to drive a wagon from Yonkers to New York City and back up to a farm twelve miles north of Yonkers. Tim would need this to get through the checkpoints, past the mounted militia that patrolled the neutral ground, and the regulars who policed Manhattan Island. He would also need a permit to cross at King's Bridge. He had heard this piece of paper cost two shillings – a good day's pay for a skilled man. But John had likely negotiated a better price for a permit to allow a wagon to make a regular run. Still, this tax would eat up a large part of his profit on the shipment.

Lastly, the blacksmith handed Tim an old blunderbuss. "It ain't loaded and I'd advise you not to try loading it. The lock needs work and it's prone to firing without your having to pull the trigger. You'll use it if you meet up with some rough characters on the road. You pull this out and you just cradle it in your lap. They won't know that it's not loaded. And anyways, if it was, you might be tempted to fire a shot. You do that and then what? The one of them that's still standing would then know for sure that it's not loaded any more, wouldn't he? And even if he doesn't take a run at you, he could go into town and tell one and all of how an innocent man had been shot dead by a wicked boy. And it'd be your word against his, wouldn't it? Yea, you'll be safer with a broken weapon, you will. And I'll be just as likely to get my horses back."

Tim had been nodding his head as he listened. When the man seemed to be finished he said, "Yea, I suppose you would be," and nodded a few more times.

The sun was high as Tim drove out, feeling like a prominent citizen. With no suspension, the wagon rattled along over the ruts and stones, but it was still a pleasure. His first stop was the worksite where the others were at their menial labor.

"Well, here he is at last!" called Josh when Tim reined in the horses. "I was wondering whether you'd ever show up." Tim knew he had no reason to question the short amount of time he had taken. Josh was just teasing him, out of envy.

"You get that loaded quick now, you hear?" said Josh with a stern tone and a wag of his finger. "You're already running late!"

Tim rushed at the loading, not because Josh had ordered him to, but because he would have anyways. If he made good time, he would be all the more likely to be asked to do the job again. He piled the bundles of sticks and split logs as compactly as possible and tied them down securely.

"Well, look at that mess," said Josh once the wagon was loaded. "My blind grandmother could stack a better pile than that! That pile will be slumping down to one side at the first rut that you hit and you'll be unloading and reloading out in the middle of the road and wasting precious time. My word, a Tim Useless you are. The minister got it right when he heard your mother wrong. Tim Useless you are and will always be, poor boy." The boys all laughed at this. It did not pay to forget to laugh at one of his jokes. It was Josh who divided up the chores and kept up the pace. Even Tim laughed.

Josh got off a few more good ones as Tim finished tightening the ropes. It was hard tying knots while everyone was watching and laughing. Anybody would be useless under that level of scrutiny. When ready to go, Tim climbed onto the seat, gave the reins a flick and called, "Wish me luck," but the horses were rattled by all the shouting and would not move.

"They know what they're in for," called Josh. "A good horse knows whether a boy's ready for driving."

"They'll get used to me," said Tim with a smile. "It'll just take a little time."

"A little! Ha! A little…" but Josh's mind had gone blank. The sight of it was too much. Tim Euston was driving a wagon down to the city, a job that should have gone to him, the eldest son.

"A little more time than you'll need to make it there before dark!" called another boy to fill the silence. Tim had jumped down, grabbed a halter and was trying to pull the horses along.

"Too little time, too small a boy!" called another.

"Do your worst, Tim Useless, you've got a reputation to uphold!"

"Mind you turn towards the south, eh? Not north!"

"No no, tell him to go north! Then when he gets it wrong, he'll get it right!"

"Worry not, my boys," called Tim, forcing his best smile. He was pulling with all his strength, but the horses were barely moving. They were anxious and at any moment they might bolt. He had to be on his guard, ready to move with them. If he could only get them round the bend in the road. That would have them out of sight of the boys. Maybe then, the beasts could calm down. One of them was now deciding to go ahead and he lurched forward, but the other still held back. When Tim thought the stubborn one was about to give in and go, he let go of the bridle, jumped aside and ran to leap up onto the wagon and into his seat. He grabbed the reins and they were off. With laughter and shouting behind them, the horses were ready to break into a gallop, but Tim pulled hard to hold them back. If they did take off, the wagon would surely tip over on the next corner and maybe break a wheel.

"Whoa boys! Easy!" Tim hissed as he pulled on the reins. One horse was still trying to pull ahead, but the other was obeying. "Easy! Easy!" said Tim firmly, but not too loudly. It worked. They both came to a halt. And at least now they were around the bend. The shouting had stopped. Tim eased off on the reins, waited a moment and then gave them a shake. The horses started off together at a walk. Tim could feel the blood pounding in his head. He had been gritting his teeth so hard they hurt. "Blockheads!" he said to himself. "It would have been their fault, but I would have been blamed!" He silently cursed them with every word he could come up with, until he realized he had just turned the wrong way. He was heading north. "I am useless," he moaned. "I'll never make it!"

Chapter 8

Pellises going and coming.

Tim reined in the horses, cursing himself for being just as useless as Josh or anybody had ever said. He looked around. No one was in sight. *Thank goodness for that,* he told himself as he climbed down. He grabbed a halter and led the horses around. One of them snorted, sounding as if he had known all along. Tim tried to ignore him.

Fortunately, the road was wide and flat. It had to be. During wet weather this sort of land would be cut into ruts by every heavy wagon that came along. Enough width was needed to allow the next wagon to go around ruts left by the last one. And the next one along would have to go further out.

Tim climbed back on and soon they were making good time. The weather had been dryer for the past few days. The clouds were clearing and it looked like the sun was still well short of its peak. If all the day's bad luck was over, he would have the load delivered well before dark. "And all is surely going to go well!" Tim called out to the cattle that grazed in a meadow. "Mark ye one and all! As sure as liberty will triumph!"

Now Tim felt good again. He could forget about Josh Gainer and start thinking about Tim Euston. Driver! Teamster! He was a man doing a man's job! A new man in a new nation! "O ye that love mankind!" he shouted out, reciting a passage he had memorized from a book. "Ye that dare oppose not only the tyranny but the tyrant, stand forth! Every spot of the Old World is overrun with oppression. Freedom has been hunted round the globe. Asia and Africa have long expelled her. Europe regards her like a stranger and England has given her warning to depart. O! receive the fugitive and prepare in time an asylum for mankind."

This was from a book he and Sadie had been reading. It was by an Englishman named Thomas Paine. Everybody was making jokes about his name, but practically everybody who could read was reading it. It was called *Common Sense* and in it, Paine preached a gospel of independence. It was pure sedition and over the past year it had been read all through the colonies – from Newfoundland to Barbados – and all men were debating its ideas. They loved it or they hated it! Tim and Sadie had gone the whole year without a chance to read it. They had got hold of short pamphlets with excerpts taken from it. They had read other pamphlets, too, with the writings of Sam Adams and Thomas Jefferson and others, but they did not have *Common Sense* – not the whole book, cover to cover – the book everyone had been talking about.

Then Matilda – Matilda Walker of all people! She had got hold of a copy down in occupied New York City – of all places! When her husband found her with it he threw it on the fire. Moses Walker was as much a loyalist as any and in his house he would not allow any questioning of Parliament's right to tax colonies, nor the use of any rude and offensive terms like "tory." Before the invasion of the previous summer, he had kept his opinions to himself and escaped the attention of the rebel Committee and Commission for Detecting and Defeating Conspiracies. Once the British had arrived in force though, he felt sure that "law and order" was here to stay.

While he and his wife were still snarling at each other, Sadie had grabbed the book out of the fire, patted out the flames with her dust rag, quickly replaced it with a book of sermons, and snuck *Common Sense* out of the room. By doing this she was guilty of three crimes. She was guilty of sedition because she had put herself in possession of seditious material, written or spoken words aimed to incite hatred of king and government. She was guilty of theft because she had taken another person's goods with the intention of permanently depriving her of it. And too, she was guilty of willful damage to property for burning the book of sermons, though likely nobody would notice it missing. But at the same time, Sadie had committed no crimes. What she did was in support of a revolution that had been made legal by the Declaration of Independence, signed in Philadelphia six months before. That document had made all acts of rebellion legal in those colonies that had voted to establish an independent United States of America. From that moment, the new nation had been in existence and had become legal authority. British law was now foreign law, even in the territory the "foreigners" had grabbed back. It was all as confusing as it was exciting.

And now that they had *Common Sense*, Tim and Sadie had been reading it almost every evening. Tim would come over when she was milking the cows and making butter. With the short days of winter, he was off work early. One of them would take a turn reading while the other milked. They had read the whole book through so many times they had lost count. It would not have been half so interesting had it not been a banned book, and not half so exciting had there not been a war in progress. They would read and discuss what it said, and then compare it with what other writers had to say and what people in town were saying. People like Amos Short, who had an opinion on everything.

Tim and Sadie would copy out the more stirring passages and carry them in their pockets so they could work at memorizing them when they had spare time. Tim would do this while he cut wood. He would take out his notes, read a line, put it back and recite the line over and over in his head. He told others his notes were from the Bible. Nobody could fault a boy for wanting to memorize passages from the Bible, not while God might be watching. Josh was happy with it because he could tease Tim for being a Methodist fanatic. Tim did not mind that, since it was not true. It was always easy enough to forget about Josh.

Today, Josh was all the easier to forget because he was back with the others cutting wood while Tim Euston was driving a wagon. A wagon! Imagine! Tim Euston was out on the open road where he could recite the words of Thomas Paine at the top of his voice. "It is repugnant to reason, to the universal order of things, to all examples from former ages, to suppose that this continent can longer remain subject to any external power. The most sanguine in Britain does not think so. The utmost stretch of human wisdom cannot, at this time, compass a plan, short of separation, which can promise the continent even a year's security. Reconciliation is now a fallacious dream." (from *Common Sense*, December 1776)

But then Tim stopped his recitation. He was coming within sight of King's Bridge. This was a strategic point where General Howe had set up a large base. Armed soldiers patrolled both sides, day and night. Tim drove up to the end of a short line – not really a line for there was only two wagons, a man leading pack horses and three more on foot. Tim stopped and waited. A sentry in a red and white uniform walked up.

"Where you headed, my boy?"

"The city," replied Tim, as he handed over his traveling papers. The man read them, handed them back, said, "Carry on," and walked on to wait for the next wagon that was just coming into view. Someone called out an order and the three wagons were allowed to cross the bridge without any further delay. On the other side, Tim passed by the camp with its rows of newly built log huts and red coated soldiers milling about. Then he was onto the rolling meadows of Manhattan Island and soon to be riding into the city.

That was easy, thought Tim. He had heard people complain about the long delays. Today the redcoats could not have seemed more at ease. There must not have been any rumors going around about smugglers. *The perfect time to be one,* thought Tim. *It's a shame I'm not smuggling something – smuggling for a rebel army while reading seditious materials. Wouldn't those two tasks just go hand in hand?*

More miles passed without any problems. The sun was shining and there was a mild breeze from the south, smelling of the sea. Another checkpoint came along and the traveling papers worked their magic again. Back on the road, Tim got out his pages of seditious material and went to work. By the time the church steeples of New York City came into sight, he could recite another paragraph by heart.

There was a lot of traffic coming and going – big wagons and small, men on horses and so many people on foot. Tim was in good spirits though and could not help but laugh when he saw the gibbet hanging from its scaffold. *The next time I pass by,* he told himself, *it might have itself an occupant. And some day the corpse it displays might be mine!*

Tim had been told to get over to Broadway, follow it past the burnt out remains of Trinity Church and then ask for directions. It was not just the grand old church that had been lost. He had heard it described, but still it was a sad sight – 500 houses burnt to the ground. It had happened when the invaders had seized the city and all that was left were chimneys and foundation stones. The poorest of the refugees, mostly escaped slaves, were living amongst the ruins. The King had offered them freedom if they escaped the rebels and joined with the loyalists. The Army had set up tents made out of old sails. Everyone was calling it "Canvas Town." Tim had heard that some of these tents had fifty people living in them. Today he could see hundreds of refugees out to enjoy the mild weather. A few boys were kicking a wicker ball around the street and little ones waddled about with dolls made out of corn husks. It was nice to see children at play, but so many of them seemed half starved. They were probably just sickly though, likely with scurvy. It was not just the prisoners of war who were doing without.

"Hey! Keep your eyes open!" yelled a man in another wagon. Tim's team of horses had seen the man coming and had stopped, but no thanks to Tim's driving. Nothing had happened, but Tim was still embarrassed.

"Now now, don't ask too much of the boy," called a man on foot as he took hold of one of the horses' bridles. "'Tis just Tim Useless here. You can't demand too much of him."

It was Thomas Pellis. *Now everyone will hear about this,* Tim told himself. *Josh will hear about it! And I didn't hurt anything!*

"Lost, are you son?" asked Thomas with his yellow-toothed smile. He could afford to smoke tobacco, but it seemed he could not afford to get the local surgeon to scrape his teeth.

"I just got here," said Tim, trying to sound calm.

"Just got here and in trouble already!" Thomas chuckled as his voice rose. "Ha! You're in fine form, you are! True to your reputation!"

"Do you know where Abe Balding lives?" asked Tim quietly, hoping he would not.

"Abe Balding? Which Abe Balding are you talking about?"

"Ah... I don't know."

"Well, you should!" laughed Thomas, almost shouting again, "since there's only one! Ha! Only one with a house in this city!"

"Could you point me the way?" asked Tim as he looked to the side. Passersby were laughing.

"Ah, but wouldn't it be better if I lead the way? Safer for all, wouldn't you say?"

"I'd be obliged," said Tim as he listened to more laughter. While Thomas led the horses along the street, he asked a few questions about where the wagon came from and why Tim was not home at work, insinuating he suspected him to be a runaway and a thief. Tim assured him all had been arranged by John Gainer, though he knew it was hardly necessary. Thomas was just teasing, like always.

"Good evening, Thomas," said a man on the street.

"And good evening, Abe," replied Thomas. "Look what I've found here, a lost boy who says he's a-looking for you. Tim Useless he says his name is."

"Tim Useless?" chuckled the man. "Not Tim Euston? I'd heard wrong then. I'll have to be getting the wax cleaned out of my ears, won't I?"

"It's Euston," said Tim as he climbed down.

"As I said, Tim Useless. And may I introduce you to Abe Balding. And if you lift his hat you see 'tis so."

"And you, Thomas Pellis," said the man. "Now what does that sound like? 'Promise Tell Us?' Promise you'll tell us you're on your way home, eh? Ha! How's that one, boy?"

"A good one," said Tim.

"And now, Tim Useless," said Abe as he put a hand on his shoulder, "I've a job for thee. A job that can't wait. You take this wagon round back of the house, unload the wood, stack it in the shed and then load your wagon back up with horse manure from the pile. Can you do that before suppertime?"

Tim said nothing. All that would take two hours. He was hungry now.

"Ah, but don't fret. There's a couple of boys there who will do it all for you. You'll eat and drink while they'll do your work. Now around the side with you and be quick about it. The rest of us are a-waiting upon thee."

"Yes sir," said Tim, who was glad to finally escape all the good humor. But as he led the horses he wondered. *What was Thomas doing here? First Nat was at the blacksmith's to see me off and now Thomas is here to greet me. Pellises going and coming!*

When *Common Sense* was published Paine was thirty-nine and had only been in America for two years. In England he had completed an apprenticeship as a corsetmaker and had also worked as a privateer, a schoolteacher, a tax collector and a tobacconist. He failed at each effort, blaming a corrupt monarchy and judiciary, along with bankers and traders. In his writings, Paine said that the achievement of liberty would require more than protests, boycotts and a few battles to improve the colonies' bargaining position. It would require a long hard war fought for a great objective. Any reconciliation would leave the King free to renew his attacks on colonial liberties. Complete independence would provide the only guarantee of freedom. The simple language and clear logic won over many and this included the commander of the American Army. When *Common Sense* first came out, George Washington had still been toasting the King in the officers' mess at Cambridge. But on January 31, 1776 in a letter to a friend, he wrote "the sound doctrine and unanswerable reasoning contained in the pamphlet *Common Sense*, will not leave numbers at a loss to decide upon the propriety of a separation."

Chapter 9

Looking for trouble.

The next morning, Tim was up and out by the break of dawn. He knew he had many miles ahead of him and he ought to be on his way north, but there was something he had to take a look at. He drove the wagon south towards the harbor to see the sight everyone had been talking about since the summer before. He left the wagon in the street and walked out to the end of a dock. There they were. They had first begun to arrive over at Staten Island on the second of July. They were the ships that had brought Major General William Howe and his thirty-two thousand red coated soldiers. Half of them still sat at anchor in the harbor and it was still quite a sight to see. Through a light mist the first beams of sunshine rose above the clouds and illuminated the lines, yards, masts and hulls of more than a hundred vessels. Most were transports and frigates, but a few were great battleships. Not the biggest ones, but still they were vessels with seventy guns and three and four decks and masts that rose two hundred and twenty feet above the water.

"Yea lad," said a red coated officer who walked up, "behold them. The guardian angels that protect the good and godly folk from rascals and rebels."

"They are," said Tim, but right away he was ashamed of himself for denying his commitment to the cause. For a patriot like Tim, these ships offered no warm feelings of security. They stood before him like a row of muskets all aimed at his heart. This royal fleet was nothing more than the brutish fist of tyranny – the enemy of freedom.

"That's the biggest of them out there, part of that group of five," said the man and he went on to brag of its cannons and crews and its service in battle. Next, he pointed out other vessels, telling of their accomplishments.

Tim stayed only for a few minutes until he began to shiver. He resented the fact that this man seemed to be as good and honest as any man. Tim preferred to think of the British as proud fools. He said he had to be going and thanked the officer with so much courtesy he must have left the man with the impression that he, Tim Euston, was as much a loyalist and royalist as any tory in New York City.

Tim gave the reins a shake and turned the wagon around. As he drove up Broadway, he could see the city was getting busy. There were large and small wagons and riders on horseback. There were men pulling carts and pushing wheelbarrows and many just on foot, going every direction. More were coming in than were going out, carrying goods to be sold that day. There were sacks of grain, peas and every sort of bean. And there were all the root crops too: carrots, parsnips, potatoes, turnips, onions, horseradish and beets. These staple foods provided the bread and soup that was standard fare for late winter and early spring. What meat ordinary folk could afford this time of year was usually cooked until almost black to maximize its effect on the flavor of soup. It was getting repetitious and everybody was looking forward to spring's first green onions.

After a solid mile of heavy traffic, Tim was back out in the countryside, passing field after meadow after field. He helped pass the time with his memorization of Thomas Paine. When he recited the words out loud, he would try mimicking the way an educated man would say them. He would have to go down to a whisper when someone was passing by, but he could go up to a shout when no one was near. "The powers of governing still remaining in the hands of the King, he will have a negative over the whole legislation of this continent. And as he has shown himself such an inveterate enemy to liberty and discovered such a thirst for arbitrary power, is he or is he not a proper man to say to these colonies, 'You shall make no laws but what I please'?" (From *Common Sense*, December 1775.)

The first checkpoint was no problem. The soldier had the unsure look of a new man on the job. When he examined the traveling papers, Tim could see his eyes were not moving from side to side. He was just pretending to read. Tim suspected he was filling in for someone else who was better qualified.

"On your way," the soldier ordered, as he turned away. Tim's first impulse was to feel sorry for him because he likely never had a chance to learn to read. *But,* wondered Tim, *maybe he had been given the opportunity and he had not cared to make the effort. Maybe he and his friends had just made a joint decision to refuse to learn.* Tim had seen that happen before, back when they were living in the city. His mother had sent him and Sadie to a woman who taught reading, writing and figuring out of her home. Tim had kept his studies secret from his friends for fear of what they might think. They regarded themselves as bold and brave for their refusal to allow book learning to be forced upon them. They might not want to have a friend who allowed himself to be pushed around by a mother and a schoolmistress. And what was more, Tim could hardly let them know he actually liked it.

When Tim got to King's Bridge, there was activity. Soldiers were walking about and there were at least ten wagons in line. A man with corporal's markings walked up. After he read Tim's papers he said, "Pull it over there." His order was not loud, but Tim knew from his tone that he would get nasty if not obeyed promptly. Englishmen were good at that sort of a tone. It hinted at more than was said – the sort of tone that said, "I'd just as soon see you stripped and flogged."

Tim drove the team as far as he thought he needed to, reined them in and waited for what seemed like a long time. Finally, the corporal spoke to an officer and pointed in Tim's direction. The officer nodded and the corporal saluted, turned and went into a hut. He came back out with a shovel.

"Pull another ten yards over that way and shovel out half your load, down to a foot deep. Then come over and find me when you're finished."

"Yes, sir," said Tim with a bow of his head. He took the shovel, set it behind him on the load, and with a shake of the reins drove the team forward and around to the spot. He got to work quickly, not wanting to antagonize anyone by looking lazy. When down to a foot – a half a foot in places – he jumped down and went to tell the corporal.

"Keep hold of that shovel and wait here."

Tim stood there, feeling out of place. Close by were more soldiers and huts built of squared logs and whitewashed. A number of muskets with fixed bayonets were lying against a post. *Ready to be grabbed hold of,* he thought, *were a force of patriot raiders to suddenly gallop over the hill.* He slowly stepped over to take a closer look. *The latest sort of a Brown Bess?* he wondered. His nose was close enough to smell the gun grease when he felt a hand on his shoulder.

"You can look, but don't touch," said a soldier's voice. It was friendly and menacing at the same time. "Not even with your pinkie finger. Someone might come bite it off, eh? Though, as for myself, I prefer them pickled to fresh off the hand."

Tim smiled at him and said, "I won't."

"Come!" said the corporal as he picked up one of the muskets. They went back to the wagon. The corporal climbed on and started poking the bayonet into the manure, stabbing down to the floorboards. He covered the box of the wagon in an orderly way, following a grid of imaginary lines. He was obviously looking for a hidden box or sack. For all Tim knew, there was one. And if there was it might be full of something illegal.

"What you looking for?" asked Tim.

"Sometimes these wagons carry more than they're supposed to. Stolen goods sometimes. And sometimes even a deserter in a box. Did you load it yourself?"

"Ah... no."

"No? Not a wise move, lad. You should never haul a wagon that you've not seen loaded with your own eyes. Otherwise, you might carry more than you'd reckoned on and then we might have to stretch your neck a bit."

Tim felt an unpleasant tingling in his neck. The man did not sound like he was joking. Tim had more questions, but he kept them to himself.

"Good enough," the man sighed, sounding disappointed. "Load her back up and be on your way."

By the time Tim made it through the lineup to the bridge, another hour had passed. The rest of the way up north went as well as could be hoped. He stopped in to see his sister and mother. They might not know about his new job. Sadie was off somewhere and his mother was tormented by a toothache. She had little to say in praise of him, but he could tell she was happy to see him entrusted with a team of horses and a wagon. As he talked, she got together a meal of cold meat and vegetables. Matilda came in and seemed sincerely pleased to see him there and to hear of his errand. "A manly task," she called it.

Tim left feeling energized by both the food and the praise. Back on the road north he kept at his memorization and recitation all the way to the farm. He had to keep quiet for a while though, when he met with a few of Colonel De Lancey's "cowboys." The colonel was from a wealthy family on Manhattan Island and he had raised a 500 man troop of light horse that had been given responsibility for patrolling the neutral ground – hunting for deserters and protecting the Army's supply routes. This group was as much a gentleman's sporting club as a military force. They were referred to by their enemies as "cowboys" because they were often seen driving cattle they had gained by plunder or secret purchase from unpatriotic farmers.

The older of the horsemen asked Tim whether he had seen anyone who might be a deserter. Tim had seen many people on the road and more than one could have been a deserter. He said no and showed the man his traveling papers that said he was permitted to continue on to a farm, belonging to a man named Felix, that was twelve miles north of Yonkers. The load of manure he carried would be spread on the fields as fertilizer. It was a long way to carry manure, but the man would understand. The carriers of firewood would rather have a low value backload than none at all.

"You're headed up into dangerous territory, my boy. We don't usually patrol that far, unless we're looking for trouble. You're aware of that, I hope."

Tim coolly shrugged his shoulders and said, "'Tis a risky task for sure, but if I'm robbed, I'll just walk back home and blame it on the robbers."

"Ha! Well, good for you then. With that sort of attitude, you might make a good soldier someday soon."

"I've been told I'm too young – maybe next year."

"Come to the city when you think you're ready and we'll put you to work for good King George. And in the meantime, you can be one of my scouts. You keep your eyes and ears open for word of deserters or smugglers. You lead me to the smoke and I'll find the fire."

"I'll do that sir," said Tim with a nod and a smile.

"Good for you then. I await your first report," he said and then signaled his men to follow.

"I'll do that," said Tim to himself as he watched them ride away, "but not for King George, I won't. Scout for George Washington, perhaps. Yea, and if this gets to be a regular run for me then I'm sure to see things that'll interest the forces of freedom. I'll just have to find me a contact to pass the information along to. That shouldn't be too hard."

At this time, "cowboy" was not meant as a compliment. The boy who tended cattle got no more respect than the shepherd or swineherd.

"Tory" comes from the Irish, toraidhe, which means pursuer. It was what the English called an Irish bandit until the 1680s, when reformers started to apply it to supporters of the King. During the War for Independence, tories were also called royalists, inimicals, the disaffected and the King's men. Continental General, Nathanael Greene, prohibited his soldiers from insulting civilians "with odious epithets of 'Tory' or any other indecent language, it being ungenerous, unmanly and unsoldierlike" (Colonel's Hutchinson's Orderly book.)

Chapter 10

Did it not come as a surprise?

The Felix farm was at the north end of the neutral ground, where a sort of law and order was imposed by armed and mounted men who often allied themselves with the American cause. Their activities included collecting an unofficial tax on residents, in the form of whatever the taxpayer had that they wanted. Their victims would joke about how the skinners would take all that a man had, including his skin. Tim, being whig, was sure the better of the skinners would never take more than what was fair. His resentment was reserved for Colonel De Lancey's "cowboys."

Tim had to wonder how good his traveling papers would be up north, since they had been signed by a known royalist. The signature that pleased a cowboy might not please a skinner. But no riders came to see if there was anything in the wagon worth taking. That was a relief, but also a small disappointment. Tim had heard a lot about them, but had never actually seen a skinner, not to know that he was one.

It was not yet sunset when Tim found the farm. It was easy to spot from John Gainer's description. "Just beyond where the road turns to go around a small pond with some young oaks on the far side of it. It'll be a clapboard house with two chimneys."

"Tim Euston!" called a gray haired man as he came round the side of the house.

"Yes, sir. How'd you know it was me?"

"I'd been told to expect a slim boy of sixteen years to arrive in the late afternoon with a team and a wagonload of manure – and here he appears as was prophesized."

"Too easy then."

"And besides, you were pointed out to me by John Gainer once when you were a-hacking away at a tree like it'd wronged you greatly."

"Ha! Well, sometimes I get to thinking about politics."

"Fighting imaginary battles, eh?" chuckled the man. Zeke Felix was gray haired, but he looked like the sort who used to be a redhead. "John said that you were a daydreamer. Said you're always imagining this and considering that and losing track of what happens before your eyes. Be that a fair assessment?"

"I don't... I suppose... ah... I can't say that..."

"Whoa now boy, you start thinking six things at once and pretty soon you be running six ways at once. Then we'll have to catch you in a net and put you in a cage."

"Oh... I don't..."

"Now, you must be hungry as a lost dog," said Zeke as he took hold of the horse's bridle. "You go around to the kitchen and get yourself a nice cup to refresh yourself. I'll have the boys shovel this out upon yonder field and we'll all be sitting round the table before you've fallen in love with the kitchen maid."

"I do thank you," said Tim as he climbed down.

"Oh, and she'll thank you too, she will. And I must thank thee for such a fine load of New York City horse manure. They say there's none quite like it out in the countryside."

· · · · ·

Tim started out next morning thinking that, with only a few sacks of carrots and beets for a load, he would make a quick trip home. It had been a pleasant stay and they had fed him well. "I could grow fat at this kind of work," Tim had said to the mistress, who had smiled and patted his head. *It was odd though,* he thought as he drove along. *She kept looking at me as if worried. Does she think I'll be murdered by highway robbers?*

Back in Yonkers, Tim returned the wagon to the blacksmith and assured him all had gone well and he had been easy on the horses.

"Good for you," the blacksmith said with a smile. "Now you'll be working the rest of the day here with me. I've hired you to do some woodcutting. Out back, you'll find a stack of logs. I've a good bucksaw all sharpened up and waiting for you. You'll be able to saw and split 'til sundown and you'll have barely gotten started, so you'd better get to it."

"I should," agreed Tim, trying to sound pleased. He wasn't. Like most boys, he preferred to work with others, even if one of them was Josh Gainer. *At least,* he thought, *I'll get plenty of memorizing done.*

When sunset finally told him he was finished for the day, Tim had gotten through all the lines of Thomas Paine that he had written down. He would need to copy out more. *At this rate,* he bragged to himself, *I'll have the whole book memorized in just over two years. Though, I suppose I'll forget what I did before, as I go along.* The minister had once told about monks who had memorized the entire Bible – Genesis through Revelation. *That's too much for me,* Tim had told himself.

When back in town, Tim heard the tinkle of cowbells. The town cowherd was bringing the dairy cattle back. Most households had a cow or two and they shared in the cost of pasturing them. It used to be a boy who tended them, but he had been replaced by a "rough looking Roger," who carried a rifle. This was out of fear of cows being stolen and it meant a higher cost for owners. It seemed the cost of everything was up. Wartime was hard times for those who could not find a way of getting rich off of it.

Tim decided to go see his sister. These days, Sadie was doing almost all the milking and other dairy work, so the return of cows meant she would be in the cowshed for hours. He could go eat supper at the Gainer's, but Tim was not that hungry. The blacksmith's wife had fed him, too.

"Good evening, Sister," he said when Sadie answered the door. She used to leave the door unlocked and he could go straight in. Now she was putting a post against it, in case a deserter or some other dangerous sort – Thomas Pellis, for example – was skulking about looking for food, shelter or whatever else.

"Good evening to you, Tim the teamster," she teased as she went back to her work. "I hear you've been down to the city and way back up north in two days only."

"My talents are in demand. And I hear you've been learning to make cheese when you're not scrubbing and scouring."

"Indeed I have been. Aren't we the fortunate ones to have such opportunities granted unto us?"

"Yea, count our blessings, we must. I've got to copy out more Tom Paine. I've been memorizing up and down the countryside."

"I knew you'd be, so I copied it out for you. I've got it hidden away right over here."

"Well, good for you, Sister. How's your memorization going?"

"Not a lot of Tom Paine. It's hard in this household. You never know who's going to look over your shoulder. If the master found a book of such sedition as that, well! I'd have to blame you for giving it to me and then you'd be back in jail again, wouldn't you?"

"I thought of what I'd do if I'm caught with my notes when I'm going across the King's Bridge. I'll just say that I can't read and that I'd found them blowing about in the street and hoped somebody would give me a reward for bringing them back."

"Good plan. And anyone would believe that you can't read, wouldn't they? You've that look of natural stupidity that's so beneficial to boys who need to avoid suspicion."

"But if only I was as dull looking as you, Sister. Think of what I could do then as a scout for the Army."

"Oh, but don't sell yourself short, Brother. Surely, you're way duller looking than me. When George Washington sends word that they're in need for a dull looking boy, they'll hear your name spoken of from the Jersies to Connecticut and beyond, for surely your fame has spread."

"Likely it has, but it's unfair, isn't it, when 'tis you who are duller looking by far."

"But I do wonder," said Sadie in a voice that had turned serious, "just what's behind your sudden good fortune. I'm wondering whether you'll be carrying more than just firewood – maybe not now, but later. Once you're a familiar sight on the road."

"Why would you think that?"

"Did it not come as a surprise to be called upon to do such a job when there's old men here in town who would do it cheaper?"

"Well… they need someone strong enough to load and unload."

"You and the boys could load it up and whoever it's shipped to could unload. They've no need for a strong young stripling like you to be doing the driving."

"I don't know about that. If they wanted an older man then why'd they come to me?"

"Exactly what I'm wondering, Tim Useless," Sadie replied, as she settled herself on her stool to start milking.

Chapter 11

You didn't see the look in his eyes.

"Now you be careful with that axe," called Josh. They were at a wooded area by the road, just south of town. "One slip and you'll chop a toe right off. And then you'll only be able to count up to nineteen."

"I'll take good care," said Tim with a smile. He was not sure whether to smile or not. Either could be taken as a smart comeback and Josh was in a sensitive mood.

"Yea," sighed Josh, "a boy's got to be extra careful when he just ain't got much of a head for numbers to start with."

"Indeed he does," agreed Tim with a nod as he kept at his work. He had just hacked down a small tree, about as thick as his thumb. Next, he would lay it on a block and chop it into lengths suitable for bundling. What Josh had to say did not bother him – not a lot. It was nothing Tim had not heard sixteen dozen times before. Or at least it would not have bothered him if they had not been working close to the road and if Becky Clark and her cousin Morgan had not come to see how they were doing. They carried baskets. That could mean they were on an errand, or simply that they did not want to look idle. The sun was warm and their cloaks were pulled back, showing one in a pink skirt and the other in yellow. Both had clean white caps and aprons with gathered edges. With each of his clever observations, Josh had the girls giggling, as much in admiration of him as in enjoyment of his humor.

Tim knew they were just a pair of ninnies and their opinions should hardly matter, but he could not force back the tightening of his scalp and the pain in his Adam's apple. Already his sister had him worrying about smuggling and jail. And now there was this. It was all too much! Something had to be done! Josh might be the master's son, but the honor of Tim Euston was at stake. Tim swallowed hard to relax his voice and shook his head to clear his mind. After the next comment on the subject of his uselessness, he looked at Josh with a confused expression. In a tone of sincere apology he said, "Oh... were you talking to me? I'm sorry, I wasn't listening."

No one laughed – no one except for Becky and Morgan. They burst out laughing, but then stopped short when they saw Josh give them a sharp look. It was not much they had done. It was just a spontaneous giggle, but the sound of it soothed Tim's spirit like a drink of warm cocoa on a bitter cold day. Tim felt restored. These girls – these high and mighty judges of the worth of sixteen-year-old boys – they had laughed out loud in support of Tim Euston. They had frustrated Josh and now they were rushing away – again giggling – at who knows what? It did not matter. This might be enough to keep Josh quiet for a half hour – maybe even more.

Josh gradually recovered and by afternoon, he was back in form. He was just through the story about the time his father had put Tim into the round storage shed and told him to go stand in the corner. He had just come to the punch line when he noticed his father, John Gainer, walking up. Josh seemed able to read the man's mind, for they only needed to give each other a look. The son turned away in disgust and John went to where Tim was still at work. Tim had seen him coming, but he wanted to be the last boy to take a break from his labor.

"Tim, we'll be needing you to take down another load."

"Yes sir," said Tim with a nod. "Pick it up at dawn?"

"Be there early and help get them hitched up."

"Was my work at the blacksmith's satisfactory?"

"He didn't complain," said John as he turned away.

. . . . .

After supper, Tim went to visit his mother and as he came through the door she saw a grin on his face.

"What is it, son?" asked Abby, who was having trouble deciding whether to be pleased or worried. "You're not headed back to the big city, are you?"

"Again already?" asked Matilda who was working with them. The supper dishes had been cleared away and the table was covered with yellow fabric. Though there were high prices for basic goods, the cost of luxuries was remarkably low for those who had money. The American Army might control the land beyond the neutral ground, but the Royal Navy controlled the seas and merchant ships kept docking at New York's wharfs, bringing delicacies like Russian anchovies, German mustard, French mushroom ketchup, Spanish olives, Italian confectionaries and Indian spices.

Matilda's husband Moses had agreed to pick up a bolt of Cathay silk for a new dress, along with everything else needed to make up a suit. He owned several patches of land and had a large crew of General Howe's regulars at work, cutting and sawing. Local workers were getting angry about the competition. All these soldiers and refugees meant thousands of idle hands. The price of labor was way down. Some who had considered themselves loyalists were now talking about going upcountry and begging the mercy of the committee, swearing an oath to be faithful citizens, so they could find enough work to feed their children.

"Already," said Tim with a nod. "And maybe until there's no more ice flowing down the river – a few weeks maybe. And... and if the people are in need of firewood, then firewood they shall have." This last part he said like a lawyer before a court. All his memorization was giving him the ability to mimic the better sort of man and here in the Walker home he had no reason to worry about putting on airs of quality.

Not unlike his Pellis in-laws, Moses Walker thought himself a gentleman and spent too much on clothing. He had inherited enough to live an easy life and was a small moneylender, distiller and landowner. He had acquired land at what looked like a bargain, only to find it was too stony for cultivation. Frustrated, he let it go back to woodland and now, with war and the price of firewood way up, he discovered it could make money after all.

"I've something for you," said Abby as she got up to go to the storage room. She came out with what at first looked like a wool blanket. "Try it on for size," she said as she let it unroll. It was a coat – a dark blue heavy wool coat. It was obviously not new, but even when bought used it could not have been cheap. Tim slipped one arm in and then the other. It was loose, but not by much. "A good fit for a boy who's likely still growing."

"Where'd you get it?"

"It was my cousin's," said Matilda. "When he was staying with us I got it for him, but then he took a spurt and grew right out of it. When your mother heard you would be driving a wagon she insisted I sell it to her. It's a bit worn but, it'll still keep you nice and warm when there's wind and rain. And that's what matters, isn't it?"

"It is," said Tim. Wool fibers thicken when damp. This makes the fabric grow so dense it can repel both wind and water. Other sorts of fabric get soggy and cold. With a heavy wool coat, Tim could drive through a long day of rain without shivering. Equipped with a proper coat, he would be even better suited for the job of driving a team.

"You'll be taken for a grown man with such a coat as that," said Sadie. "They'll think you apprenticed to a silversmith."

"Oh, and I've got something else," said Matilda and she went to the next room and came back with an old hat – the sort of ordinary wide-brimmed felt hat that almost every man was wearing with the brim pinned up on three sides. Again, it was worn and unfit for a gentleman, but it was as good as the hat John Gainer usually wore.

"I don't know that I can afford it," said Abby.

"You paid me too much for the coat!"

"No, I didn't!"

"I could pay for it," said Tim, who had a few pennies saved. "I could start anyways."

"Can't I give away my husband's old clothes?"

"Well…"

"It's yours, Tim Euston, in exchange for all the lovely music you and your sister have given us."

During their better times back in Boston, Tim and Sadie's father had paid for music lessons. They had started by learning simple tunes on the tin whistle. Later, they each got a violin. When they performed together, Sadie would usually play a simpler base line. When Matilda had guests over for dinner, she would borrow Tim and the two of them would provide the entertainment.

To prepare for the event, a teacher would often be hired to help them learn a new piece. They usually practiced in the evening, out in the cowshed, after other work was done. Matilda did not realize just how much she was demanding, but the two of them never complained, thinking they had little choice and that they ought to be grateful for the opportunity to better themselves. "There!" she said, turning to Abby. "Now I no longer feel in debt to your son."

"Oh you..."

"And not another word about it!"

"I just hope my workmates will forgive me," said Tim. He and his fellow woodcutters usually wore smocks or other more humble attire. The boys would have opinions about Tim's coat. Clothing made a statement. The sorts of tradesmen who were better paid and worked indoors, like silversmiths and gentleman's tailors, dressed up as a show of their higher rank in society.

"Just use it for driving," said his mother. "It'd be too warm for woodcutting."

"You ought to dress for the job," added Matilda. "You don't see coach drivers in smocks."

. . . . .

It was the day after next when Tim found out how badly he needed to dress for the job. The ride to the city went well, with sunshine and dry roads. The trip back north was not too bad either, not until he was within six miles of the Felix farm. Black clouds rose in the northern sky and Tim was hit by a cold wind that came right out of the mountains – rain, sleet and then snow. His face was cold, but he still was not shivering. Were he dressed in his smock, he would have been soaking wet and chilled to the bone.

With bad weather came glum thoughts. And it was Sadie's fault, too. She had him wondering why they chose a boy to do the driving when a half lame old man would do it for less. Tim might be small, but he was a good woodcutter. Three years at swinging an axe and pushing a saw had made him strong. The cost of his labor would be better spent on that sort of work, rather than driving a wagon. Tim knew if it were up to him alone and, if he were working at a day rate and not as an apprentice, then he surely would have chosen woodcutting. Sure, it was a step up in stature to drive a wagon, but money's money. *So why,"* he asked himself, *would John Gainer want to make Tim Useless happy? And why would he want to make his own son suffer from jealousy?*

Tim was able to forget his doubts once he got to the farm. Again, he ate while others unloaded the manure and reloaded the wagon with sacks of wheat. *Good thing it's just a few sacks,* thought Tim, remembering that the soldier at King's Bridge had warned him about making sure he knew what was in his wagon. Tim could peek between the sacks. Were they to reload the wagon with a big pile of something then he would have had to unload and reload to see what was underneath. And he would have to do it after he was well down the road and far enough away. He would not want to offend them with his suspicions.

·　·　·　·　·

"God speed thee, boy," said the gray haired mistress next morning as Tim climbed on the wagon.

Again she had the look of worry – almost dread. It was irritating for Tim. It was scary. It was like she knew he was doomed to some great misfortune. *Could you save it for your sons?* thought Tim as he drove off.

Now it was Tim who was worrying. He tried to cheer himself up by reciting some Thomas Paine, but that was hardly cheerful either, with all his calls for war and self-sacrifice. Finally, as he rounded a pond, Tim decided to do it. He reigned in the horses and got down from the wagon. A quick look one way and the other reassured him that no one was watching. He walked to the side of the pond, broke off a willow stick and brought it back. He held the stick inside the box of the wagon, using it to measure the depth. With his finger to mark the point, he held the stick on the outside. Sure enough, it was a few inches deeper. That meant the box had a false bottom, concealing a hidden compartment. It would be about a hand's width deep, just enough for muskets or cannonballs or whatever else that could be bought from dishonest soldiers who were supposed to be guarding the King's munitions and not selling them.

Word of corruption had been going around. There had been rumors of John Gainer being somehow involved with the patriots – or the "rebels" if it was a tory talking. John had always been out for training with the militia and he had sounded as angry at unjust taxes as most others, right up until Billy Howe and the British Army in North America had won a string of victories that had taken them right up to his doorstep.

Probably, wondered Tim, *his wife just wore him down with all her lecturing on his duty to his family. But maybe he's still trying to help the cause behind her back. Maybe he's smuggling in muskets for the Army – bought from crooked regulars and sold to good patriots.*

The middlemen in this exchange would not likely get silver coins, not from the American Army. Likely they would only get some of the Continental dollars that the Continental Congress had been printing for the previous two years. Officially, the "Continentals" were hard currency, but right from the start, they had been trading for less and now they were down to half their face value. And they would be rendered worthless if the King's invasion force prevailed and the patriots lost heart and gave up. All they would need to accomplish that would be the winning of a few more battles to wear down the will of the people to resist – wear them down with bad news and high casualty rates and high prices.

But still, thought Tim, *this puts me in the thick of it, doesn't it? If I'm carrying smuggled goods then I'm part of the struggle and I'm risking my life for the greater good of the liberty-loving people of America, aren't I? I'm taking chances and I'm risking all for the good cause! Though, it's demanded no great courage so far, has it? I'd never chosen to take any risk. It was forced on me without my ever knowing. I'm just an ignorant apprentice sent out on an errand. 'Tim Useless' has been given a risky mission, but he's too simple to be entrusted with any knowledge of it. And who better for dangerous work than 'Tim Useless', the boy who has no future in carpentry because he keeps making stupid mistakes?*

Tim climbed back on the wagon and drove off, wondering how soon he would be met by a patrol – one of Colonel De Lancey's. *If I can find a false bottom with a stick then why haven't the soldiers? And what about the cowboys? They'll search me and I'll be arrested and led down to the city, walking behind a horse with a rope tied round my neck – there to be tried, convicted and hanged. Well, likely not hanged. They'd likely believe me when I said I didn't know nothing about it. And then I'd be offered the option of serving time aboard a ship of the Royal Navy, like Jack Lauper and Dan Eliot. Or more likely I'd be put on a chain gang, cutting firewood, out in the woods somewhere – likely far away. In Nova Scotia, likely. That's what I'm good for. I'll do the same as I do here, only for worse food. And with no chance to read the writings of Tom Paine.*

After he left the wagon at the blacksmith's shop, Tim decided to stop to see his mother so she would know he had made it back safely. *And if I'm called upon to take another load then... then this will likely be the last time I ever see her, other than at trial. She'll see me in chains behind the prisoner's bar and then after it's all over, she'll see me led back out the door. And what then? There's many who die in prison, aren't there? Who's to say I won't die?*

"I'm back," said Tim as he came through the door. This time he came with no smiles or false modesty.

"Oh Tim," said Abby. "God be praised. The drive went well?"

"It did. No trouble at checkpoints. The coat kept me warm when I was going up north and the weather hit. I would have been frozen without it."

"Oh, I'm glad. Matilda will be pleased to hear it's being put to good use," she said, looking down at her work. She seemed distracted and her brow was in a knot.

"Toothaches worse than usual?" asked Tim.

"Oh, it's not that bad."

"Do me a favor, Mom and get them all pulled. I lay awake worrying about you and your teeth."

"Oh Tim, don't be a pain yourself."

"Where's Sadie?"

"Out in the yard chopping up sticks, or maybe she's in the cowshed. The Widow Kayhill has been teaching her to make cheese. She'll make a fine dairymaid before long."

"And a fine dairywife for a fine dairyman. Little and good like a Welshman's cow."

"Don't you go teasing her!"

"I'd never tease her, not my sister! Now remember, you promised me to get them all pulled," he said while reaching for the door latch.

"I never did!"

· · · · ·

Tim knocked on the cowshed door and called "Sadie!"

"Around here!" he heard her call from outside. He walked around and found her with a hatchet, cutting up sticks on a chopping block. They were from a bundle just like the ones he hauled. "All went well?" she asked.

"No holdups. I could have got back last night before dark. Maybe I shouldn't have stayed there."

"You might as well have stayed," said Sadie, "You'd just be back for more work."

"Better useful than useless."

"Well, you'll always be that."

"They call you 'Sadie Useless'!"

"Just because of you!"

"No no, Sister! You've got your head in the clouds as often as I do."

"You're worse by far!"

"But you're just never tested like I am, with all my having to take measurements."

"I am so tested! Last week, I added the salt twice and the master said the soup tasted like seawater!"

"No no no girl, you're supposed to be countering my point with a counterpoint, not supplying me with supporting evidence."

"Oh! Don't be too smart or I'll stop feeling sorry for you."

"Well..." said Tim, but suddenly he recalled the hidden compartment and his likely future as a convicted criminal.

"What is it?"

"It's nothing."

"Well then, nothing's got you all a-looking like you've just seen a ghost."

"But I have! Right behind you he is! Can't you feel his cold hand upon your shoulder?"

"Don't even talk that way!"

"But I'm only telling you what I see before my eyes!"

"Tim!"

"All right, I'll... but take a look at that man over there," he said, pointing over the fence and across the street to a thin man with sharp features. "Doesn't he look like he could be a demonic spirit? He's maybe the killer of Amos."

"Where?"

"Right there!"

"That's just Abner Wall," says Sadie. "He always looks like that. He's a trader from down in the city."

"Does he always look like he thinks he's being watched?"

"Indeed, like he's always on his guard. Maybe he sees ghosts."

"You suppose he might have been the one who killed Amos?" asked Tim.

"No! And why should I? And anyways, it likely was Jack who killed him. They were both drunks, weren't they – Amos and Jack both? And haven't they each been in a hundred brawls?"

"They have but... but that Abner Wall, he gave me such a dirty look the other day. It was the day after we got back up from the city. I was looking for you at the Pellis store and when I came round the house, he was there, looking like he'd caught me with...'with the knife in my hand' as they say."

"He's likely just a friend of Thomas's who's preferring to believe his friend's side of the story. And why shouldn't he? The judges did."

"You think he was staring daggers at me just for wronging his dear friend Thomas?"

"Staring daggers?"

"You didn't see the look in his eyes," muttered Tim as he wondered whether the King's regulars and the loyalist militia were the only forces he needed to fear.

Chapter 12

Have I said too much?

"Josh, whose coat is that?" asked Eustace Gainer with a dark tone of motherly disapproval. She was coming home and the boys were out in the street.

"Just Tim's," Josh replied, as he gave her one of his lovable smiles.

"Give it back to him!"

Josh was wearing Tim's new coat and had been amusing the other woodcutters with a story about what Tim had to do to get such a gift from old Thomas Pellis. Now his mother had spoiled all the fun. And just when he had been getting to the good part. He sighed and shook his head as he pulled off the coat and tossed it over. Tim caught it and carefully examined a split seam under the armpit, to bring it to the attention of Eustace.

"Did you do that?" she asked, knowing from the expressions on both faces that there was only one correct answer.

"It must have been that way already," Josh replied, innocently.

"Give it to me," she said to Tim. They all knew she would repair it before anybody got their supper and that Josh would be made to regret his sins.

"To your chores! All of you!" she ordered, as she turned towards the door. Tim followed her inside without a look back at Josh. Tim knew Eustace would more than even the score on his behalf and he did not want to appear to be taking more than his fair share of pleasure in it. Josh might have torn his coat and teased him, but the first born boy was suffering under the belief that a valuable reward had clearly gone to the wrong boy. Tim now realized how wrong he was. He knew that when John Gainer had given the job to him, he had committed nothing less than an act of cruelty. What could be worse than selecting a boy for a mission that would probably cost him a long sentence of imprisonment – false imprisonment – unjust penal servitude during wartime – a virtual death sentence! Tim understood this, but for now he was willing to take the bad with the good. And it was sweet pleasure to see Josh Gainer suffer the torment of an envious fool.

"Hand me my kit," Eustace ordered, once they were inside. It was a normal speaking voice, but she could project it. She could project it so far, the old woman across the street likely heard it. If only she had been born a man, Eustace Gainer could have made so powerful a preacher.

Tim stepped quickly towards the sewing kit, picked it up gently and brought it to her. Without waiting for further instructions, he started setting up the table. The folding frame and planks rested against the wall when not in use. This was the first of several tasks that Tim did in preparation for supper. Tonight he would demonstrate his gratitude by doing his duty with all the speed and silence he could manage. Tim had been assigned indoor work when he might have been sent out to the barn to fork hay or shovel manure. There was a reason why the woman of the house called upon Tim to help inside. He was a natural play-actor and, when doing this, Tim would straighten his posture and speak in the refined voice of the blue-coated servant of a wealthy household. He had got in the habit without realizing he was doing it. It had just seemed appropriate for the job. Eustace liked it. Combined with his solemn expression, Tim cast an aura of refinement over the evening meal.

"Josh, your father's good shoes need polishing," said Eustace without looking up from her needle.

"Yes Mother," he replied, after a pause. Tim could hear the frustration in Josh's voice – almost pain. Shoe polishing was the job of the youngest son. And the shoes did not even need polishing. And Josh would be expected to keep the shoes on the floor while he polished them. This would put him on his knees before both his mother and, even worse, before his primary adversary. And it would not end there. After he had polished them once, he would be told to polish them again. She would say "and this time, do a proper job." And all the while he was doing it, he would receive a sermon on respect for personal property. Even the elder woman servant by the fireplace frowned in agreement, while the red haired girl-of-all-work smirked. With all this happening, Tim could, for just a little while, forget he would probably soon be contemplating his future while sitting in a New York City jail.

When supper was over and everything put away and ready for the morning, the Gainer household, as always, gathered around the fireplace for stories, songs and handiwork. While the boys knitted or carved, Josh read from a book of sermons. Next, Tim was asked to play a slow and mournful tune on his violin while Eustace accompanied him on a dulcimer. Finally, John read from the Bible. It was after a long passage from the Book of Job that John delivered the final blow to his son. "Tim," he said while getting up, "I'll be needing you to take down another load." The room went silent in sympathy for poor Josh. If he had looked up, he would have seen everyone staring at him.

. . . . .

The weather was good and Tim got his load of wood to the city and exchanged it for another load of manure. The next day it was cool and windy on the road north and Tim had to push himself to keep up with his memorization. He even found himself wondering why he was bothering to spend so much time on so pointless an effort. How many elegant phrases did he need to have ready to use in debates on the topic of loyalty versus freedom? *Am I planning any career that demands an education?* he asked himself. *And besides, you have to have a schooling to truly have an education. Nobody was ever hired on the strength of what he learned on his own. I'm being trained to be a carpenter and I'll never even be that! I'll be the best-spoken woodcutter in the Colony of New York. Yea, that's what I'll be, for sure! I'll work side by side with bound servants and slaves. And if I ever have a wife, I'll keep her in a shack barely fit for cattle. I'll likely marry an old maid who's given up hope for a better man. And as the years pass she'll even the score against me by belittling my every move. It'll be like I'm married to Josh! And that's assuming I don't die first, doesn't it? Die of jail fever in the city, or more likely die of cold – shiver to death – way up in the wilds of Nova Scotia where I'll be wearing a ball and chain while I saw planks for good old King George.*

With that mournful lament repeating in his mind, Tim found himself arriving at the British encampment at King's Bridge. He felt his stomach tighten. Somehow, he knew that today would mark the end of his career as a smuggler. *No, don't be stupid!* he ordered himself. *Just look bored and irritated by the delay and they'll suspect nothing.*

Tim pulled up to the end of the line of wagons. A red coated soldier walked up, looking at Tim as if he recognized him.

"Good day," said Tim. "Keeping you busy, looks like?"

"Pull it over there," the man replied, in a Scottish accent, sounding angry.

Tim did what he was told and waited. It did not take long. Another soldier came out with a shovel and told him to dig it out. This time, he stayed to watch. Tim hurried, thinking this would show the man he did not dread finishing the task.

"Down to half a foot?" Tim asked when he thought he was finished.

"All of it," replied the soldier.

All of it? wondered Tim as he glanced around, but then he noticed something strange. Over by the larger of the log huts stood Abner Wall, talking to an officer. Abner had his hands up in the air as if he was troubled by something. *What's he doing here?* Tim asked himself as he turned back to his shoveling.

"That's enough," said the officer, who had just walked over after his talk with Abner.

"Yes sir," said Tim and he looked at the soldier and saw a puzzled expression, as if what the officer had said had come as a small surprise.

"Come," said the officer to the soldier and they walked away towards the hut.

Tim wondered what he should do next. *Wait? Refill the wagon?* He decided to wait, for now at least. Abner Wall was gone from sight, but he might be inside the hut.

Another wagon pulled up and another soldier took charge of it. It was loaded with manure as well. *The city's primary export,* thought Tim. He watched the driver unload it. The soldier climbed on to poke about. Nothing was found. The driver was told to reload and go on his way.

Finally, Tim made a decision. He started to reload his wagon, thinking it might at least get somebody out to tell him to unload again. He finished, but still no one was taking an interest in him. He sighed, got back in his seat, took the reins in his hands, gave them a shake and started off, pulling around to get in the lineup.

"Hold on!" snapped the soldier, who had emerged from the hut. Tim felt his flesh creeping beneath his skin. "Let's see your papers again," he ordered. Tim pulled them out of his pocket and handed them over. The soldier glanced at them and gave them back. "On your way, boy," he said, this time giving Tim a knowing look before he turned away.

At first, Tim hesitated, unsure about whether to take what the soldier had said seriously.

"Move along!" called another soldier. Tim obediently gave the reins a shake and the horses started towards the bridge, obviously more confident than their driver. Tim felt certain that at any moment he would hear the shout – the order to stop – the capture – the iron cuffs on his wrists. But nothing happened. *What are these doings?* he wondered. *Why was Abner Wall here? Is it a coincidence? Has Abner paid a bribe? Is Abner my secret employer? How could it be, when Abner had looked at me with such suspicion in his eyes?*

· · · · ·

Darkness was falling when Tim made it to the Felix farm. This time one of the old man's sons came out to take the wagon. With a smirk on his face he asked how the trip went.

Tim shrugged a shoulder. "For a while there, I thought I'd been caught until I saw..." Tim hesitated and looked down.

"Good boy," laughed the man. "You might know more than I need to know. Now you just leave me to unload while you go in and get yourself something to eat. A long day on a rough road in a cold wind – it can wear a man out, can't it?"

Tim agreed and said something about his mother's good cooking, but all the while, he kept wondering about his comment: "You might know more than I need to know."

"Made it back before dark?" called Mrs. Felix from the door.

"All went well, except for the weather."

"I've a nice stew set aside."

"I was hoping for that."

"Come now and wash up. We've all eaten. I was wondering whether you'd even make it at all, what with the delays. We've heard stories of folks having to spend more time waiting than driving."

"We have, too," agreed Tim, though he was not really listening. John Gainer had never told Tim he was carrying illegal goods. But now, Tim had all but admitted to the son that he knew about the hidden compartment. *Have I said too much?* Tim asked himself as he came into the kitchen.

Chapter 13

Maybe I'm just dreaming.

To spare poor Josh the torment of his presence, Tim was sent a half mile north of town to cut wood by himself. The day passed slowly, as Tim kept trying to think of something other than hidden compartments, army tribunals and hard labor in the cold rain of Nova Scotia. The cloud cover was heavy, so he was only able to tell evening was coming once the light grew so dim that he found it hard to see what he was doing.

As he slouched into town, Tim heard the clanging of cowbells. That meant he had missed supper. It would not matter. Mrs. Gainer would have set aside something for him. In fact, she probably saved an extra big helping and would likely serve it to him right in front of Josh.

I'll stop by the cowshed, he thought to himself. *That way Josh will be hungry again by the time I'm home.*

Tim felt his shoulders straightening as he walked through town. The rain was starting, but was still a light drizzle. *Snow by morning,* he thought, imagining bright sun on white snow.

"Sadie, it's me," he said, tapping on the door.

"Is it raining yet?" she asked as she pulled it open.

"A bit," he replied. He sat down on a stool and leaned back against a post. Sadie went back to her milking.

"How's Mom?" asked Tim.

"Worse."

"Oh."

"Sick in bed now. Her face is all swollen up."

"Oh," he sighed and shook his head in frustration. The thought of her toothaches and her refusal to accept proper care was enough to give him a headache. And this was on top of the burden of worry he bore already – criminal conviction and hard labor.

"What are you sighing about?" asked Sadie.

"Nothing," he muttered. He knew that under no circumstances could he tell his sister about the threat that hung over him.

"You're looking like a sad dog."

"No, I'm not."

She waited for him to say more, but he did not. Finally, she said, "I know how to make cheese now."

"There's a false bottom in the wagon!" Tim blurted it out, as if she had forced it out of him. "I don't know what's in it, but I probably would have been caught and jailed if Abner Wall hadn't been there."

"Where?"

"At the King's Bridge."

"What'd he do to stop you from getting caught?"

"I don't know! He was there and talking to an officer and then the same officer called off the soldier who was about to give the wagon a good going-over. He would have likely found the hidden compartment and arrested me for a smuggler."

"What do they pay you for doing this?"

"I... I get the same pay as always…"

"And what's that? Room and board?"

"And clothing! And training! And two pence a week!"

"And you get to look like you're a grown man with your own team and wagon."

"And I can do some trading on my own account too!"

"So you labor all day and place your life in great peril for that much, only. Well, it ain't much for..."

"I eat a lot!"

"I suppose it's plenty then."

"If I don't get caught, it's plenty," said Tim, after a pause.

"Why didn't they tell you about the false bottom? You were just told you'd be hauling wood down to the city and then picking up manure for a backhaul."

"Well..."

"How'd you find out about it?"

"With a stick. The inside of the box isn't as deep as the outside. There's room enough for muskets. After me getting through like that at the King's Bridge... well... it all seemed too strange, so I started to wonder."

"Maybe you're not so stupid as you're supposed to be."

"Maybe I'm not," said Tim, half to himself. They sat in silence, broken only by the squirting of milk into the bucket. Sadie was getting good at milking. With all her carrying of water and milking of cows, she was growing stronger than many boys her size.

"Maybe that's what Abner suspects," said Tim. "That I'm not so stupid as I'm supposed to be. And maybe that's what got him looking so nervous."

"Maybe."

"But the look he gave me when he saw me come round the side of the house, last week. If looks could kill, I'd have been dead."

"Abner's often in to see Nat," said Sadie, "and when there's no one else in the store, they'll talk in hushed voices."

"I saw Nat up at the blacksmith's, the first morning that I drove the wagon. He came out and begged apology for doubting my innocence."

"Good for Nat."

"But when I was first walking up to them – Nat and the blacksmith – they took a look at me and laughed."

"Laughed? At what?"

"At me! Or that's what I thought at first. Then I told myself I was... I don't know. I figured it couldn't be me. What'd they have to laugh at me about?"

"The stories that Josh tells."

"I suppose."

"And I've been wondering whether Nat Pellis was up to something," said Sadie as she got up to pour the full bucket into a crock. "Him and his Uncle Thomas, too. Thomas is wearing new clothes these days and how's he paying for them? That's what Matilda's been wondering. Thomas buys for the store down in the city and along the river, but what's he or Nat selling these days that'd be letting either of them prosper? Sure, prices are up, but the countryside is half empty of people. She says Thomas has no hand in the cropping of wood or anything else. Where's he getting the money?"

"Thomas was down in the city the first day I got there. He helped me find the house that I was looking for. In the morning, Nat was there to see me leave and Thomas was down in the city to see me arrive. It's an odd chance, ain't it?"

"As if Thomas was there to watch out for you?"

"I don't know! He was there and he knew the house. That's all I know."

"But of course!" whispered Sadie. "If he's in with the others on some illegal trade, then they'd figure they'd have to have somebody down there, wouldn't they? A 'Tim Useless' would be too stupid to find the house himself. And they wouldn't want you lost and asking one man after another and making folks start to wonder who you are and what you're doing with a wagon and team. And they'd be hoping that 'Tim Useless' was stupid as that too, for otherwise you'd be smart enough to figure out that something's going on and that the wagon has a false bottom. Then you'd be demanding more money."

"But... I don't know," sighed Tim. "It just doesn't make sense. Both Nat and Thomas – they both just seem like such a pair of tories. And what smuggling would there be coming out of the city and up through here besides stolen muskets and ammunition on their way to George Washington?"

"Well, I don't know that Nat truly is a tory – not at heart. That's what Mom says, too. When he's over to visit his sister, he'll sound like he's as much a tory as the best of them. He'll belittle the 'rebels' and the 'republicans' and he'll speak so well of 'loyalists'. But he knows the master won't hear a word said against good King George. And when he's back at the store and talking to a fellow that he knows is leaning the other way, then we'll hear him say 'patriot' or 'whig,' instead of 'rebel' and 'tory' instead of 'loyalist.' He can change his politics as fast as he changes his hat, just to suit who's listening. And even if he was loyal to good King George, so are all the redcoats who are out a-stealing the goods that are sold to the smugglers."

"But... but it ain't neither Nat nor Thomas who's ordered me down to the city. It's my own master, John Gainer! And I just can't see him mixed up with the likes of Nat and Thomas and Abner."

"Well, I don't know," said Sadie.

"In with smugglers he might be, sure. But not with any of them. And anyways, they all say John's been refusing to take sides."

"Or refusing to admit what side he's taken."

"And besides, maybe the false bottom is empty," said Tim as he sat back down. "Why would Abner want me to drive his goods when he gave me such a look of suspicion… that time by the store?"

"I don't know."

"Maybe John had just rented a wagon to haul firewood and I was chosen because he won't miss me if I'm shot by a horse thief. Maybe I'm just dreaming up vile conspiracies and slandering an honest man. Maybe I've got nothing to worry about, other than my own uselessness."

"Maybe."

"And it might even be that under the false bottom is just bottles of rum and the man who loaded them is off somewhere in jail or dead, and it's been sloshing around in there for who knows how long."

"That might be," said Sadie, "or maybe you're hauling contraband and you're headed for a stay in prison."

"Or worse," said Tim as he stared at the floor.

How much was Tim's room, board, clothing and training, plus two pence a week? The value of his labor in coin would usually have been about ten or fifteen English pence a day. The raw cost of food for a working man was usually four or five pence, or about four hours labor. Today, this could be paid for in an hour, making food far less expensive. Food then, would have been much cheaper after fall harvest and very expensive in late winter and spring. Coins were even more scarce, so the two pence in spending money would likely have been paid as a credit at a local tavern. This would be no great cost because apprentices could be relied on to spend it on beer and calories drunk down at the tavern offset calories eaten at home. Back then, calories were expensive and the poor were skinny.

Tim could expect his earnings to double if he completed his apprenticeship and found steady work as a carpenter. He could then afford a wife, especially if she was useful around the house. A man with children was paid more, not for working harder, but because he needed more. If a man did dangerous work, like a sailor, a logger or a miner, he would earn more and get more of it in coin. These better paid men usually spent a lot more on liquor and tobacco.

Prices varied widely, depending on season, weather and availability. Compared to today, transportation, law enforcement and financing were highly unreliable. A very large part of trade was done by barter, making it easier for the average person to estimate the true worth of what he was buying and selling. A skilled tradesman could often be hired for twenty or thirty pence a day. This sounds cheap, but it was not. A merchant or farmer would not earn much more and, for them, the tradesman's twenty or thirty pence was expensive.

Twelve pence equaled a shilling and twenty shillings made one-pound sterling. Before war broke out, the military's "Brown Bess" musket would have cost at least two pounds (480 pence.) A rifle good enough for hunting would have been at least twice that. A skilled tradesman could often buy a new rifle if he was paid in coin for two months work. Unless he lived where there was wild game to hunt, this would be a major sacrifice, when so much was needed for basic necessities. In spite of laws requiring gun ownership, when the militia was called out, sometimes only one in four arrived with a firearm.

Along with English currency, there was a wide variety of local and foreign coins in circulation, along with various types of paper money and promissory notes. The most popular international currency was the one ounce silver Spanish milled dollar, called the 'piece of eight'. In 1775 the Continental Congress had created a Continental dollar that was initially worth one Spanish dollar, or fifty-four English pence, but had since lost half its value.

Chapter 14

Keep on strutting.

"Good morning, Bessie," said Matilda to the woman coming through the backdoor and stamping the dirt off her shoes. Bessie was a tall, thin young mother with curls of black hair sticking out from under her cap.

"Mornin', Mrs. 'Tilda. I've come to borrow your girl-of-all-work, if you don't mind. Take her back to help at the store, if you don't mind."

"If you wouldn't mind," corrected Matilda as she turned towards the door to the front room. "Sadie!"

"Upstairs still, I'd imagine," said Abby, who was by the fireplace stirring a pot. She had a cloth tied round her head to keep a bread poultice against her swollen cheek.

"Sadie!" Matilda called again through the door after she pushed it open with her elbow. Her hands were sticky from cooking. "And what will you be working on today?" she asked Bessie.

"Just cooking and washing and such. And I've got the oven hot for baking." The Pellis store had a large oven built into a massive stone chimney. Bessie had been over at dawn to build a fire. When it had burned down, she shoveled it full of glowing embers to warm the oven. By now, the bricks would be hot enough to maintain a good baking temperature.

"Here she is," said Matilda as Sadie came through the door with a broom and dustpan. "Bessie's needing you. Take a chicken over to roast."

"Yes, ma'am," said Sadie. She already had one bled, plucked and gutted. It was the one she had seen pecking away at a poor little duck. The big chickens were always bullying the small ones and the small ducks got it even worse – pecking them half to death sometimes. Before the execution, Sadie had called over some of the neighborhood children to help officiate. She recited a litany of its crimes before the whole flock. A black cap had been stitched together for these occasions, just like the one the judge wore when he sentenced a criminal to hang. They would then draw straws to see who got to wield the axe. All except Alice Bender, who always wanted to read the prayers and call upon the miscreant chicken to make a final confession. After the sentence was carried out, they would hold a funeral for it, with as much high church pomp as they could think of.

. . . . .

A while later, over at the store, when the oven was full and nothing needed to be done, Sadie found some sewing and sat herself down. While they worked, they talked about which neighbor was sick and what they were taking for it. Bessie never tired of this topic and she was developing a reputation for dosing and curing. She grew medicinal herbs and gathered more in the forest. Store-bought medicines were available at reasonable prices in the city, but many could still only afford the local fare.

Bessie was talking about a heated debate she had had with her mother when Sadie heard the voice of Abner Wall out in the store. She moved her chair closer to the door. Bessie kept talking about her mother and the issue of her granny's sore hip. In spite of her talking, Sadie was able to make out a few words. Abner said something about "blockheads," "the King's Bridge," and "be of little use." Sadie got up and put her ear against the closed door. Bessie gave her a look of disapproval, but kept quiet to allow her a chance to hear.

"We can't evade all risks," said Nat.

"So long as it's his risk and not ours," said Abner. It sounded to Sadie like he had been looking away when he said this – maybe keeping an eye on the front door.

"But it's our pawn that's doing all the talking to the little one, isn't it?" said Nat with a smile. "And that leaves the bulk of the risk to them, doesn't it? And especially the little one, who so bravely takes the lion's share."

"Good for the little one then," said Abner. "Better him than me."

"He's a good one for the task too, he is – in need of the sort of employment where there's not much risk of making too many errors. Error prone and inattentive, they say he is. We're not likely to do better than that."

"Perhaps not."

"And, if by some misfortune, he is lost," said Nat with a shrug, "there'll always be another like him to take his place, eh?"

"No, there'll never be a shortage of inattentive boys."

"But 'twould be such a sad loss, though. Such a pretty boy."

Now Sadie was almost certain they were talking about her brother. He was a pretty boy and they would surely think he was inattentive if they'd heard about it from Josh. And that would explain what they meant by the "risk." But who was their "pawn"?

"A pretty boy, you say?" she heard Abner snicker. "Now now, don't you start growing fond of him – not a hometown boy. You and your uncle..."

"Oh no no no, worry thee not. I'm just a caring sort who fears..."

"But what I am wondering," interrupted Abner with a tone in his voice that gave Sadie a chill, "is whether he's just not dull enough. What if he has suspicions, eh? He may try to sell them, mightn't he?"

"No, not him. Simple boy, simple suspicions. He'll do nothing…"

"Let us hope that they're simple! He doesn't seem all that simple to me, not to look in his eyes."

"No, he's a Simple Simon, he is. A Simple Simon."

Sadie had heard enough. Her brother was surely facing grave danger. She told Bessie she would be back shortly and went out the door. She headed north of town to where she thought she would find Tim.

· · · · ·

"You're too young to be taking such risks," snorted Tim. "Listening in! Ear to the door! Nat could have come through that door and you'd have been knocked on your backside."

"You're one to be talking about the taking of risks!" said Sadie. "Look at what happened to Amos Short! Wasn't he driving a wagon? I saw him come into town on a wagon and it might have been the same one you're driving now."

"When did you see him driving a wagon?"

"I don't know. Not long before he died."

"I thought you were convinced that it was Jack Lauper who killed him."

"I… I don't know!" moaned Sadie. "Maybe what got Amos killed wasn't his defending you and accusing Thomas. Maybe that was just the last straw. Maybe he'd got himself a willow stick too and measured the depth of the box. Maybe he knew too much and then he went and talked about it. He was a drunkard. They always talk too much."

"That's a lot of maybes."

"Well, maybe it is." They stood in silence. The clouds had grown darker and in the distance they could hear the cawing of crows.

"I don't know," said Tim as he started to pace back and forth. "What do I do? Do I go and tell John that I don't want to be driving the wagon any more and that it's only fair that somebody else gets a turn?"

"I don't know! Wouldn't you think that'd just get him wondering why you wanted out of the job, and whether you knew something that you weren't supposed to know, and that you weren't as simple as you're supposed to be?"

Again they stood in silence.

"I guess I could ask Josh to vouch for me," Tim joked.

"Good old Josh."

"If there are stolen muskets and powder hidden in there and, if it's on its way up to their enemy, then they're into a profitable line of trade that they won't want out any time soon."

"And if they are," said Sadie, "and they get suspicious of you knowing too much, then what? You'll be a threat to what's likely their only profitable line."

"And the boys know I'm proud as a rooster sitting up there on that wagon with my blue coat and my felt hat. I've been a-strutting around like a fool, I have. Now nobody'd believe I'd ever not want to keep on doing it."

"Like the fool you are?"

"Exactly. So... what do I do?"

"Keep on strutting, I suppose, and hope that we're just imagining things."

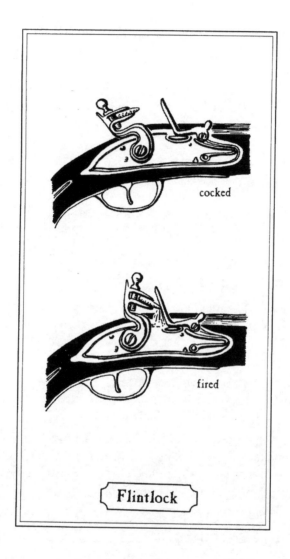

cocked

fired

Flintlock

Chapter 15

Talking too much.

Three days passed. Tim began to hope it had all come to an end and that he would no longer be called upon to risk his neck for the benefit of who knows who. This hope ended when new orders were served to him along with supper.

The next morning, he was back on the post road to the city. The sun was out and he was being waved through checkpoints like any red coated officer. But other wagons seemed to be receiving the same treatment, so he could not draw any conclusions. On his way back north the next day, the soldiers were just as easygoing and the nice weather was holding. Maybe spring fever was making them lazy.

Tim was just past King's Bridge when he came up behind a man on foot who looked familiar. He slowed as he passed. Sure enough, it was his former cellmate. "Dan Idiot!" he called.

"Tim Useless! Why! And look at this! Just barely out of jail and here you've already stolen a wagon and team! Lack-a-day boy, you'll surely hang for this!"

"No, it's not! But what're you doing walking free?"

"Not free! I'm still serving out my term. Still the property of the Royal Navy," said Dan while climbing on the wagon to take a seat next to Tim. "And with the fleet still at anchor, there's not much to keep us busy and half us convicts have been rented out. I'm on a farm just a couple of miles south of Yonkers, cutting wood mostly."

"Everybody's cutting wood."

"'Tis the season for it. Get a good stock piled up before there's field work. And they've got me a-working all on my own – all alone! The solitude's worse than the hard labor."

"I know what that's like! I'm being shunned myself. My master's son's so envious of me – of my getting to drive a wagon – it pains him to look at me. So I'm kept away, out of sight. Where's Jack Lauper? Out too?"

"He's still on the boat and he'll likely stay there too, him being a murderer. It'd scare the womenfolk to see him out and about, wouldn't it? They'd fear for their babes. But he's not so bad off though, for the carrying of the label of 'murderer' makes his fellow prisoners wary of him. They're showing him respect, even though he hasn't earned it, him being innocent. But all that extra elbowroom is making him a bit like an officer. Like a rich boy just out of school with his purchased commission and his fancy new uniform. Only Jack ain't neither rich nor fancy."

"Yea, a lesser sort and a convict, too. Worse than a slave."

"But now I'm a-wondering, Tim Euston. What's a mere boy like you doing with a man's job like the driving of a team? Why do you get to flatten your backside all day instead of working like the rest of us?"

"It just happened that way. My master told me to get the wagon and load her up and drive her down to the city. Down there, I get loaded with manure and I drive north, almost all the way to the Croton River. This has been my fourth trip down and up."

"And the master's son envies you so much that you're forced to work on your own and keep away from him?"

"That I am. He wants the job, but he's too busy overseeing the boys. He's a good overseer, too. He could boss a gang of convicts."

"He just watches over you, or does he swing an axe, too?"

"Oh yea yea, he does his share."

"While Tim Useless drives a wagon down to the big city."

"Ain't it odd?" chuckled Tim.

"It is."

"Maybe because it's dangerous. A man could get robbed and killed."

"Robbed maybe," said Dan. "Not likely killed, though. You could be killed by a falling tree, just as easy."

"You could. A woodcutter got killed last fall, up north, east of White Plains. They said a gust of wind took the tree down before expected. And it wasn't a big tree either. He was speared by a broken branch."

"And look at you in this fine coat, like you're driving a stagecoach."

"No, it doesn't take much. A human life's a fragile thing, as they say."

"What is it?" asked Dan with a grin. "They've got you running contraband or something?"

"You've always got to take care, as John's always telling us," replied Tim, now talking too fast. "Razor sharp axes and falling trees – it's a risky job, cutting wood."

"I'll bet you there's a false bottom under this," said Dan, as he turned to look at the mound of manure.

"No no no, just manure and nothing more."

"Let's pull in up ahead where I'm a-working. Nobody comes by this time of day. We'll shovel it out and have a good look. Who knows what we'll find?"

"How... how... how in blessed name did you figure it out so fast? It took me and Sadie a week!"

"Well, that's why they call you Tim and Sadie Useless. So your master's a true-blue patriot then? Or is he just buying and selling for the easy profit?"

"He is a patriot. That much I know. But the others who seem to be in on it too, they look... well... more like tories to me. Sadie and I are just about certain of who two of them might be. And we're suspecting that your old friend Thomas Pellis is in on it, too."

"Thomas Pellis ain't no friend of mine, not no more! You just tell me if he goes after your little Sadie again and I'll go after him with a skinning knife!"

"Sadie figures for sure there's his nephew in on it too – Nat Pellis. And likely a trader from the city called Abner Wall."

"Abner? Now that doesn't surprise me a tick, unless you tell me he's doing it to defend our liberties. Have you opened it up to take a look?"

"No. There's a couple of likely looking knotholes in the planking, though. It looks like you'd just need an iron bar with a bit of a hook on the end."

"Turn in to the right, just past the rise there, just so long as nobody's close by that can see us," said Dan as he looked back.

"They figured I'd be too stupid to ever suspect a thing."

"Well, they figured you for a Tim Useless who'd just have a Dan Idiot for a friend. Only you ain't useless and I ain't no idiot. I'd bet some would have driven six dozen times and never suspected a thing."

"I suppose they would have," said Tim as he stood up to look up the road and back. No one was in sight so he turned in. The road went through some dense woodland and took them to a fork. They took the less used way and went as far as a clearing. Dan had a good-sized pile of bundles cut and tied.

"The farmhouse is back down the other leg. I'll fetch a pair of shovels and we'll go to work."

"Won't they wonder about you taking shovels?"

"They won't see me. There's three women living there along with an invalid man in bed. They like to keep warm by the fire. And if they see me, then I'll say I'm on orders to dig groundnuts when I find them."

Dan ran down a path that cut through the trees while Tim waited. It was not long before he was running back with two shovels and a broom. "Get digging boy! The sooner we're finished, the less likely we'll have a visitor coming along and asking questions."

"I thought you said nobody ever came," said Tim as he went to work.

"You never know. Now, dump it into a tidy pile or we'll never get half of it back in."

In no time, they were sweeping away the last of it. Dan had brought a pair of hooks with eyelets tied to light ropes. They hooked them into the holes, stood on the sides of the box and pulled on the ropes. After some tugging and wiggling the bottom rose. They lifted it up and set it aside. In the compartment were objects wrapped in canvas. They unwrapped one and found a musket. There was nothing special about it – the ordinary Brown Bess the gunsmiths of London turned out by the thousands. Tim and Dan kept opening the packages and found two bolts of cloth and about twenty leather bags containing either musket balls or gunpowder. There were also two saddlebags full of more balls. A closer inspection of one of the saddlebags revealed a hidden pocket containing sheets of paper covered with numbers, printed in pen and ink.

"Well, look at this!" said Dan with gleaming eyes. "A spy's intelligence being sent to – likely direct to George Washington himself!"

"Do you think so?" asked Tim, as he felt a shiver run up his spine.

"Yea, I've heard about this. Each number is a word. Here, this '233' might be a ... a 'when'. Who knows what? The more common words might be mated to one, or two, or three different numbers. This '536' here might be a 'when', too. Or it might serve for both 'when' and 'there', to make it harder to crack the code. Which number is used might depend on... whether the second word before begins with a letter that's one of the first ten letters in the alphabet. That sort of thing. Who knows? Without knowing the key it'd be near to impossible to decode the message. Decode means translate it back to words."

"I know that!"

"Good for you. But just think. This message could be warning of... well, of who knows what?"

"Indeed. Who would know?"

"Or it could be a red herring and be nothing at all. Just put here to waste the time of the poor clerk who'll be called upon to try to break the code."

"I guess we ought to put it all back now. I should get going."

"You should," said Dan with a nod, and they went to work, placing everything back neatly and refilling the wagon. "You know, it just don't make sense. This is surely on its way north – and likely on to Morristown."

"It must be."

"But why's Abner Wall and Thomas Pellis behind it? They'd only work for good money. The Army's poor, they all say so."

"It is," agreed Tim. "They say they can only pay in their Continentals."

"So I have to wonder why the likes of Abner and Thomas would be into the supplying of arms to the Continental Army. Isn't everybody saying that a Continental dollar doesn't buy half what it used to? And where are they gonna spend them? And if peace is signed and the war's lost, they'll be worth nothing, won't they?"

"I don't know. But… I don't know that there'll ever be peace talks. If Washington went to talk peace, they say there's many a Continental soldier who will defy him. They'd break away and form another army, headquartered out of Boston, most likely."

"And if Abner and Thomas want to spy and smuggle, then why wouldn't they be laying their necks on the line for the British, who would pay them in hard coin?"

"Well," said Tim. "maybe they just haven't had the opportunity. Maybe they've found themselves a chance to get these things to somebody who will pay something and they've nothing to sell back to Billy Howe."

"Maybe… but still, it just don't add up, does it?"

"No, it don't," agreed Tim as he climbed onto his seat to pull away. "I'll come in here for a visit when I'm going past next time so you won't be so lonely," he called, as he urged on the horses with a shake of the reins.

· · · · ·

The next afternoon, Tim was back to his lonely little patch of woodland, cutting, sawing, memorizing lines and waiting for the hours to pass. When he heard the sound of cowbells, he went directly to the cowshed, eager to tell his sister the news.

Sadie kept him waiting as she talked of how their mother's face was even more swollen and her breath stunk worse than ever. "I fear for her life, I do."

Tim was reluctant to change the topic too quickly, wondering whether a lack of proper fear for his mother's grave condition might work against her. "Perhaps a prayer would be best," he said, and started into one, but he was still impatient to tell the news. As soon as the adoration, confession, thanksgiving and request were adequately discharged, the news burst out of him. "The wagon carried a musket. And there's balls, powder and encrypted messages!"

"What?"

"I met up with Dan Eliot on the road yesterday. He's the fellow from jail you saw convicted at trial. The one with curly blonde hair and..."

"I know who he is!"

"The Navy's farmed him out and he's working a couple of miles south of town, cutting wood. I told him as little as I could and... and he just put two and two together. He figured I was surely carrying contraband and then he insisted we take a look in the wagon."

"You didn't tell anything..."

"He'd guessed it all! And we opened it up and we..."

"But he'll likely go and tell everybody! I've seen him in town and he's the type who likes to talk."

"But he won't tell..."

"What if he does?"

"Well... he likely won't. He knows the danger I face. There's muskets and powder..."

"I'm not surprised there is. What else would they..."

"There's more! There's a saddlebag and in it was papers covered with numbers and Dan says it's in code. And it might be secret letters sent to George Washington himself!"

The two of them thought about what it all might mean and what messages the letters might carry.

"Or it might just be a smuggler's orders and receipts," said Sadie.

"It... it might be. And Dan thinks it might too just be there to waste somebody's time when they try to decipher it."

"But it might be something important," said Sadie after a pause.

"Indeed it might."

"Something the whole war may turn on," whispered Sadie as she held her hands to her heart. "Yea, something that'll mean the difference between freedom and slavery!"

"Yea, something."

"'There is reason to apprehend'," said Sadie, quoting from George III's proclamation of August 1775, " 'that such rebellion hath been much promoted and encouraged by the traitorous correspondence, counsels and comfort of divers wicked and desperate persons within this realm...' "

"Yea, and now I'm one of them 'persons'," said Tim with a big grin.

"This at least explains a few things," said Sadie as she turned her attention back to her milking. The cow let out a low moo, sounding annoyed. Sadie was pulling too hard.

"Indeed it does," agreed Tim. "It tells us that our suspicions were correct."

"It does that, for sure. But what it doesn't tell us is who you serve and just how much risk you face – whether it's a hanging offence."

"No, it doesn't," said Tim, after a sigh.

"You'll have to be careful not to say anything that betrays how much you know already."

"Well…"

"What?"

"I did sort of let it out, up north at the Felix farm. I didn't say much. I just said to the younger fellow that I'd thought I was almost caught."

"Oh, you didn't!" moaned Sadie.

"He might not say anything about it. He didn't seem to be surprised. It was like he thought I ought to know what my real mission was."

"Well, of all the…"

"It likely doesn't matter!"

"Well… I don't know about that! But what I wonder is… if Abner did help you get past the King's Bridge and, if Abner is in on the smuggling, and if he did hear from those up north who might now suspect that you've guessed your true mission…"

"Yea, it could be that he has."

"He might just decide to keep you on as driver anyways, just because you're getting the job done and not demanding extra pay for risking your neck."

"That might be," agreed Tim.

"And maybe he's asked around and knows you're a good little whig and that you'll probably think you're serving your country like a brave little soldier."

"Well, I do!"

"So your odds of staying alive are likely better if you keep right on taking load after load down to the city and up to that same farm – better than if you cut and run."

"Maybe."

"But on the other hand, by sticking with it you might be committing suicide."

"I might be."

"But no more than if you were to join up and fight in a few of their losing battles."

"Or winning battles!" protested Tim. "We won at the Harlem Heights and at Trenton and..."

"Those weren't battles. They were skirmishes and ambushes."

"That was one big ambush at Trenton!"

"Yes yes yes. So what are you going to do?"

"I... I don't know! What do you think I should do?"

"It's not for me to decide," said Sadie. "Likely I'm going to end up with a mother who's dead of a toothache and a brother who's hanged for a rebel spy. And it may be that all this will come to pass within just a few more days. And then I'll be cast out of this tory household for being kin to a traitor."

"You might be."

"Then what should I do?"

"I don't know. You could marry Thomas and bear his babes."

"Indeed I could and... and just thinking about it all," she said as she sat on her milking stool, slouched over, her hands still, "it sort of makes you start to feel like... like...like your insides are rotted and filthy, doesn't it?"

"I haven't noticed that," said Tim after a pause.

"You never have?"

"No! I've... I've just been thinking of freezing my toes off in Nova Scotia while cutting firewood for good King George."

"That's all?"

"And it makes my toes hurt. But... for now... don't we both have a house to live in and three square meals a day?"

"We do have that."

"Yea, we've much to be thankful for."

"So we do," whispered Sadie. They sat in silence until one of the cats started mewing. "Thomas has a new suit again," she added.

"Good for Thomas."

"He'll be wearing a powdered wig, next."

"It'll suit him," said Tim with a shrug.

"And how else could he be getting the money except by your efforts? You're his trusted courier, likely. Facing all weather and all danger so he might pay his tailor."

"Or maybe I'm not!"

"No, we don't know all of Thomas's doings, do we?"

"Well, he was down in the city the first day, the first time I brought a load down. It was like he was there to meet me."

"If he's in on it... then if he had been worried about Amos finding out too much and talking too much, then Thomas would have had two reasons for killing him, wouldn't he have?"

"Maybe he would, but I don't know about him being the killer, I just can't see Thomas Pellis with courage enough to kill a man.

"Or a boy," said Sadie.

Chapter 16

If only we knew who to trust.

"Come along now girl, drink it up nicely," said the woman, as if talking to a child. Old Clara Campbell had been there for the past two hours, telling how life had been so much better since the last of her rotten teeth were out. She was encouraging Sadie's mother to drink another cup of soothing compound. It was an excellent concoction that Tim had bought from an apothecary in the city and Matilda had mixed it half-and-half with rum.

"I'll have them all out in no time at all," said the surgeon with a smile. "First I'll pop out the loose ones and they'll hardly hurt at all. No more bother than losing a baby tooth when it's dangling loose."

Abby was not listening. She was staring at his little leather case as he took out his polished silver tools. When he laid a pair of pliers on a red cloth, she stopped breathing and her hands started to shake.

"You won't miss them once they're gone," said Clara as she reached to take Abby's hand. "You'll just have to get used to cutting up everything small. Teeth are naught but a vanity, you'll find."

"No, I can't!" sobbed Abby as she hid her face in her hands.

"Mother, don't say that!" ordered Sadie. She had been standing behind her mother and now she took hold of her shoulder and leaned to look into her eyes. She was determined to be a soothing and reassuring presence and help her mother through the experience with gentle encouragement. "Think of the soldiers in battle, Mom. You always praise them for their courage. And now you can show us some courage of your own."

"No no, I can't," Abby sobbed again and shook her head as she tried to turn away.

"Sure you can," said Clara.

"Indeed, listen to her," agreed the surgeon. "It'll be over... "

"No no no no..."

"Get up and get on with it!" shouted Sadie. Her mother stared at her in shock. Sadie backed away, surprised by her outburst. "Forgive me," she whispered, but she still stared at her mother with angry eyes.

"Really you must," agreed Matilda. She was glad Sadie had acted so boldly. "Let's be on with it!" she said, wanting to make full use of the drama of the moment. The surgeon took hold of Abby's other hand and they pulled her out of the chair. The biggest of the helpers slipped around and scooped her up in his enormous hairy arms.

"No! Please! Please!" Abby whimpered, but with little conviction. They got her laid out on the table. Sadie pushed her mother's head down with her hand and stared – her face in her mother's face – her furious eyes in her mother's terror-stricken eyes.

"Ah!" Abby shrieked when the surgeon gave her a severe pinch on the muscle on the underside of her upper arm. That gave the man at her head the opportunity to wedge a dowel into the side of her mouth, rendering her unable to utter more words of refusal and allowing them all to presume she no longer wished to express any denial of permission. Four of the five helpers were British soldiers who had been in Yonkers to cut wood for Matilda's husband. They assumed their positions as automatically as in cannon drill.

"Loose ones first," said the surgeon. He started by wiggling a tooth with his fingers and then pulled it out with the pliers. All of Abby's teeth had thick plaque going right up the root where it had eaten into the bone. That meant most were loose so the surgeon could pull one after another and hear only a small yelp for each. He went down the row "like pulling carrots," but he left three for last. They were badly inflamed. He knew the pain would be as intense as pain could ever get. The expression in his eyes communicated his expectation. Abby saw this and writhed and shrieked in terror. The men wrestled with each appendage and one almost lost hold of a leg.

Sadie ran for the door. She could not bear to watch. Out in the garden, she paced up and down the path, stamping her feet on the brown earth, pulling off her cap with one hand and grabbing a fistful of hair with the other. She turned and went back around the house and stopped. As if called forth by the Devil, there in front of her was Thomas Pellis, coming across the road and straight for her.

"What's all the shrieking about?" he laughed. "Have pirates sailed up the Hudson and are the innocents of Yonkers under attack? My faith, if I didn't see you before me now, I'd have thought it was you, sweet Sadie, in the sweaty hands of buccaneers!"

Sadie turned away and went to the kitchen door. She had never imagined herself capable of as much hatred as she felt for him at this moment. She wanted to kill him. "Oh, for pistol loaded and primed," she muttered.

Back inside, everyone was still. Only then did Sadie realize the screaming had stopped and her mother was no longer on the table.

"Finished," said the surgeon in a low voice, with a glance at Sadie while he wiped up his tools with a rust red towel.

Sadie stood there, her hands crossed and her shoulders in a rigid slouch. *Finished?* she wondered. *Finished off? Dead? And... am I now an orphan – alone in the world with no one...*

"I'm wondering," said the surgeon with a half smile, "whether you might have suffered more than your poor old mother."

Sadie stared back at him through squinted eyes. She wanted to kill him, too.

"She shouldn't be working for a couple of days," he said to Matilda. "The bad teeth were quite inflamed and the poisons will take time to drain, but she'll soon be fitter and better than ever."

Shouldn't work! wondered Sadie. *Be fitter and better! Is this the way you talk about one who is dead? What crass and callous words...*

"Yes, just let yourself rest a couple of days," he said to Abby, who was back in the armchair. Clara had hold of an arm in case she fainted and fell forward, banging her head on the floor.

"Yes yes," continued the surgeon, "and within a week you'll be saying that you've never felt so good, not in years. And soon doing the job you've done," he said with a smile to Clara, "and spreading the good word of the wonders that can be done by a capable surgeon."

"You know," responded Clara with a smile, "I still hate the man who pulled my teeth."

"But... that was me!" gasped the surgeon with mock astonishment.

"No it wasn't! He's down in the city these days. Yea, I hate him and I love him, too. It had to be done and it should have been done sooner, only with more soothing compound than I was given!"

"It's a blessing, isn't it? Last fall, at one battle after another, I was helping with the sawing off of arms and legs. And often with nothing at all to ease their pain. I still have nightmares about it! So much blood and screaming. What a thing to live through."

"We don't pay you enough," said Matilda.

"Well, you can still pay me more."

"I mean during battle!" she laughed. "I'm paying you plenty, today."

"At least you pay me more than promises," the surgeon said, as he put his pliers back into his case. "Now, here's a fine soothing compound that will make all the difference in the world," he said loudly, pulling a bottle out of his bag and hoping to make a sale.

"Oh, tell us about it!" said Matilda, speaking even louder – almost shouting. They wanted to drown out a fresh outburst of sobbing. Abby had lost consciousness on the table and was gradually coming to.

"There are eighteen ingredients in it," he said, loud enough for the neighbors to hear, and he went on extolling the virtues of the mixture with the flowery language of physicians and apothecaries.

Soon Abby's sobs were replaced by sniffles and her terror eased as her mouth went numb. All the medicine she had drunk was having its effect and her eyes looked very drowsy. They helped her over to her bedroll, which had been rolled out for her in the pantry. Within minutes, she was sound asleep.

· · · · ·

Tim had known this was the day of his mother's ordeal. As soon as the winter sun was setting, he came to Sadie to ask how it had gone. She met him on her way to the cowshed.

"She's well enough," she said without waiting for a question. "She was scared half to death and they loaded her up with so much medicine she'll likely sleep for two days."

"Good."

"Three days would be better."

"So, he figures she'll soon be up and well?"

"Probably," said Sadie as she looked away, sounding angry.

"And how are you?" he asked, after he had followed her out to the cowshed. The cows were at the door waiting. As soon as the door was open, they would shove by and each would go to her usual stall, and then turn to look back. As she got to work, Sadie described the procedure to Tim. The cows could tell something was wrong and they offered long low moos in sympathy. Sadie patted one in thanks.

"I'm just glad it's over with," she sighed. "The surgeon said it went well."

"He'd hardly admit to doing a bad job," said Tim as he sat down at his usual place by the post.

"How's your memorization going?" asked Sadie.

"Good."

"Are they sending you down again?"

"Again," he groaned. Sadie knew he did not want to go, even if he was serving the cause of freedom. They were both thinking about the mysterious death of Amos Short. They knew that if Tim were to refuse the job or even ask questions, he would only put himself in greater danger. The risk of getting caught and charged for smuggling might be small in comparison to the risk of being silenced for knowing too much.

"I've been doing some thinking," said Tim. "We've never wondered whether the killing of Amos might have been done by somebody else, someone who came to collect on a debt. Maybe he was killed to set an example for other debtors. They say it happens. And maybe he was in on some crooked deal and he came out of it owing more than he could pay. It could even have been some crazed deserter on the run who was inside his house and stealing. And then Amos surprised him. It could be anything."

"Indeed, it could," agreed Sadie.

"And Abner or Nat might never have done anything. When I saw Abner at the King's Bridge, maybe he didn't even know I was there. Maybe he was just angry because they were hinting that they wanted a bribe from him and he thought they wanted too much. Even if he and the others are in on the smuggling, maybe they're all good patriots – as good as John."

"Well, they don't look it."

"No," sighed Tim. "But as they say, you can't judge a book by its cover."

They sat in silence while Sadie kept milking. When she finished one cow, she poured out the bucket into a crock and went to the next.

"And," said Tim, "it could be that all three are loyal to the King and they're happy to trick the Continentals into believing they bring good intelligence. The redcoats might be writing up false reports, just to throw them off."

"And the letters might not even be going to the Army at all. They could just be to other smugglers."

"But if they do go to the Army," said Tim, "then what they send might be the cause of great mischief. The lives of good patriots might be the cost of us doing nothing."

"Well... you could go to Morristown and talk to somebody."

This was a town in a hilly region of New Jersey. After the victories at Trenton and Princeton, Washington had taken his troops there to pass the winter. Hill country was hard to attack and easy to defend, and winter was not the season for fighting battles. Besides, many thought General Howe was going to hold off well into the spring and summer. They suspected he did not want to inflict total defeat on the American Army. His goal was to bring the colonies back into the empire and persuade them to pay taxes. He wanted to generate goodwill. If Washington and other patriots were quietly thankful for not being crushed, they would probably be more agreeable. But who would ever know what Billy Howe's plans might be? Every sort of rumor was going around.

"I could go there," said Tim with a shrug, "but what would I tell them when I got there? If I went into town and said I had information, I'd be taken to some officer, wouldn't I? I wouldn't go straight to Washington, even if he happened to be there. They say he's always traveling about so he probably wouldn't be. And what if I go to an officer who just happens to be the one who's supplying information to Billy Howe? There must be one, at least. There's word going around about peace talks, isn't there? Once there's peace, then those who helped the royal general to impose the King's will upon the colonies, he'll be rewarded – well rewarded! Surely, the Continentals aren't free of men who are looking to prosper, no matter which side comes out on top. It's only human nature. And what if I go to just such a scoundrel and I end up exposing honest patriots? I'd get Abner caught and hanged along with whoever else. Maybe John Gainer."

"But... do you really think it's so great a risk?"

"I don't know! There must be at least one officer who's serving both sides. There's maybe two or three."

"I suppose there likely is."

"If only we knew who to trust," said Tim, sounding hopeless.

"We could ask around and... maybe see who's who and... who can be counted on."

"We could," sighed Tim. Nothing more was said as Sadie finished the milking and other dairy work.

The hope that the American Army could count on its officers to keep secrets had ended the August before with the arrest of its Surgeon General. Dr. Benjamin Church had been an outspoken whig and member of the Massachusetts Provincial Congress, but all the while, he had been communicating in cipher with the British. A young woman caught with a letter had confessed. Church was tried and convicted.

In November of the same year an Army staff officer named William Demont defected to the British, bringing plans of Fort Washington. Fourteen days later the fort was captured along with three thousand prisoners.

Chapter 17

A fool's errand.

"No, it was not a pretty sight," chuckled Dan as he sat next to Tim on the wagon. As he had promised, Tim stopped to visit him on his way to New York City. The ground was covered with wet snow and the wagon was the only dry place to sit. "Yea, when me and the man that brought me here arrived at the door, and when he told the three women that I was to be living with them and them feeding me, well well! They looked at me like I was a Hessian mercenary with goat's feet and a dragon's tail. Them six beady little eyes, full of fear and hatred – they chilled me to the bone, they did. All I could do was look down at the ground in shame, though I'd done nothing to deserve it."

"Sure you did," said Tim with a smile. "You're a convicted criminal. You beat that poor boy black and blue and were justly punished by the powers that be."

"I suppose I was – charged and convicted by a wise judge – three wise judges! How could I not be guilty? But the man who brought me didn't seem to like the reception any more than I did and he wasn't in the mood for a lecture from angry women either. He pulled me out the door and took me straight over to the woodlot. There he says I'm to start cutting and keep at it 'til I've cleared every stick of wood. Well, no man could cut that much wood in six years, so I was to prepare for a long stay. Then he takes the axe he brought and he cuts a stick. He says that each day, I'm to keep at the cutting of firewood and the binding of it into bundles – enough to make a pile as wide and as high and as long as the stick that he cut. Well, I've done me a deal of woodcutting in my time and I know this to be no great task for a day's work – not for me – but I'm not going to let him know that, for then he'd just go and cut a longer stick, wouldn't he? So instead I let my jaw drop and I looked at that stick like it's my favorite dog run over by the wheel of a wagon. Then I just said nothing. Always a wise option, don't you think?"

"It is that," said Tim, remembering the scolding he got from his sister for talking too much.

"So, he hands me the axe and tells me to start by cutting a couple of bundles and taking them over to give to the women, to buy their peace. And I'm to tell them I'm going to be supplying them with extra firewood to sell, to cover the cost of feeding me. That'd make them happy, don't you think?"

"It ought to."

"So, I decide to go at it hard and fast and I cut them some good bundles – four big ones. I bring them over and I stack them in front of the door, and I knocked on the door. And when they come I say they're for them to burn or to sell, to pay for feeding me. And that I'll bring four or five bundles for them every day."

"Did that make them happy?"

"It should have, but no. They still looked at me like I was a dangerous criminal. Didn't believe me, I suppose. And I suppose I could hardly blame them, so I had to think of something else to get myself into their good graces. I have to live with them, don't I? So, when supper came they gave me a bowl of the stingiest vegetable soup – mostly hot water and cut up parsnips and carrots and not enough meat to make a rat happy. Well, they were all pretty skinny so I suppose that's what they'd been eating themselves. So I spoon it up like a good boy and then I stare at the empty bowl. I sighed me a long sigh and say that it's just the way my Momma always used to make it the last winter. 'The last winter?' the younger one asks. 'Yea, the last,' I says and I stammer a bit and say that it was a couple of years ago now and the winter had been a hard one up in Massachusetts and we were eating whatever there was to be had. But we were always hungry enough so it tasted good. And we knew that she was doing her best and that she was always able to find enough to make a good bowl of soup so we didn't never..."

"What?" Tim asked, after Dan's voice trailed off.

"I didn't say any more after that. I just stared at my bowl, like I've been choked into silence by a lump in my throat."

"What about?"

"Well, about nothing. I just wanted them to believe that I'm a-thinking about a mother that's now dead and gone and that I'm fighting back tears for the memory of her."

"Did it work?"

"At first I didn't know. I just got up and without a word I go to the door, my face down. I fling it open and then I run off, back into the woods, only now it's dark out and I've no reason to go there."

"And?"

"I wait a while and I came back. I say thank you for the supper and I keep my eyes on the floor. I go to my bedroll and I roll it out and I make like I'm tired and I'm going to bed. Then I hear it."

"What?"

"The old one asks if I want some more of that soup. Well, I kept my eyes on the floor, except when I glanced up. And then what did I see! Three women all a-looking at me like they're ready to be bawling their eyes out. Well, my eyes are back on the floor again, for now I'm feeling ashamed of myself."

"Were you really?" asked Tim.

"Well... to be honest, I was. A-toying with the sentiments of kindly sorts – that's the worst kind of naughtiness as some would say, as my own mother has said. But now I can't back out, can I? So I get up and I go and sit at the table and they serve me a big bowl of soup, only now with a deal less water and a deal more meat. Well, I lap it up like I was a starving dog. And that wasn't no pretense, for I was hungry! Then they ask me how the rest of my family is, and I tell them the truth, about my sisters and my older brother, at least."

"And your mother?"

"Well, I can't tell them the truth about her. She's up in Boston and she's married to a ship's chandler now. And with the port open now and with the equipping of one privateer after another, I suspect they're doing well enough."

"She's married to a merchant?"

"And why not?"

"You said you were poor!"

"Aye, well I am now. But we used to be of the middling sort, back before my dad died of a fever and times got tough. I even studied in Boston Latin for two long hard years."

"Of course!" said Tim. "I'd thought I'd seen you before somewhere."

"You were there, too?"

"Yeah, but I'm two years younger."

"Oh… yes…" said Dan as he tried to imagine Tim as a boy. "Well… well I was there, I was. And I was a good student too, but once we were without a father, it was off to work for me, instead of schooling."

"And your mother's well and prospering now?"

"Yea, I fear she is, fat and happy as they say."

"And you told them she was dead!"

"Not directly!"

"Lying by omission, thou art!" said Tim in mock outrage.

"To a degree."

"Thou conniving scoundrel!"

"Nay nay, say not that! I feel guilty enough without your shaming me deeper."

"And you're not going to tell them, are you?"

"Well! I can't now! They've all but adopted me as their own! I can't now go and shatter their faith. Besides, I'm the best thing to come into their lives in... well, since last October when the old man was shot in battle. He's getting better, but slowly. He's not really as bedridden anymore as he's been making on. He was a Continental and he'd be in prison with the others now, had the doctor not said he'd surely die. Instead, he's mended and got his strength back. But he can't be seen at work, so he sits around the house carving wood and knitting and whatever."

"You're doing all the heavy work?"

"The outdoor work. There's not much, not until spring. I can cut my quota by early afternoon and after that it's all for them, either cutting wood or doing something else. I've always found the time passes quicker when I'm rushing away at something. So they're getting all this firewood and they're a-selling it here and there – and for good money, too."

"But if you're giving them more than the landlord expected" asked Tim, "then aren't you and they both overstepping the spirit of the agreement?"

"No, not at all!"

"Playing Robin Hood, are you?"

"Nay, I'll steal from no man. The sailor who gave me my orders told me to cut some extra for the women to cover the cost of feeding me. He did not specify how much to cut. And the landlord hasn't bothered to come out and supervise me, has he? It's fine cooking they're providing for me, now that they can trade wood for meat and pepper. And it's served up in great style by a gracious hostess. There's value in the presentation, as they say. The worker's worth her hire."

"Well well," sighed Tim.

"Now you keep this under your hat now. It'd be a shame if what you say was to be exaggerated in the retelling."

"Yes, I promise not to tell them that your mother lives and prospers, and they're getting more wood than their landlord had in mind."

"Might have had in mind. He's yet to speak his mind."

"Thou art a good and generous man, Dan Eliot."

"As thou art as well, though not as good as I."

"Well," sighed Tim, "I suppose I ought to be off to the city. Off to perform another act of generosity for old Thomas Pellis and whoever else."

"Back to your life of crime, eh?"

"Not crime. It is in the service of the Continental Congress that is now the lawful authority in all the colonies that have bound themselves under its just and proper rule."

"Nay, treasonous defiance of our anointed King is what it is," joked Dan as he wagged his finger, "but I suppose only when you're off of the neutral ground and onto the island."

"No no no. The Continental Congress claims the City of New York too, right down to the saltwater. And that makes my carrying of captured muskets just and honorable."

"How many honorable muskets will you bring back this time?"

"Who knows? My advice has not been asked, has it?"

"Any more evidence of who precisely you do serve? And who the encrypted messages are going to?" asked Dan quietly, while climbing off the wagon.

"No! But Thomas is going about town in a new suit, so he's likely out shopping with money I've helped earn for him."

"Old Thomas. It would surprise me not a tick if he was master of the whole operation. He knows a lot of men and he can tell stories about every one of them. Good stories, too! I shudder to think of what he tells about me."

"But really," said Tim. "How could a drunken sot like him manage to keep a secret?"

"He probably can't! And his talking will probably be the death of you all."

"The death of them, but not me! They'll hang, but I won't, for I'm just a poor stupid boy."

"Now, don't sell yourself short, boy. You'll get the credit you deserve and hang along with the best of them – brothers all!"

"No, I suspect… I suspect I'll just freeze my toes off at hard labor up in Nova Scotia."

"Well, but at least if Thomas does start to talking, then word will get back to you. And that'll be how you find out for sure who you serve."

"Probably so."

"A good bottle of rum would have the truth out of him, likely," chuckled Dan. "And a lot more too. I should get me a bottle and go pay him a visit. The women wouldn't stop my going out. They don't see themselves as my jailor. As their benefactor – that's how they're seeing me these days."

Tim looked interested. "I could get you a bottle down in the city. I've got money. There's women in Yonkers who sell me a sack or two of carrots or potatoes to add to my load and I sell them in the city and pocket the difference."

"Good for you, Tim Euston."

"And my master, John Gainer, he knows I'm doing it and he don't mind. He calls it 'initiative'."

"Better for you. And you can take a couple of my bundles of wood."

"I'll be back tomorrow with a bottle of the good stuff – Barbados Brandy they call it."

"I'll be here. Now don't go getting caught before you're back again."

. . . . .

On the evening of the next day, Nat Pellis was in the store holding a candle while he put together an order for a local farmer. He made note of what goods he was out of, or would soon be. When finished, he went around the back to his uncle's to ask him to go to the city and do some buying.

Outside, it was clear with a rising moon. With its light reflecting off the new snow, the path was easy to follow. Thomas's hut was next-door on land belonging to Nat's father. If, in the spring, General Howe was to win another battle or two and extend his control beyond the neutral ground, the value of land would surely rise. It could rise a lot. New York City would likely boom the way it had during the French and Indian War. And when the City of New York boomed, Yonkers was sure to prosper, as well. Nat Pellis would prosper like never before. If his father died, he would inherit the store and emerge as a man of wealth and stature.

Nat was about to open the door. He never needed to knock for Uncle Thomas. But then he heard a voice. Thomas had a visitor. Nat opened it a crack and listened.

"And he's a loyalist too, I'd bet," said the voice. It was a young man. Or was it a boy?

"Oh, I don't know, I don't know," replied Thomas. "He's six of one and half a dozen of the other, like a lot of us, eh? Loyalist on Monday, patriot on Tuesday."

"Indeed a lot of us are," said the voice of Dan Eliot. "I wonder sometimes what I am. When one of them Sons of Liberty types get to talking of democracy and the rights of man, he can sound pretty convincing and I'll get all fired up for the cause of freedom. But then, when I think of all that old England and her colonies have accomplished under the old order, then I'm ashamed to have even thought of rebellion."

"Well my boy, you are wise, you are wise. Yea, that be a wise thing, you say," slurred Thomas. Nat could smell rum and knew it must have taken more than a small amount to get Thomas talking like that.

"You know what I got?" asked Dan. "It was just last month, just before I'd got me into trouble. I got me an offer to deliver a package. The man said it was a family heirloom going to a cousin upriver. From his old auntie, he said it was, but I knew better. I'd heard a rumor that this fellow was active for the rebel cause and I reckoned that that parcel likely contained a secret letter or some such thing – encrypted messages maybe. Had I taken it, I might not be here today, for if I had been caught, well, I'd be starving behind bars – in with all those poor soldiers – or maybe dead even. But it was good money the man was offering me and he assured me that it'd be no trouble at all. Well, I knew then that it was likely a secret message for the rebels.

Wouldn't you think so? But ever since I've been a-wondering, why I didn't take it? Where'd the harm be?"

"Ha! Where? You should know boy, being you're a convicted criminal at hard labor!"

"Oh, but we've all got to take a few risks from time to time, don't we now? Otherwise, we'd lose the joy of living, eh? Do I want to be a humorless old toad like that... who's the fellow down the street?"

"I know what you're saying. A man's got to take a few chances every now and then, just to keep his mind sharp."

"Does he? Well well Thomas, old man, it sounds like you've been a-keeping your mind sharp."

"No no no. Never by a wrongdoing. A good boy I have always been and you've got my mother's word of honor on that one."

"Yes yes. Ah, but it's hard not to, isn't it? These days with war and rebellion – who's to know what's lawful and what's not when there are two lawful authorities at competition with each other? And there's so many opportunities, ain't there?"

"Ah yes. Wartime! A time of opportunity," laughed Thomas. "Goodness be to war and profits!"

Nat stayed there, listening. The young man kept to the same topic, sounding as if he was trying to get something out of Thomas – an admission. *But maybe not,* Nat wondered. *And who is he? His voice sounds familiar, but from where?*

· · · · ·

"I've news," said Tim to Sadie, the next day in the cowshed.

"What?"

"It is very unlikely that Thomas Pellis has any involvement with the wagon."

"Doesn't he?"

"Dan Eliot and I came up with a plan to find out some more about who does what. I bought a bottle of rum in the city. Then, just last night, Dan paid Thomas a little visit. Just a friendly social call. They drank it down and talked about this and that. Dan led him along, confessing to his own temptations. He poked and stroked, as they say, but he got nothing out of him. We figured Thomas could never resist the temptation to do some bragging when the opportunity would present itself. But the old man confessed nothing at all. And Dan's all but certain that he knows nothing at all about the operation. Not likely, anyways."

"Did he come right out and ask him?"

"No no no. He just danced around it – waving a baited hook to see if he'd bite."

"And he didn't?" asked Sadie as she sat down to start milking.

"Nope."

"Oh," she responded, after a pause to think it over.

"You don't think so?"

"I don't know. They say Thomas has been trading all his life and that he's a sharp trader, too."

"I suppose so," said Tim with a shrug.

"He might have suspected that Dan was getting nosy."

"But he was drunk."

"I don't know that a Dan Eliot is more clever than a Thomas Pellis."

"Maybe not."

"Can we truly assume that Thomas is part of it or not, just on what he does or does not tell to Dan Eliot?"

"I don't know." Tim hated it when she came up with good questions.

"Dan might just have raised more suspicions."

"Maybe."

"Does anybody know you've been talking to Dan?"

"No, just you."

"Well good! You don't need more suspicions directed your way, do you?"

"No," sighed Tim as he shook his head. He was now wondering whether they might have only made Thomas suspicious of Dan. He now remembered that Thomas would have seen both Dan and himself convicted at the same trial. And he must have suspected that Dan had gotten to know his fellow prisoners. *Have I just made more trouble for myself?* Tim wondered.

173

Chapter 18

Curiosity killed the cat.

Sadie was coming down the street with a basket under her arm when she saw him. Abner Wall was on horseback, riding into town, looking the way he usually did with his eyes shifting back and forth as if in fear of hidden enemies. She looked away, not wanting him to think he had been noticed. At the gate she turned to glance back. Their eyes met. His had a sharp look of suspicion. She wondered whether her eyes had revealed any less.

Once into the kitchen, she unloaded half the onions from her basket and said she needed to go help Bessie. Ignoring her mother's call, she went out, slamming the door. Slowly, she came around the house, trying to scan the street without being too obvious. No sign of him. With her eyes on the ground, she crossed over. When at the back door of the Pellis store, she stopped, took a deep breath, went up the steps and through the door. Bessie was at work. *Thank goodness,* thought Sadie.

"Goo'mornin', girl," said Bessie.

"We've too many onions. Could you use a few?"

"Sooner or later," Bessie replied, wondering why Sadie had a peculiar look on her face.

"Let me help you with that," said Sadie with a false smile.

"All right."

Sadie looked at what Bessie had in her hands – a knife and a potato. "Or I could do some sewing," she said as she turned to the sewing bag. Bessie was always behind with the sewing. Sadie took a pair of old John's breeches that had been pinned for taking in. Since his health had been failing, he had lost weight and all his clothing needed work. A needle and thread was ready so she was able to pick it up and carry it with her as she crept over to the door that led into the storefront. Bessie watched and said nothing. Sadie put her ear against the crack of the door and listened to the voices coming from the store.

"And it took some begging to get him up out of bed and down here," complained Nat. He had been telling the other voice about all the bother he had gone to the day before, starting with the need to get his father to mind the store while he was out. "The old fellow's better than he was, but he's still not well. One day at the counter and he'll be in bed with a headache for two, so it took some begging on my part. And then, once I was out and on the road, driving through rain, I still had to waste half the day at checkpoints waiting to get through. They enjoy their power, they do."

"Oh, you can't blame the poor soldiers though," teased Abner. "'Tis their only joy, wielding power. You'd be doing it, too, I'd think, were you in their place. Just imagine yourself standing guard all the day long – impatient civilians in your face and anxious officers looking over your shoulder. Having to be watchful for deserters and smugglers and spies and saboteurs and at the same time having to calm the honest and ordinary folk who just want to go about their business. I know what it's like, having done it myself in the last war. And I've now the greatest patience for the boys who are doing the job. Unpleasant duty, it is – boredom and fear together, for you never know when a pistol-carrying loony might lose his nerve and take a shot at you. Put a hole in you, in what he imagines to be his self-defense, eh? And all the time you're a-worried about that, everybody else is fuming because you won't let them all ride right past."

"Well, pity the poor boys," sneered Nat.

"But once they get to know you, they'll single you out and wave you through. Just give them a little present every now and then. A penny or two to buy themselves a small beer."

"Yes yes yes. And when I finally did get through – dripping wet, practically – you're not even there! Not last night and not this morning, either!"

"I had business to conduct," said Abner. "A man's got to make a living. And anyways, I got your note and here I am. So what's this all about?"

"It is our Old Goat again, I fear. He had himself a visitor, the night before last. At first, I didn't remember who it was, but then it came to me. 'Tis that sailor boy who was sent down from here to be tried for battery and was sentenced to hard labor. He was there with him and all the time talking of how a man could profit from the current state of affairs. The same sorts of opportunities that have been of interest to you-know-who."

"What sailor boy is this?"

"The one that young Toothless spent some time with down in the city," said Nat, who paused and then whispered, "In jail with him, while awaiting trial."

"He's out already?"

"They're always letting them out these days. They've no room for them all. The city's got more prisoners than rats."

"You suppose he learned anything from him?" asked Abner.

"I don't know, but I doubt it. Last night at least, the Old Goat seemed to be capable of restraining himself from his usual boasting. I must have stood there for a half hour. I almost froze my toes off! I had to sit before a fire for a good long while before I stopped shivering."

"And he didn't admit to anything?"

"Nothing that concerns you or me – not while I listened," replied Nat, with a nervous glance to the front door. "Not that I overheard, anyways."

"And 'sailor boy' kept pressing for answers?"

"Well, not exactly pressing for them. He was just on the topic, telling of what he might be willing to do, were he to have the opportunity to make some easy money. He said that, not long ago, he got a chance to take a package upriver. And he said he had suspected that it contained a secret letter written in code. Well, it was all very much of a coincidence if he was not informed by someone. And if he was not wanting to hear a confession."

"It does seem a bit suspicious."

"Yes, it does!"

"But it could be nothing at all," said Abner, with a shrug.

"Or it could be something!"

"Well, I don't know. What can we do? We can't shoot at every shadow. We'll just have to keep our eyes and ears open and if this amounts to something, then... well, if it does, then perhaps he'll come to the same end as 'our famous torte.' "

Nat grunted in response.

"And you came all the way down to the city just to tell of this?"

"Not that alone. I took a small wagon loaded with roots and was able to do enough selling and buying to make it worth the effort."

"A profitable day's work, I'd wager."

"A long cold day's work for a small profit," said Nat, and he started to complain about the prices he got.

Sadie had heard much of the conversation, but she could not make sense out of it. *Who's 'Toothless'?* she asked herself. *My toothless mother? And what's a 'famous torte'? A German cake that's much talked about?* She walked back to the table, wondering about it all, and had just taken a seat when Nat burst through the door.

"What did you pay for those potatoes?" he asked Bessie.

"Them? I got them from my Aunt Annie in trade for work done," she shrugged, and started into a long explanation of all she had bought and sold lately, to establish what the going price was for potatoes, parsnips, turnips, onions, horseradish, beets and carrots. Sadie, whose heart was pounding, kept her eyes on her sewing, except for glancing up at Bessie once or twice while she went on about "the prices these days."

"Well... all the better for those who are selling," said Nat finally, but in a tone that made Sadie wonder whether he had something on his mind other than root crops. It felt like he was watching her. Nat finally turned and went into the store. Too anxious to sit still, Sadie got up again to listen at the door.

"Come out front for a moment," said Nat to Abner. Their footsteps crossed the floor and the door hinge squeaked.

Sadie looked in and saw the front door swinging closed. The two of them were outside. *What for?* she wondered. *What are they saying out there that they couldn't say inside?* Without thinking, she crept across the squeaky floorboards and up to the front door.

"What's she doing in there?" she heard Abner ask.

"She's often over," replied Nat. "She's my sister's girl-of-all-work. I hire her to help when Bessie's in need of it."

"And now, I suppose, she's doing his nosing for him, as well?"

"That's what I don't know."

Sadie had heard enough and was heading back towards the kitchen, trying to step lightly to ease the floorboards' agony. She had just made it through the door when she looked back. Nat and Abner were coming in the front. Did they see her? She had no time to take a look – not enough time to tell.

Doing his nosing for him, Sadie repeated in her mind as she sat back down. *Why would he say that? Do they suspect us?*

"Curiosity killed the cat," whispered Bessie, who was busy with her work. Sadie looked at her. Bessie was smiling and looked as if she intended to keep this secret.

"I've got to be back," said Sadie.

"Do you now? Back to what?"

"Oh… nothing," she replied, and took her basket and went out the back door. Just outside she hesitated and wondered what kind of a fool she was to take such risks with men who might be killers.

Chapter 19

Which is more dangerous?

Sadie went to look for her brother. It had rained off and on during the day and the road was mucky and it stuck to her shoes.

"Tim," she called when she found him at the woodlot north of town. He had his mitts off to tie a bundle and he looked cold.

"What?" he asked as he lifted the bundle on top of the pile. It was at least a wagonload.

"Abner's been in town and he's been to see Nat. And Nat says he listened in on the 'Old Goat.' That must be Thomas, I figure. He said it was the night before. And he says a 'sailor boy' had been out to visit, who sounded like he was trying to get him to admit to something. They were using code names – like they're up to something. And they were talking like they might be suspicious of me and you."

"Why'd you think that?"

"Because he said something about somebody called 'Toothless' and 'Toothless' rhymes with 'Useless'."

"That doesn't tell much."

"And then Abner said somebody might come to the same end as 'our famous torte'."

"What?"

"'Our famous torte'," she repeated.

"What's that supposed to be?"

"I was hoping you'd know. A torte's a German dessert. Matilda makes it and it takes about a dozen eggs. Then Nat comes into the kitchen, and I'm just sitting there. And then, after he finished talking to Bessie, he goes back and takes Abner out front. I snuck out after them to listen at the front door and I heard Nat a-wondering to him whether I was there to do 'his' nosing for him."

"You followed after them?"

"To do 'his' nosing for him, is what he said!"

"You followed after them? In through the store?"

"And right up to the door, but I got to the kitchen before they came back. At least I think I did."

"You think you did?"

"Well, I don't know! I don't have eyes in the back of my head!"

"What would've happened if they had caught you nosing?" asked Tim, sounding angry.

"Well…" said Sadie, unable to think of what to say in her defense.

"I don't want you going and taking such risks!"

"Me! I'm not the one who's a-pulling a wagon over the King's Bridge with a load of stolen muskets and who knows what all else!"

"That's different."

"How's it different?"

"I'm a man!"

"You're a boy! And if Nat and Abner think you're onto their game, then the life of a Tim Euston ain't going to be worth much more than the life of an Amos Short!"

"I thought you were sure it was Jack Lauper that killed him."

"Well now I'm not so sure! And now if one of them has killed a man and got away with it, then... then the killing of another will come easy."

"If you're so scared of getting killed, then you should take care not to get yourself killed – or worse!"

Sadie huffed, looked away and said, "You're the one they'll want to kill!"

"I ain't scared!"

"You ought to be scared!"

"You can be scared for me!" said Tim with a sneer.

"You! If you ain't scared then you're a blockhead! You're out riding your wagon and taking great risks for the profit of those who don't care a whit about whether you'll live or die. You're a fool! You're what Josh Gainer says you are and no more and no less!"

"And maybe you should take yourself home to where you're safe behind your Momma's skirt. And maybe you should keep yourself there!"

"And who's going to keep you out of harm's way?"

"I'll take care of myself, just fine!"

"Well, then you keep up with it, Tim Useless!" said Sadie as she turned to walk off, her hands in fists and her shoes splashing in the puddles.

Tim went back to his work, but now he was so tense he could not aim his axe properly and was taking twice as many swings to cut through the tree. He tried not to, but he kept thinking about Abner Wall. He was wondering about "our famous torte" when he should have been thinking of which way the tree might fall. It missed him, but still he got a good scare.

"How could I be so stupid?" Tim said out loud as he stared at it. If he had been pinned under a branch, there would have been no one to help him. "This is too dangerous. Everything is too dangerous! It can't... I've got to do something!" Tim turned, leaving the tree for later and started towards town.

. . . . .

"What brings you in here?" asked John Gainer. Tim found him alone at work in the shop behind the house, cutting parts for a pair of wooden door hinges.

"My arm was getting sore and I figured it needed a rest."

"Best way to rest an arm is to go at your work a bit slower." John had noticed Tim working too fast in recent days.

"I ought to. But I'm wondering about something else. Who do I drive the wagon for, besides for you?"

"Well... the roots you take down come from Nat, aside from your own that you get from..."

"I know that, but... what about the stuff hidden under the false bottom?"

"How'd you... why are you asking that?" asked John, with a look of worry in his eyes.

"You're for the patriots, aren't you?"

"It pays to be neutral when you're living on the neutral ground."

"I don't mind my risking getting caught and jailed for the cause of liberty," said Tim, while looking to the side. "I... I tried to sign up for the Army last summer, but they wouldn't take me for being too short."

"So I heard. You know you did wrong by not asking my permission."

"I didn't think of that till later," lied Tim, as he looked at the ground, feeling ashamed.

"I let it go. I might have signed up myself had my wife not been against it," said John with a half smile.

"Well… maybe if we had fought, we'd both be down in the city now, sitting in one of them prison churches and praying for food."

"Yea, we might have been that or..."

"So where does the stuff in the hidden compartment go to?" asked Tim.

"It goes north and then west and it goes to serve the cause."

"And Abner Wall's in charge?"

"Come now, boy. You know better than to ask that. These are dangerous times we live in and we've all got to take care. The fewer who know who's who, then the fewer stories will be going around. It protects you, too."

"I won't tell nobody."

"Well, I'll take you at your word, but… you know that you or anybody else will talk, once they've got your feet a-roasting over a slow fire." They both chuckled at this.

"I suppose," said Tim.

"You know, it was because you had tried to join up that I offered you for driver. I figured that since you were willing to risk your… your… that since you were brave enough… I figured it wasn't so unjust to send you off on a dangerous task… doing it for your country."

"I didn't mind. I was proud to do it, even after I knew."

"And you weren't scared?"

"Oh, I was plenty scared."

"But still you did it," said John as he looked away. "I don't know that I could have."

"Well… well, I guess my arm's got enough rest," said Tim as he turned to go.

· · · · ·

Once Tim was back at cutting wood, he found his aim was no better than before. He hacked away like a beginner, haunted by thoughts of roasting over a slow fire. He kept busy, rushing around, hoping the activity would drive the thoughts out of his head. It helped. He had the tree limbed and a section of the trunk cut small enough to lift onto a pair of sawhorses when he heard footsteps coming up behind him.

"What … what are you back here for?" he practically shouted when he saw it was just his sister.

"I came back to say I am sorry for calling you a blockhead."

"You nearly scared me out'a my skin!"

"Sorry."

Tim turned his back on her and picked up the bucksaw. It would take the rest of the day before he had the tree cut and ready for splitting.

"Famous torte rhymes with Amos Short," said Sadie.

"What?"

"Abner said that somebody might come to the same end as 'our famous torte'."

"So what does that matter?"

"I figure that somebody must be you."

"You don't know that," said Tim as he started sawing.

"Well, neither do you!"

Tim kept sawing. A one foot length fell off. He put down the saw and stepped over to pick up the log and move it another foot along the sawhorses. He picked the saw back up and started another section.

"What were you doing in town?" asked Sadie.

"What makes you think I was in town?"

"I saw you walking through."

"I went to see John."

"To ask him questions?"

"He wouldn't tell me nothing."

"But now he knows that you know?"

"He says it's for the cause! He's a patriot! I don't doubt it now! I never doubted it! He's in this for the cause of freedom and justice!"

"And now he knows, that you know, what you weren't supposed to know!" said Sadie with a voice that had hardened.

"He... well... he didn't seem surprised."

"And you figure he just doesn't know what sort of people he's got himself mixed up with?"

"Do you know more than he does?"

"I get to listen in on them, don't I?" she replied, sounding like she could not believe his stupidity.

"So... you figure it's likely just the four of them?"

"There's not been any mention of other names, but that doesn't mean much, for I've not heard that much. And we know there's the blacksmith, and those that you go to down in the city, and there's those others up at the Felix farm."

"But it's maybe only the four of them that I'm driving the wagon for."

"Maybe four. Maybe fourteen."

"And... just one of them might be willing to kill to keep their secrets and keep them earning..."

"Earning the King's money is what," said Sadie. "It's good King George and his General Billy Howe who have money to spend."

"They all have money. The King just has more."

"A lot more. And all the while you and John are supposed to keep thinking that it's just the Army that benefits."

"We're just guessing," said Tim as he turned and took two steps away.

"We are that," sighed Sadie as she shook her head.

By this time the sky was a deep blue and the evening star was bright in the western sky. They walked home together. Tim made it to his place in time to help set up. Josh seemed almost unaware of his presence. All was quiet and Tim started to hope it was all over with and life was about to return to normal. This only lasted until John told Tim he would be needed to deliver another load the next morning. Tim nodded his head and tried to reassure himself that he had little to fear, now that the soldiers at King's Bridge knew he was supposed to make it through. *Or perhaps,* he wondered, *I've got a lot to worry about! Which is more dangerous, taking the wagon or refusing?*

Chapter 20

We should go tonight.

Driving the wagon was a dismal task now that Tim could no longer feel certain it was done in service of the cause of liberty. The wind felt even more bitter and the road seemed bumpier. At King's Bridge the sentry waved him through, giving him a look that said, "I know who you are and what you're up to."

That puts him a step ahead of me, thought Tim as he continued on. Darkness was falling by the time he made it to the city. On the edge of town he did not notice the gibbet until he was practically under it. This time it was occupied. Tim squinted his eyes to get a good look at the corpse, just when the setting sun peaked a yellow beam through the clouds to light up the poor miscreant's face. Tim felt his stomach flutter. *Zookers, it's me!* Or at least it was a young man who looked like Tim. It was hard to tell with his face half hidden by the steel bars of the gibbet. Tim looked down, having realized that other onlookers might notice the similarity. He gave the reins a shake and kept on going. It was only after he was well away that he realized that just looking like some felon would hardly reflect suspicion back on him. He felt angry at himself for being so easily frightened. His anger made his head ache and he started to shiver. The fright had made him break out into a sweat and now he was even colder. The sun was down and the sky overcast and he was driving into the city in near darkness. He might never find his way to the house.

Tim stopped by a street vendor. "Would you give me a light?" he asked, holding out his lantern.

"For a farthing."

That seemed like a lot for nothing. The woman was selling potato pancakes. "How much for one of them?" he asked.

"A halfpenny. And then I'll light your candle for free."

"All right," he said, handing her the lantern and reaching into his pocket to find a halfpenny coin. He had to get off the wagon to examine the coins under a better light. He chose one and gave it to her. She took a look at it under a very small magnifying glass that she held up to her eye. She gave him a pancake and he took a bite. It was cold and greasy. Once she had the candle in his lantern lit, he took a look around. He realized it would do him little good. The lantern could not light up a whole street. He felt foolish for wasting his money.

Tim walked on, leading the horses and trying to make out the buildings. The street was going from crowded to deserted. Soon though, he would be able to see "canvas town" because the roofs would be lit up by open fires underneath. He knew it would not be much further and maybe someone could help him. He counted his steps to estimate how far he had gone past the first tent and then turned up the side street. He led the horses along, calling the owner's name until a familiar voice said, "There you are, boy!"

Supper was good and after, Abe Balding read a book to the family members who sat around the fire. It was a mostly true story about a man's travels through Europe. He would get himself into the funniest predicaments and everyone was laughing at his misfortunes.

· · · · ·

Next day, the trip north went well with only brief stops and mild weather. Tim began to feel optimistic, hoping all his troubles would start to grow small and disappear. He pulled out his notes and started back at his memorization. It was a passage he had worked on before and he soon had it down pat. "It is the violence," Tim called out, "which is done and threatened to our persons, the destruction of our property by an armed force, the invasion of our country by fire and sword which conscientiously qualifies the use of arms; and the instant in which such a mode of defense became necessary all subjection to Britain ought to have ceased, and the independence of America should have been considered as dating its era from and published by the first musket that was fired against her" (from *Common Sense* by Thomas Paine, December 1775).

. . . . .

Tim's good mood lasted the whole day and into the next, until he was back at work cutting wood. As if to warn him the sky clouded over and the wind picked up. Then a gloomy-faced John Gainer came walking up the trail.

"It's coming along," he said, looking at Tim's pile of wood.

Tim did not reply. He knew John had something troubling on his mind.

"A fellow I know was out to see me today," said John. "Up from the city he was. And he tells me that he had seen Abner going around back of a house, just a couple of days before. He says it was the house of a tory so he got curious and he walked up and down the street a couple of times and kept an eye on the house. He says he saw others – gentlemen – going in the front. They weren't wearing uniforms, but there was at least one of them he recognized as an officer in the regulars. All the while, Abner was inside with them. It's probably nothing, but it's got the two of us wondering."

"I... I saw Abner talking to an officer at the King's Bridge, right when I was going through – the second time I went."

"You suppose it's any cause for concern?"

"Could be," said Tim, wondering whether he should tell John about his and Sadie's suspicions without having to worry that he might go off and tell Nat or Abner. "When I saw him there, a soldier had just finished telling me to shovel all the manure out of the wagon. The first time I'd been through the man had just wanted me to shovel out most of it so he could poke around with a bayonet. This time it was all of it he wanted out. Then an officer came out and said "that's enough" and he took the soldier back with him. I was left alone for a while and then I was told I could drive off. Since then, I've just been waved through and the looks in their eyes have been different. Maybe Abner paid a bribe or maybe he said I was a good tory or... or maybe Abner's got them thinking he's working for them to cover his working for the Continentals."

"Yes, it's probably that."

"But Abner doesn't really have the look of a patriot to him, does he?"

"Well," sighed John, "you can't tell all that much just by the look of a man."

"No, but... but he... he just doesn't seem the type who would risk his life for any cause other than getting himself some easy money."

John responded with a sad, bewildered expression and a faint "No... no he don't."

"Sadie can hear them talk sometimes – Abner and Nat – at the store. It doesn't sound like much when she retells it but... but she's getting worried that they might be in the pay of Billy Howe, and that I might be getting myself into the same sort of trouble that Amos Short did."

"You've told all this to Sadie?" asked John, sounding worried.

"Just to her."

"Well... don't go talking like that around town or you'll make problems for yourself... and for me, too."

"We've not been talking to anyone else. She's only talked to me and I've just talked to you. Well... you and Dan Eliot. He's the sailor who was jailed for beating up..."

"I know that. He's cutting wood south of here."

"He is," said Tim, and he explained about his and Dan's plan to ply Thomas with rum, and about what Sadie had overheard two days after from Nat and Abner – about their suspicions regarding Dan's visit. And about their code names for Dan, himself and Amos Short.

"She figures you could be the next one dead?" asked John.

"She's worrying, but she's just a girl."

"It could be nothing at all – all in her head."

"Probably," agreed Tim.

"But you've got to stop talking to people."

"There's been nobody else, except for you."

"Well, she might be right about Nat suspecting you've been talking to Dan about something."

"Why?"

"A few days ago Nat asked if the sailor who got convicted the same day as you was out already."

"Why?"

"Somebody had thought he'd seen you giving him a ride."

"Oh."

"And then he was wondering whether you might be smarter than you let on." John tried to chuckle when he said this.

Tim said nothing, but his stomach was twisting up again.

"Well well well!" sighed John. He paced a few steps one way and then the other. "I suppose I should ask around. It was Amos who was driving the wagon before you."

"It was."

"Not for long, though. It was usually old Saul Kane."

"You figure Jack Lauper was likely the killer?" asked Tim.

"I had been preferring to think that it was him, after he was convicted. Everybody was. It's only natural to want to think the killer was caught. But now with... I don't know. And I don't like it that I don't know. Maybe we should try to find out more about Abner and... and Nat... and about Thomas, too. Maybe we could set a trap of some sort."

"We could but... well, but what if it turns out like it did when I got Dan to go talk to Thomas? We didn't find out nothing and then Nat went and found out about it. And what if Nat and Abner – or maybe even Thomas – what if they're doing good work for the Army? They could be some of the best spies that George Washington's got and we'd be messing things up."

John stopped to think about this for a moment and shook his head. "Paul Revere and Thomas Pellis," he said with a smile, "kindred spirits – heroes of the revolution."

Tim chuckled at the thought of it.

"Well," said John with a shrug, "maybe I ought to go up north – to the farm where you take the manure to. Or maybe across the river to someone who's up in the ranks. And maybe you and your sister ought to come, too. We could say all that we've got to say and then leave it in their hands. Surely, they know far more than you or I."

"But... well... who do we know that could be trusted with a certainty? Even if we went all the way across to Morristown and talked to the top men and then... and what if we're seen going there? And even if we do make it there safe and sound, we won't be taken straight up to a general. We'd have to explain our business to the first officer that we're taken to. And what if he can't be trusted? What if he's in secret communication with Billy Howe? With all the rumors of peace talks going around... anybody at all could be hoping to have friends on the other side if there's a settlement. And even if he's a good and true patriot to the end, what do we say to him? That neither Abner nor Nat nor Thomas seems much like the type who'd serve a noble cause?"

"No," sighed John, sounding hopeless. "Well... what all did your sister overhear?"

"Not much. They're using code names, like 'Toothless' that might mean 'Useless', so it might be me."

John sighed again and said nothing. He paced in a circle. Off in the distance they could hear the clucking of chickens and the barking of dogs. "Tim... we're probably just all a-worried about nothing."

"Likely so."

"Maybe we should just start showing some courage and hope for the best."

"I suppose we ought to."

· · · · ·

John walked home and Tim went back to chopping down another tree. It was young growth, ideal for firewood. Years ago, a farmer must have ribbed the old trees to kill them and then had not gotten around to clearing a field after the dead trees had been blown down. Between the remains of rotted logs the new growth had come in dense. Once Tim had the tree down, he began to saw off the limbs. He was going to wait until milking time to tell his sister, but he started getting impatient. It was still mid-afternoon when he picked up his tools and went into town. He had been working hard and needed a rest. He could be there and back in no time and would still get in a good day's work.

"You shouldn't have told either of them!" said Sadie after hearing the news. Tim had found her carrying water back from the town well and they had gone to the cowshed to talk while she worked on making cheese.

"But... Dan had all but guessed it anyways."

"That Abner and Nat and Thomas were likely all in on it?"

"No, just that I must be carrying stolen goods."

"You could have left it at that."

"I suppose," said Tim.

"And you shouldn't have told John either. Right now, as we speak, he could be off telling Nat or Abner."

"Maybe."

"Who knows! And maybe John should have had sense enough not to admit anything to you. What did he have to gain by it?"

"Well... he'd been talking to somebody else and he was worried that Abner or Thomas or whoever might be helping the regulars by sending bad information to the Continentals."

"Maybe that's what he was thinking when he came to you but... but he's trusted Abner up until today, hasn't he? He might decide to trust him again."

"Who knows?" said Tim as he stared at the mud floor.

"But what we do know is that he doesn't care a whole lot about you. He sent you out to drive the wagon, didn't he? If they're not working for Billy Howe and if you are caught at the King's Bridge by someone who hasn't been bribed, then you'll end up in prison. And then what? John will go and choose the second to most useless boy to replace you and business will go on like you'd never been there."

"Well... maybe he's felt bad about offering me to them. Maybe he had just been talked into choosing me by Nat."

"Maybe he was."

"And maybe not," said Tim as he turned away.

"And maybe not."

"There's a lot of maybes."

"There is," said Sadie as she shook her head.

"And maybe Tim Euston is going to end up joining Amos Short in a graveyard."

"Maybe you should go tell John to keep quiet about all you've said!"

"I could."

"And don't tell him that I've been listening in on them," said Sadie as she pointed her finger.

"Ah... I already did."

"What did you tell him?"

"Just that you'd heard them talking and that it might be nothing at all."

"Might be?"

"It probably won't matter."

"Probably!"

"Well! You've got to trust somebody, sometime!"

"We're both going to get killed!" moaned Sadie as she cast her eyes heavenward and pressed the back of her hand to her forehead in a tragic gesture.

"Maybe not!"

"We've got to run and hide!"

"Where?"

"I don't know!" gasped Sadie. "We'll cross the river and go tell the Continentals all that we know and... and then we'll just keep on running."

"To where?"

"I don't know! Just keep going south. Philadelphia maybe."

"We could," said Tim, nodding his head. "I always wanted to see Philadelphia."

"Good. We could find work. You can cut wood and I'll do household service. We won't ask much and we'll take what we can get."

"We'll need a boat. I can likely pick the padlock on Clay Boodle's boat. We'll leave him a note telling him that we left it on the other side. And we can leave money to pay for its use. I've money... but... we should hold onto it. We'll need it on the road. I could leave an IOU. He'll be able to get his boat back again within a day and we'll owe him for its use."

"We should go tonight," said Sadie, whose voice was shaking with fear – fear of what might face them on the road.

Chapter 21

A mindless pawn.

Before she and her brother could make their escape, Sadie felt obliged to carry water and do other chores. Otherwise, her mother would be left with it all. *I hope Matilda hurries up and hires someone right away,* she thought as she crossed the street with her yoke and two buckets. *And it ought to be easy enough to find somebody.*

When she got back, her mother was coming out, on her way to a friend's house. That was good. It would allow Sadie a chance to get together food and clothing, wrap it in a cloth, and get it out to the cowshed. *And my bedroll too!* she realized. She had almost forgotten about it. *What a tragedy that would have been,* she told herself and started to wonder what other necessity she might be stupid enough to forget. She would have to get the bedroll out of the house without being seen. Matilda could not suspect anything because Nat could drop by at any moment. If she told him she, "had caught the girl making to run off," then he would know the reason why.

· · · · ·

"We'll still need more water," said Abby later on, when Sadie was coming up from the shed.

"Yes, yes," muttered Sadie, trying to sound in a bad mood. Her mother ignored her. It never paid to encourage her daughter to talk when she was in one of her moods. Sadie picked up the buckets and yoke and went back out into the cool evening air. The sky was clearing, with just a few clouds on the western horizon. There would likely be a nice sunset over the wide river and that would mean good weather tomorrow. *"And the next sunset I'll see will be somewhere far away,"* she told herself.

"Ah-ha, the girl-of-all-work heavy burdened with buckets," sang Thomas Pellis. He looked elegant in his new suit and he wore the stupid grin he always had when drunk. "Growing up so fast, eh, Sadie my dear? Soon to be heavy burdened by full breasts and a fretting babe, eh? Oh, but as a properly married mother, though. Or so we'd hope? Sure you'll be." He said this as he followed her along. Sadie could only keep quiet, her eyes down, and wait for him to finish having his fun.

"Oh, but I mustn't keep you, though. All the chores you're forced do, eh? On pain of a whipping, eh? So many chores, all to be done before they'll feed you, eh? Business before pleasure, eh? Ah, but I'll be a-waiting for thee, my love." This last line he sang and he walked off singing the rest of a mournful love ballad.

At least when I'm far from Yonkers I'll be far from him, Sadie told herself as she imagined him coming at her with a knife.

Sadie and Tim's plan was to take the boat after dark. By then, there would be a half moon rising and just enough light to get them across the river. On the New Jersey side they would follow the shore until they saw a light in a window. There, they would knock on a door and ask for directions to an inn. If asked, they could say they were on their way to work for a farmer, north of Newark. Whoever answered the door would likely say, "No no, stay here. Better you give your pennies to me than to another." Next morning, they would be warm and well fed and ready for a long day's walk. It should all go off with no difficulty.

. . . . .

"Sadie!" whispered Tim from where he was hiding behind a shed close by the waterfront.

"Did you get it open?"

"I found where Clay Boodle hid the key," he said, holding it up. He looked around as he came up to her. No one was about. "I've written him a note and left him a penny and an IOU for another five. He'll know I'm good for it."

"He'll hope you're good for it."

"It's his boat against our lives! He'll know some day what we were facing and he'll forgive us." Tim went to the boat and crouched to find the padlock. Earlier, he had unlocked it and then locked it up again, in case someone came along while he waited.

Sadie turned to take a last look at the town. In the evening gloom, the roofs were almost hidden against the gray-brown of distant hills. The faint flicker of candles could be seen behind wavy windowpanes. They had only been there for three years, but it was as much of a hometown as Sadie had. And she might never see it again – or her friends either. She might never see her mother again. "No, don't!" she ordered.

"What?" asked Tim, looking up. He had the chain off the boat and was about to start pushing it down the muddy slope into the river.

"I cannot be a thief!"

"But we're just borrowing it!"

"We'll likely just get caught and then be sent back," she moaned, shaking her head. She was a bound servant and he a bound apprentice. By law, they were obliged to serve out the balance of their terms – that or find money enough to buy their way out. Servants were always running off and

208

being forcibly returned. Any watchman or constable would ask for traveling papers and expect them to be written in good handwriting. Sadie had quickly forged one, but she knew it would still look suspicious. Their youth and ordinary dress would be enough to make anyone suspicious. And that would give them cause to arrest and jail both until enquiries were made.

"But what will we do if…"

"We can take our chances!" she snapped. "And we shouldn't worry about John. He'll likely not talk. He'll know the risk that we face. If we're brought back in chains, it will just be an admission to Abner and Nat that we believed ourselves to have good reason to fear them. And what would that say? It'd tell them that they've reason to fear us – for what we could tell. Our chances are likely just as good staying put as they are running."

"But we don't know that…"

"We don't know otherwise, either! We don't know anything! We don't know who killed Amos or who Abner serves. And besides, if either of us faces any great threat, then it's you and not me. If you want to run, you can run on your own and you'll not have your little sister tagging along to slow you down."

"Well… well… well, then that's what I'll do," said Tim, but he was feeling no great enthusiasm either. For all he knew they were being watched right now by someone in the shadows – someone who would raise a hue and cry as soon as he saw him pushing the boat towards the shore. If it was this easy to steal boats, they would be stolen all the time. Besides, if Tim wanted to demonstrate his courage, then he could just as easily demonstrate it here in Yonkers rather than out on a field of battle. And anyways, if there was peace, then there might be no more battles to fight – not for years. If Abner and the others were spies for Billy Howe, then this might be Tim Euston's only chance to serve the cause before peace talks began and the cause was lost.

Tim sighed, relocked the padlock and took the key back to its hiding place in a chink between two logs, just under the eaves of the shack. He took back the note and penny, and looked at Sadie. She turned and they started back towards town.

. . . . .

Sadie made it back without anyone having noticed she was gone. She went straight to the cowshed, where the cows had been kept waiting. They were now irritable. One of them kicked her.

Tim got home late for supper, but no one asked why. He quickly ate his cold meal. Afterward, he still felt restless. He was about to go out again when a frustrated looking John Gainer came through the door to tell him he would be taking another load down to the city the next day.

Tim nodded and said, "Yes sir," on his way out. In the empty street the wind was up and it was getting colder. The moon was high enough to let him keep to the road, but not bright enough to allow him to avoid frozen ruts, so he kept stumbling. "Too scared to run," he said, belittling himself. "Yea yea, used and abused I am. A mindless pawn is what I am and serving who knows what cause."

Tim kept walking until the last house and then turned back. He considered stopping by the cowshed to see if Sadie was still at work, but felt he could not face her now. He walked past and then changed his mind and turned back. At the door of the cowshed, he hesitated, then knocked. She opened it and let him in, but said nothing. One candle burned. She was skimming the cream. He pulled a stool over and started skimming off the other crock.

"What've you been memorizing?" asked Sadie.

"More Tom Paine."

"I've copied some more out for when you're finished."

"Good," said Tim, sounding discouraged and wondering why they were bothering with all this study. What did they need it for?

"I've been working away at it too, memorizing," she said, half to herself.

"Good for you," snorted Tim.

Sadie sighed and recited a passage that she thought might encourage him. "These are the times that try men's souls," she said, quoting Paine. "The summer soldier and the sunshine patriot will, in this crisis, shrink from the service of their country; but he that stands it now deserves the love and thanks of man and woman. Tyranny, like hell, is not easily conquered; yet we have this consolation with us, that the harder the conflict, the more glorious the triumph. What we obtain too cheap, we esteem too lightly" (from *The American Crisis*, December 1776).

Tim said nothing and they kept up with the work until it was finished for the night. Together they walked up to the back door. Tim said goodnight and continued on home.

Chapter 22

Go forth in courage.

Tim woke up from a dream of being trapped inside a sack that someone had just thrown into a river. He gasped a few breaths of air before realizing he was still in bed. Up on his elbows, he stared into the darkness, expecting at least one angry voice to tell him to keep quiet. No one spoke. They had all slept through it.

To cope with the winter's cold the five boys had to cuddle together spoon-style, under their five wool blankets stacked one on top of the other. Whenever one woke up and decided it was time to turn over, he would poke and prod the others awake and they would all turn over together to face the same direction again. Come spring, each would be on his own straw filled bedroll. On warm summer nights they would often sleep outdoors. But once winter was back again, they found they needed warmth more than elbowroom.

Tim knew he would never get back to sleep. He might as well get up. The gray-blue light of dawn was just starting to show through the small windowpanes. It had been his turn on the end of the row so he did not rouse anyone as he got on his feet. He slept in his day clothes with a wool nightcap. He took his shoes off, but wore all his socks, one over top of each other. Most of these socks he had knitted himself. On a windy night in January, the house could get bitterly cold and he would need all six pairs and more. This morning was not too bad, though.

Tim crept to the fireplace, careful not to kick any iron pots. He found the poker and dug about to expose live embers. A big piece of oak would almost always last the night. He sprinkled on dry shavings and then twigs. This was the job of the first person to wake and see light in the window. At least, it was supposed to be. Some boys would wake up and then just lie there with their eyes closed, waiting for somebody else to do it.

As Tim crouched before the fireplace, staring into the orange flames, he had a feeling that today would be a day when something decisive would happen. Lately though, he had felt that way a few times. He would have to wait and see. By tonight he might be in jail, or he might be dead, or he might be spending the night down in the city again. The three possibilities seemed equally likely.

. . . . .

The day passed. He drove the wagon and nothing happened. At least not that day. The next day in the early afternoon, when he was almost all the way up to the farm, Tim was met by four men on horses. They had scarves pulled over their faces and their pistols and carbines all pointed at him. Tim held up his hands, not knowing whether he was being robbed by thieves or "taxed" by skinners. He wondered what kind of reception he might receive when he got back to Yonkers and walked up to the blacksmith with neither horses nor wagon. The town might see him chased down the street by a blacksmith shouting and waving a stick.

"Tim, you're coming with us," ordered one of them. His voice sounded familiar – likely one of the young men from the Felix farm.

"Hop down, boy!" said an older voice.

With his hands up, Tim jumped off, took two steps towards them and stopped. He kept his eyes down and said nothing. Someone came up from behind and tied a cloth around his eyes. He tied Tim's hands in front of him in a complicated knot that ended with a loop around his waist.

"You keep your hands right there in front of you now," the man said. "It won't draw tight unless you try to wiggle your way out. And you don't want to do that because you don't want your fingers to turn blue and start to drop off." He grabbed hold of the back of Tim's belt. "Now boy, I'm going to help you up and onto this here horse." He pushed Tim ahead a few steps. "This leg up," he said, taking hold of Tim's ankle to guide his foot up and into the stirrup. "And up you go," he said as he gave Tim's belt a lift to help him. Both horse and man acted like they had been through this procedure a hundred times. "Now you grab hold of the saddle so you don't fall off and break your neck."

"Let's go," ordered another and they rode off.

Tim could hear the wagon following behind. Maybe, he wondered, *I'm being pressed into service with the regulars. That's unlikely, though. There's been no word of press gangs, other than the navy taking sailors last summer. And what would they want me for this time of year? They must be bandits, taking me for ransom. Are they thinking that Tim Euston has family that can pay ransom enough to make it worth their bother?*

They had not ridden far when Tim could feel they were following a trail down a steep slope. That meant down to the river. As soon as he could smell water they stopped. The same man who had helped him up was guiding him down, again with his hand under Tim's belt.

"Down we go, same way as we got up. This way now," he said once Tim had both feet on the ground. The man placed his other hand on the back of Tim's collar, like a tavern keeper giving a drunkard a quick escort out into the street. "Take care now," he said as they went down the steep slippery bank of the river. "Now, you're going into a boat." One hand went down to grab Tim's ankle and place his foot onto the edge of the boat. "Up and over." Tim's foot landed on the edge of a seat and slid off. He stumbled, but the man still had hold of his belt and was able to pull back enough to ease his fall and get him into a sitting position. Tim wondered whether the man had strength enough to pick him up and toss him in the river. The sense of complete helplessness along with the thought of ice-cold water had Tim's heart pounding with fear.

"Heave off," called the older man. Tim heard the last man splashing in the water and jumping into the boat. Next came the sound of oars creaking in oarlocks. They were either crossing over or traveling along the Hudson River. Tim dared not ask why. He felt droplets of water hitting his cheek, but could not tell whether it was rain or the splashing of oars.

"How's that mare of yours doing?" asked one of his captors.

"Still a bit stiff," said another and the conversation was about horses for as long as they kept rowing. They seemed at ease for a band of thieves. Tim wondered whether they might be Continental soldiers. *That might explain the one with the accent,* he told himself. It could still be kidnapping for ransom, though. Or maybe they were bounty hunters and he was being taken down to the city to be charged and convicted for smuggling. Maybe Abner had failed to pay his bribe and the operation was being shut down. And Tim would now join John and Nat and the others in a jail cell. These considerations kept repeating themselves in Tim's head as they kept rowing. As soon as they hit the muddy bank, Tim was manhandled out of the boat, onto the shore and up onto another horse. As they traveled, they alternated between a walk, a trot and a canter depending on the quality of the road. Wherever they were going, they needed to get there fast.

After hours of this punishment, Tim began to feel the rise and fall of hills. The call of woodland birds and the smell of rotting leaves told him they were into a forest. Through the fabric of his blindfold he could tell it was close to dark. He heard voices and smelled wood smoke. He guessed it was a large town with many houses, every chimney belching smoke from fires cooking supper.

They came to a stop and Tim was taken inside a building. His hands were untied and the blindfold taken off. It was a small room with walls built of squared timbers. The window was very small and right up at the ceiling. It was a jail cell.

"Here's a pot of stew for your supper," said a man, "and there's a bedroll and a good blanket. Eat your fill and try to get some sleep."

"What's going to happen to me?"

"Oh, don't you worry now boy, so long as you behave yourself and cooperate. You're just going to be asked a few questions."

"Why am I here?"

"I just told you, to answer a few questions. Now don't you fret, now. We'll take good care of you so long as you take good care of yourself. Get yourself some sleep, why don't you?"

He left Tim with the pot of stew and a wooden spoon. The door slammed shut and Tim was in complete darkness.

. . . . .

The next morning the man was back with a bowl of porridge. Tim had been lying awake for what seemed like hours. Later on, the man returned again, this time with a blindfold. With his hands tied behind his back, Tim was led outside and towards another building. He heard the voices of young men joking and laughing. One was daring another to do something.

Once inside, a hand pulled Tim down onto a stool. The voice of an older man started asking questions, first about who he was and where he came from, then about what work he did and for whom. Tim remembered the story John had told about his cousin – the one who was kept awake for four days while being questioned. Next came more questions about John Gainer, Abner Wall, and both Nat and Thomas Pellis. When the man got to the issue of the wagon and the deliveries into the city, Tim stopped telling the truth. He said he just hauled wood and roots and brought manure back up to a farm. He was expecting them to start beating him in hopes of getting some more useful information when someone took hold of the blindfold and pulled it off. He saw a short man with white hair at his temples.

"Let me introduce myself, Tim Euston. My name is Sam Baker. Now, I'm told you tried to join the Army last summer and were turned down for being too short."

Tim said nothing. He was still not sure whether he was being interrogated by a patriot or by a tory.

"Now," continued Sam, "I'm going to assume you still sympathize with the patriot cause and you're willing to help us."

"You're with the Continentals?" asked Tim, sounding suspicious.

"I am," said Sam, and then he paused. "Why don't we take a walk outside?" He untied the rope that held Tim's hands. The door was already open, allowing in warm March sunshine. Sam gestured for Tim to step outside. Tim went ahead, half wondering whether he might be shot the moment he went through the door. He was not. He saw a wide street and an ordinary sort of town with a few dozen houses, but there were a lot of young men going about. Two of them walked by wearing felt tricorn hats with cockades of black ribbon. Another wore a uniform – a brown coat and vest, with orange cuffs and lapels. A pair wore fringed buckskins and others, little more than rags. There were a variety of colors, though more a lack of color – a lot of grayish-brown leather and the dingy white of well worn cloth. Tim knew where he was now. This was Morristown and these were soldiers of the American Army.

"Soldiers everywhere," said Sam, "and not a redcoat to be seen."

"No," said Tim with a smile.

"Can I now assume you're willing to help us out in our struggle for independence?"

"I am, if you'll be willing to let me."

"Well, we don't need you to take up a musket and march into battle – at least not yet. What we could use you for is information. Have you ever fancied yourself as part of a network of spies?"

"It might be that I am already, if Abner Wall and Nat Pellis and his Uncle Thomas are working with you."

"Have you wondered which side they are on?" Sam asked with a smile.

"I just drive the wagon. They don't tell me nothing."

"But you know that you carry more than firewood and potatoes, don't you?"

"I've figured out that much by taking a close look at the wagon and... and a look inside."

"Well then, maybe together we'll figure out more and... and now is maybe the time to meet your new master," Sam said while looking the other way.

"Yes sir," said Tim, wondering whether he meant a new carpenter in place of John Gainer.

"Come along," said Sam and Tim followed. They went between two houses and crossed a large field where soldiers were being drilled, marching up and down in rank and file to learn how to follow orders without stopping to think. Further over were other groups. Two men stripped to the waist were wrestling while their instructor complained about their poor technique. Tim had heard wrestling was an important part of military training. Once all muskets were fired and soldiers were too close to jab a bayonet, then the battle's outcome could be determined hand to hand.

Sam led Tim towards a large house. There, a group of officers, handsomely attired in wool coats, were pitching horseshoes while enjoying the sunshine. One stood a head taller than the others. Tim hoped that Sam would not disturb them. Sam said, "Wait here," and walked straight up to an officer. Sam stopped, said nothing, and waited for the gentleman to turn and acknowledge his presence. When he did, the two of them spoke a few words, then turned and came straight for Tim.

"This is Tim Euston," said Sam, "and he's volunteered to help me gain some valuable intelligence." Tim immediately looked at the gentleman's feet, out of respect for a man of high rank.

"So boy, you've earned the trust of Sam Baker, have you?" he asked quietly. "Quite an accomplishment, I'd say." Tim glanced up for just a moment and shrugged. "Not too sure, are you," the gentleman asked with a smile, "or just too modest? Well, you can take my word for it then. Sam's a good judge of character and if he sees an honest patriot in you, then an honest patriot you very likely are."

"No more than many," said Tim. Right away he wondered whether that was the wrong thing to say.

"No, likely not, I suppose. And that's especially true here in Morristown where the best of the best are assembled. Now, you'd like to meet our commander, would you?"

Tim shrugged again. He thought he was going to meet a new master. He had never heard a carpenter called a commander before. The officer turned to go back towards the others. Tim wondered whether the man might be referring to a captain in the Army, or maybe even a colonel. Tim saw the officer go over to speak to the tall man. He nodded and they started back. Tim looked down, not knowing what to do.

"Sir," said Sam after they had exchanged greetings. "I'd like you to meet a boy who is helping us out with a tricky little issue. I've inquired into his background and it seems he's a woodcutter who likes to memorize the words of Tom Paine and practice his oratory on the gophers and squirrels of the neutral ground."

"Are you now?" the man replied, with a chuckle. "Well, I've an enthusiasm for that man's writings myself."

"And," said Sam, "we're told that the boy volunteered to fight with us just last summer, but unfortunately he was turned down for being too short."

"Well, good for you for trying, son."

"But he's grown since then," said Sam.

"Well my boy, I'd expect that by this coming summer we'll be considering you more than tall enough."

Tim was flustered and he held his hands together to stop them from shaking. "Perhaps," he said with a shrug and a glance up at the man's face. He had reddish-brown hair, scarring from smallpox, a large straight nose and he was smiling with his blue-gray eyes.

"His name is Tim Euston," said Sam. "He'll go into action this very day and he has not shown a hint of hesitation. In fact, he has persuaded me to act faster than I might have."

"Ready, able and eager? Good, good," said the tall man as he placed his hand on Tim's shoulder. "Be brave, my boy. Thy country hath need of thee and thou hast answered to a noble calling. Go forth in courage for thou dost fight to preserve our liberties." He then patted Tim on the back.

Tim glanced up again and said, "I will, sir," but it came out as a whisper.

"I thank thee for taking the time, sir," said Sam as he came to attention and saluted. The men wished them well and turned back to their game. Sam said, "Come along Tim," and they started back the way they came.

"You handled that well," said Sam once they were out of earshot. "Just the right amount of humility and the right number of words. Good boy."

"I thank you," said Tim who was shaking. He looked over his shoulder at the man whose hand had touched him. He had recognized him right away, having seen him ride through New York City over a year and a half before, when he was on his way up to Massachusetts to assume command of the American Army.

Chapter 23

I'm one of them.

Tim followed Sam to a tavern where they were met by the familiar stink of stale beer and tobacco smoke. This morning, many of the young men were drinking coffee. Sam bought a cup and a meat pie for each of them. Tim's was filled with a delicious mixture of beef and onions, and the coffee was as good as any he had ever tasted.

"Excellent, is it not?" said Sam. "One of our privateers took it from an English vessel. And doesn't that just make it taste all the better?"

"It does," chuckled Tim. It seemed odd to feel so warm towards the man who, just a half hour before, had interrogated him while bound and blindfolded.

"Who knows," said Sam, "King George himself might have held a share in the cargo of that very ship."

"God save the King, but send us his coffee," said a man who sat further down the long table. He wore buckskins and talked like he came from far away.

"Indeed," agreed Sam, "and along with it, a few of his colonies."

"Coffee ain't the only tribute that's been paid by the King, recently," said the frontiersman as he slid down the bench to join them. "Me and a few of the boys are just back from a little huntin' yesterday. The locals have been keeping an eye out for redcoats who come a-foraging," he said, looking at Tim.

"They're at it again?" asked Sam. "I'd thought they'd been driven out of these parts."

"Oh, they have been. This wasn't but a pleasant stroll from Brunswick town, but still not close enough though, not for their sakes."

"There's some who just can't learn."

"Sadly for them, no. And when we got word that a party was out a-buying up tory livestock with royal silver, well, we couldn't let them have an easy time of it. We've some farmers hereabouts who claim to be tory and take their money, but will still inform us of their whereabouts. We had them watched until they started looking like they were loaded up and on their way back. Then we took ourselves over to where they were likely coming. And just in the nick of time we got ourselves lying flat and hidden down behind a hedge that followed alongside a stretch of road. Hidden even from their flanking guard by sod and twigs we'd dug up and gathered up, just enough to hide us. Then, when a party of cavalry rode up, we had a jolly old fellow of ours who had stayed back. He was walking alongside them declaring his loyalty to the King and telling them where they could likely find some of them dastardly rebels."

"He demanded payment for his information, I hope," joked Sam.

"He did, but they just laughed at him. But not for long, for just as the wagons were catching up, at a signal, we all leaped up – muskets and rifles and pistols aimed – armed to the teeth! Well! You should have seen the looks in their eyes! Ha! Two hundred men we were and appearing right out of nowhere! We didn't even have to shoot one of them – wasted not an ounce of powder! They were caught and they dropped their weapons and held up their arms. As clean a haul as any you could ask for. But had one of them pulled a trigger though, well! It would have been a bloodbath! But no, it seems even redcoats are sometimes capable of wisdom. We captured the whole blessed wagon train! Thirty-nine prisoners we got and fifty-one horses, along with sixty-eight head of beef. And a few dozen sheep and goats too. And nine big wagons piled high with sacks of grain, crocks of lard, chickens, ducks and geese! You name it! What a haul!"

"You'll feed the whole Army for a week," said Sam.

"We will, Captain! Aye, we will!"

"Yea, we saw a turn of the tide last Christmas," said Sam to Tim as he got up from the table, "and it's still flowing with us."

"Aye, one victory after another!" said the frontiersman.

"Indeed. Well, boy! To business," said Sam to Tim.

"Another set of eyes?" the frontiersman asked Sam as he glanced at Tim. Sam just gave him a wink.

Before following Sam out, Tim looked back at the soldiers. Their eyes seemed to express both acceptance and admiration. Tim had never seen grown men look at him that way before. *I'm one of them,* he thought, as he went out the door into the bright sunshine.

Other men passed them on their way. Tim looked at them differently now. He was one of them – an equal. He was not a mere boy in the presence of men – of soldiers. He was now a scout for the Army. Tim Euston was a real scout and he was willing to go deep into enemy territory. And they would admire him for it. They might even envy him his courage, some of them. *My my, ain't this an odd feeling?* he thought as he pulled back his shoulders and stuck out his chest.

"Now let me get to the point," Sam said with a sigh, when they were back to the house where Tim had first been questioned. He sat down on a stool and waved his hand towards another. "Both you and I are unsure of Abner Wall and Thomas Pellis."

"You've talked to John?"

"He takes your concerns quite seriously and he trusts your judgment. John tells me that they just don't seem, to you, like the sort of men who would risk their lives for any cause other than their own enrichment. Well, I must say, I've been feeling the same way. And right from the start, too. In our business – military intelligence – we cannot afford the luxury of saying 'you can't judge a book by its cover'. You start giving every man the benefit of the doubt and you'll soon find yourself dead."

"I suppose so," said Tim. It felt good to hear that Sam Baker was scared, too.

"Now, as you may have guessed, Abner has been sending us encrypted information which he claims to get from someone within Billy Howe's staff."

"Does he?" asked Tim, with a doubtful tone.

"He does. And what we have been receiving does not always jibe with the information that comes from other sources. I am wondering whether Abner has made a deal with them and is being paid to deliver misleading information. Fighting season is coming fast upon us and we need reliable intelligence. Confusion will cost lives – the lives of those boys you see out in the street. And maybe yours and mine as well. Now, what I am hoping, is for you to tell me something about Abner or Thomas that I don't already know."

"Well… what me and my sister have been wondering is whether old Thomas might be deeper into all of this than what might seem. He's had good money coming in lately. He's a-wearing a nice new suit and it seems he's drunk every time you see him. Maybe he's the one with a friend in high command. And maybe he's getting a larger cut of the King's silver than the others."

"You think so?" asked Sam. He spoke in a flat voice, but the look in his eyes suggested this was new information.

"He's been seeming quite pleased with himself, lately. They say he's always been proud and putting on airs and expecting more than he has due, but now he's got worse than ever. My sister fears him, she does. And so do I – for her sake. He fancies her."

"Yes, I was at your trial."

Tim was not surprised to hear this. Court day was a big event and most men came out. "You saw Jack Lauper get convicted, then," said Tim. "He's innocent, you know. Almost for sure he is. I was in jail with him. And what we're a-wondering is whether Thomas or Abner was behind the killing of Amos Short – and not just because Amos was going to testify in my defense and make Thomas look bad. Amos was hauling wood for John Gainer, just before I started. And we've been wondering whether the others thought Amos knew too much and that he couldn't be counted on to keep quiet about it."

"And what makes you think that?"

"Well... we were just wondering. When I saw Abner, just after I got out of jail, he looked like... well, just so angry and so wicked. I, right away, wondered whether he was the killer. He looked like his heart was so full of something and... and not full of the love of the Lord either."

"You've nothing more than this to make you want to suspect him?"

"Well... I'm sure it wasn't Jack. They were friends! They'd fought before, but not to the point of killing each other. He wouldn't knock him over the head like that and then lie about it. It isn't like him!"

"Well," said Sam, "I don't know who killed Amos, but I can recall Abner saying he doubted whether Amos was the best choice for a driver."

"And he likely wonders the same about me, too."

"He has from the time you started."

"And there was my friend, Dan Eliot, who you got to see convicted the same day as me, on a trumped-up charge of battery." Tim explained how Dan had got involved, how he had gone to ply Thomas with drink. And how Sadie had later doubted the quality of Dan's effort.

"You've trusted Dan Eliot with all this?"

"Well, yes. Maybe I shouldn't have. He's a clever one though and he had it all figured out in no time – my being hired for a task I didn't deserve. Not till I was older than I am now. He figured it was likely not so much of a plum job and that there must be a catch. And that likely I hauled contraband. Dan had it figured out in no time. Like he says himself, he's smarter than he looks. But he's a good patriot too – truly he is! He was at sea all last summer and fall and he was frustrated to find that so much fighting had gone on and that he didn't get a chance to be in on it and be fighting along with you in the Army."

"Was he now?" asked Sam with a smile. "Well, you tell him to stay where he is for another month and then come to me. We'll likely have some fighting for him to do before too long."

"There's not gonna be any peace talks?"

"Not any chance of it. Things were looking dismal for us last December, but it's all changed. There's been no great battles these past three months, but there's been many a small skirmish. Poor Billy Howe lost himself nine hundred on Christmas Day alone, over at Trenton, and he's lost well over two thousand since. And what's likely been worse for him has been the loss of forage. His horses have been half starved. Every time they've come inland for to find themselves forage we've been there to chase them back, at a cost of a few men each time – sometimes a few dozen. It's been adding up."

"So the rumors..."

"Ignore the rumors, boy. That's just the wishful thinking of your 'loyalists'. No boy, there'll be no peace talks."

"Oh good! Ah... well," stammered Tim, "I suppose that's unfortunate."

"We all pray for peace, but if the war must go on then let it last long enough for Dan Eliot to show us his best."

"Indeed!"

"Now then, the day's a-wasting, boy. I must give you your orders and get you back onto the neutral ground. What I want to do is to lay a trap and you can help me with it. You've no doubt wondered about your ability to pass so easily through checkpoints. What I suspect is that they are deliberately allowing them to make a good profit on the sale of stolen muskets. And why would they do this? Because they want them to keep at it and to keep on looking like a valuable asset for the Army, bringing arms and seeming to bring good information from a reliable source. And I suspect they would only want this if they are deliberately sending a mixture of good information and bad."

"Enough that's good to keep you interested and enough bad to lead you astray?"

"Indeed. Now, when you get back, I want you to go on taking wood down to the city. And don't go showing yourself to be any more or any less reluctant to do so. We don't want you raising any more suspicions. Then, on your next trip down, I want you to open up the false bottom and add in an extra letter. John Gainer can help you get it opened up."

"You don't know where he, or Thomas, gets the letters from that they bring back?"

"Tim, I'm likely telling you too much already so don't you start asking questions."

"Of course."

"Now, this letter is written to Abner and it's in a code that he and maybe Thomas can decipher. It will tell the name of another of our spies in the city. It will be a false name though. And if this information is handed over to high-command, then... well, we've a fellow who claims to... well... let's say the same information might come back to us."

"You've a spy in the office of Billy Howe?"

"That's another question, Tim."

"Sorry."

"If this false name is passed along and actually does make it to a second source and back to us, we'll know that it has been leaked by Abner or Thomas. Now, do you think you can get the job done without raising suspicions?"

"So long as they don't catch me and John red-handed," said Tim with a shrug. He was relieved to hear his task would be a simple one. All he and Sadie had to do now was to survive the next few days. Abner, and maybe Thomas too, if they both fell into the trap, would be taken away and the threat they posed would be lifted.

"Good then," said Sam as he stood up. "I've the letter ready to go and you should be on your way back down to Yonkers before they start wondering where you've been off to. Your wagon will be waiting for you. Oh yes, I've some news you can share with your friend Luke – Jack Lauper's son – so long as you don't tell him where you heard it."

"What?"

"Jack has escaped. He was with some prisoners who were doing some pick and shovel work. We were told there were prisoners working there every day and that they weren't too heavily guarded. On a foggy morning we sent over a small raiding party. They surprised the guards and brought them all over to the Jersey shore – the prisoners still wearing their balls and chains. They're all here in Morristown now and Jack has enlisted."

"Won't Luke be relieved to hear that! He wants to enlist, too. He wasn't old enough either last year. He's sixteen now and he'd make a good soldier."

"Tell him to hold off for a month or two and bring him along when I come for you and Dan Eliot."

"And I can tell him not to worry about no peace talks," said Tim with a smile.

Horses and an escort were waiting for Tim and again he got the looks, the expressions of approval. This time, on the ride back, he got to see the countryside while they traveled along at top speed, in fear of an enemy patrol that might show up at any time. *This is so bizarre,* he told himself. *All this fuss for little Tim Useless.*

· · · · ·

They made a fast crossing of the river and he was back on the wagon in time to get it home by mid-afternoon. The blacksmith asked no questions, assuming Tim had met with the usual delays. Tim was on his way to tell his sister about the adventure when he met up with Thomas Pellis.

"Tim, my boy! Back home safe and sound, are we?"

"All went well. Another trip just like the others – bumpy roads and long waits at the King's Bridge."

"Oh, they are the devils, those redcoats, always a-keeping us good folk a-waiting. Everyone's vexed complaining, aren't they? Old Hans says he had to fork a load of hay off his wagon not an hour after he had loaded it up, and then he had to unload it a second time, down by Harlem town. Imagine that! How long must we endure?"

"Indeed, how long? Well, I'd best be back to my work."

"Ah yes, indeed you should, my boy. Better sweat than tears, eh?" said Thomas as he patted Tim on the shoulder and continued on towards the tavern.

Tim forgot about visiting his sister and went home to get his saw and axe, to get back out to do some work before sunset. Thomas had him worried. There had been a look in his eyes, like he knew something. *But don't he always look sneaky and don't he always talk in riddles?*

· · · · ·

Tim was very tired by evening. All the turmoil of the past day and night had his nerves twisted and frayed. He had slept so little the night before. Then all the nervous energy had forced him to work too hard. He ate his supper with droopy eyes and had nothing to say. Josh was as talkative as ever, until he heard his father tell Tim he would be driving the wagon the next morning.

Back on the wagon again already. Is that good news or bad? Tim wondered as he got out his knitting and took a stool over to the fireside. Mrs. Gainer started to read from a book about the ways of farming in Holland. Tim hoped it was interesting enough to keep his mind off what might happen to him were Abner to find out about his trip to Morristown.

Chapter 24

He's seen and heard more.

Next morning, Tim waited until the other boys had left so he could tell John he needed help getting into the hidden compartment. Before he could, a farmer came to the door asking about getting a lean-to built on his barn. The two of them were hardly through with greetings and gossip when John asked Tim what was keeping him from his work.

"I'm just on my way now," said Tim. It did not matter. Dan Eliot was likely cutting wood and could help. If not, Tim would come back into town and interrupt John.

"We'll be needing those hooks and ropes again," said Tim when he found Dan at work, and after looking around to make sure they were alone. "I've got something to add into the saddlebag."

"What?"

"And I fear I cannot tell you what or why."

"I can understand that," said Dan with a shrug. "You wait here while I go fetch them."

Tim was surprised at how easily Dan accepted his refusal to share the secret. *Maybe*, he told himself, *he's thought it over and has come to realize the importance of keeping secrets from all, including your trusted friends, when they have no need to know.*

Dan came back running and they went straight to work, unloading the wood and opening the compartment. He asked questions and made a couple of guesses as to what it was that Tim could not talk about. The conversation went longer than Tim had planned and he made the mistake of mentioning Jack Lauper's escape. The next thing Tim knew, Dan had pried even more out of him. And soon Tim found himself begging for a promise not to repeat anything about his getting to meet the General himself.

"You'd seen him before, hadn't you?" asked Dan.

"Just when I saw him a year ago, last summer, down in the city. We all went down. That was before Congress had signed the Declaration. That's when Mrs. Gainer decided she was against them."

"You never saw him when he was marching up and down these parts, fighting battles?

"I might have! But not to know that it was him, for sure."

"Why not?"

"Well... it was just out west of here, a few miles, if it was him that I saw. It was out by the White Plains road, last October, when the whole Army came marching past and headed upcountry. First we saw a few strangers riding past. They weren't all dressed alike, but no red coats, anyways. We couldn't tell who they were. We were well back from the road. Then we saw more coming past. And then even more. I ran up to ask what's happening. Josh was yelling at me to get back to work, but I made like I couldn't hear him. I asked who they were and they told me."

"No uniforms at all?"

"Not one in five wore any sort of a uniform. In my blue coat that I've got now, I look like more of a soldier. So I asked them where they were headed and they laughed and said 'north'. Stupid question, I suppose. But then down the road I looked and I saw more men and horses and wagons and more following them. And the line was stretching along down the road and across the valley and up the hill. A whole mile long I could see. And who knows how far beyond! The whole blessed Army was on the move! And they were keeping on coming. So I ran back and told the boys and then we were all a-dropping everything and a-running up to watch – even the boys who've got tories for fathers."

"And Josh let you?"

"He went and climbed up on a haystack and we all went up after him to see the Army coming across the hill. Then one of us started singing 'Yankee Doodle' and we all joined in and we were all waving. And then the soldiers started all waving back and they started into singing, too. Then we were jumping up and down and we were falling off the stack and climbing back up and just a-singing like a flock of jaybirds! You should have seen them! They were pulling cannons and big wagons and they were all laughing at us and waving! We must have sung Yankee Doodle a thousand times! We didn't get nothing done, but when we got home and John finds us tired and hoarse from singing, and he hears that we've wasted near the whole day away and done next to nothing."

"What'd he do?"

"We were ready to be lined up for a whipping, but instead he just laughs and says 'Good for ye, boys.' And he said it must have been a tonic for tired soldiers, just to see and hear us. It was then that I knew he was still a patriot, deep at heart."

"And you saw Washington go by?"

"Halfway through it all, Josh said he thought he saw Washington waving to us, but he wasn't sure. He didn't say so until after he was already passed by and on his way. We'd been so daft we weren't even watching. It was surely a bunch of high ranking officers for they were all up on horses and all in fine uniforms. I was tempted to run after them, but there were more soldiers a-coming and we had to keep on singing."

"Where'd they all go to?"

"They went on up to White Plains, the county seat. They took a stand there about a week later. It was just ten miles north of here that they fought. We didn't know what was happening, but on a Monday we started hearing thunder. But we couldn't see any clouds. Then Josh said it must be cannon fire. And it went on for hours, off and on. We kept working, but it made you feel strange to think that some of those same fellows who'd been walking past and waving were the ones being shot at and killed. They said afterwards that there were over a hundred Continentals carried off the field, dead or wounded."

"Indeed," said Dan with a nod, "too many defeats."

"But we got them back at Trenton and Princeton, didn't we?"

"We did that! And I remember when I heard the news about Trenton! We'd just got into harbor, down in the city, the day before. It was late, but we'd had trouble. It was a tory shipmaster we had so he'd been glad to come home to see a hundred ships in the harbor and redcoats everywhere in the streets. The tories and the redcoats were all smiling, but just for one day. And then the news came up the street – a thousand Hessians captured. After that, all of New York City was glum and sorrowful. Or almost all. Me, and a few of us that I knew were for the cause, we were bubbling inside – smirking and winking at each other."

"And come summer there'll likely be more battles to fight," said Tim with a nod. "Sam Baker says there's not likely to be no peace talks and he said to tell you to wait here another month and then he'll come for us. Luke too. And me, likely. It depends. Sam Baker might need me to stay around here, gathering intelligence. I'll go where he sends me."

"And I'll be there to fight, I will, this time. And I'm thinking of getting me some better clothes, too. To be ready for any weather. I'd reckon the women will cut and sew some for me. And I'll get extra soles for my shoes, to take along. I've heard too much about barefooted soldiers. The women, they're all patriots. And they've money to spare, what with all the extra wood I'm cutting for them. Come April, I'll be ready and I'll be a-crossing that river if I have to swim it."

"You won't have to. Sam Baker will see to it you're ferried across and taken straight to Morristown."

"Good! I can't swim!"

"We could see action by May or June probably. Soon as the weather's fine and the roads are dry."

"The sooner the better! You know, I've never yet even got to hear a battle, not even from far away."

"We all but got to watch the battle down south of here," said Tim. "Me and the rest of the crew. They fought again at Fort Washington. But this time, when we heard the cannons they sounded so near! It started right first thing in the morning and went on and on. We hid our tools and we ran south to see what was happening. We didn't make it a mile before we came to a roadblock and we were told to turn around and go back. Well, we just went back as far as a patch of woodland and then we snuck around and back down again along the river. We followed cow paths along the bank down to where we could see the great men-of-war out upon the river, blasting away. Smoke like a forest fire!"

"And you watched it all?"

"Well, we heard it all – gunfire. We could see the ships, but there wasn't much to see for it was too far away. We could hear all the musket fire and cannon fire, though. And we could see smoke. Finally, the noise died down and we

242

decided it was over. We went back and got our tools and went home for supper."

"I'll be seeing more than smoke, come the next battle," said Dan with a nod.

"It won't be long to wait either."

"And that's still too long!"

"But when it finally comes, it'll be way too soon, won't it?"

"Yea, perhaps. Well, I guess that for now we ought to be getting this wagon opened up and you on your way."

They rushed to pull off all the bundles of wood, lift open the false bottom and slip the letter into the saddlebag. It was just in time, too. Tim was leaving when one of the women came to tell Dan it was time to come in and eat.

· · · · ·

Two days later, when Tim was back from delivering manure to the Felix farm, he went right away to look for Sadie to tell her all the news. She was not home, but he found his mother up and at work. It was now two weeks since her teeth had been pulled and the swelling was down.

"You're looking well," said Tim.

"I am well," she said with a toothless smile. "In fact, for days now, I've suffered no pain at all. And that's for the first time in two blessed years!" She looked old, but the sparkle in her eyes made up for it.

"All the fever's gone?"

"And it's all healed up nicely. I really should have had them out a year ago, shouldn't I have?"

"When it's time for mine to go, I'll not wait. Where's Sadie?"

"Out. That's all I know. She comes and goes without a word spoken, that girl."

. . . . .

Once Sadie was back and had heard Tim was home, she went looking for him. Four days before, she had seen him ride through town with enough daylight left to be back the same day. The next morning, she saw the Gainer's hired girl at the pump and found out that Tim was still not home. Sadie had said nothing, but she had assumed the worst. Now she wanted answers and went to where Tim was cutting wood, carrying a basket to make it look like she was on an errand.

When Sadie passed the tavern, Thomas was just coming out. Their eyes met. With a gallant wave of his hand, he pulled off his hat and bid her a warm "Good-day to thee, Maid Sadie." She looked away and kept going.

Thomas chuckled and started to follow her. He had no specific intentions, but there were images in his head of satyrs chasing wood nymphs through the forests of Arcadia. "Ooo, not so fast, my pretty," he cooed to himself. He had coins in his pocket again and was wondering whether her frosty frown might melt at the sight of silver.

Thomas allowed Sadie to stay far enough ahead of him to prevent anyone from wondering about the two of them leaving town at the same time. Once beyond the last house, he could catch up and make an attractive proposition and see if she might desire a profitable exchange. He knew she would likely stop at some farm and his hopes would be crushed. He knew this, but he also knew that where nothing's ventured, then nothing would be gained. His heart leaped with joy when he saw the object of his desire turn down a narrow road that led to nothing but a field and woodland. "Ah ha!" he muttered to himself. "And where's she off to now? Maybe there's some herb or root that she's after or… maybe she's noticed me following. Maybe she's heard that I've money to spend. And maybe she's decided she wants a part of it! Indeed, likely she has, likely she has, but not so fast my little nymph. I'll be needing my energy for more important things."

Thomas was getting winded by the pace Sadie was setting. Once down the forest path, he lost sight of her and had to run to catch up. But then he was stopped cold. There, beyond Sadie, was Tim, swinging an axe.

Just in time, Thomas tiptoed off to the side to hide behind a thicket of undergrowth. But now he was curious. *What's bringing her out to visit her brother?* he wondered, remembering that Tim had been up north a day longer than he should have been. He crept through the woods, taking care not to step on any sticks, and he was able to sneak up close to the two of them.

"They came for me!" said Tim. He was whispering, though he had no reason to think anyone was close by. "They took me across the river, bound and blindfolded."

"To where? You went to Morristown?" asked Sadie. She was pleased to hear something was happening. And that somebody from the Army might be sharing her and Tim's suspicions.

"And I met him!" said Tim in a low voice, but with his eyes wide.

"Met who?"

"Him!"

"Washington?"

"Himself!"

"Zookers," she whispered. "What's he like?"

"Uh… tall."

"I know that!"

"Ah…"

"What else was he?"

"He's forty-four years old."

"No! He turned forty-five two weeks ago!"

"Well… when he throws a horseshoe… well. I doubt he's that good at it."

"They're not paying him to throw horseshoes!"

"He don't take no money!"

"I know that!"

"Well … he seemed pleased to meet me."

"Oh! Can't you tell me anything about him?"

"Well… what I can tell you is that we may soon be safe from danger." Tim said this last line loud enough for Thomas to hear.

"Why will we be?"

"And likely sooner than later, too. I've talked to a man, who's looking into things. And you and me know that he'll surely find what he's a-looking for, don't we? And he'll have the ways and means of doing something about it, too. Now, I can say that much, but I can say no more."

Sadie did not press, doubting whether Tim truly knew as much as he thought. "Well, good for you, Tim Euston," she declared, "for keeping tight-lipped like you ought to. And don't you go and tell anyone else about it either!"

"No, I won't," he said, as he thought back to how he had already told Dan. He hoped she would not find out.

After Sadie had left, Tim picked up the saw to cut off smaller branches. The noise he made allowed Thomas to creep back through the woods without being heard. Once into town, he went straight to see Nat. His nephew was busy with a customer, so Thomas went into the kitchen to see if Bessie was there.

"Are we alone?" Thomas whispered when he came back into the storefront.

"Why?" asked Nat.

"I've news."

"News of what?"

"News that's worth something to you, Nat Pellis."

"You've already spent all you've got?"

"I'm barely scraping by. And besides, this bit of information would be worth paying for, even if I was a rich man – and I am not."

"What is it?"

"Our little Toothless One," he whispered as he glanced to the side, "has been out somewhere and doing something. It was four days ago, on his trip back it was, when I saw him a-riding up through town upon his wagon. Well, I was expecting to see him back down again the same day, in time for supper, if not sooner. But he was not. He didn't get himself back until after the noon of the next day and he was looking like he'd missed a night's sleep. Then, when I asked him how the trip had gone, what do you suppose he had to say? Eh? Well, he had no explanation. He just agreed that there are long delays at the checkpoints. But the checkpoints are almost always south of here, not north. Now, that alone wasn't enough to cause me concern."

"Not a lot."

"After all, he could have been lazing away up at the farm. No, it was not until I overheard him just now, a-talking to his sister. I couldn't make out all that was said, as I was a fair distance back, but I could see him standing tall and bragging, Yea, like a little rooster he was. And what I did hear? Well, he claimed that 'we' – meaning him and his sister most likely – may soon be 'safe from danger'. And next, I hear her praising him for being tight-lipped. Now, I ask you, what have they got to be a-whispering about? And why should he be keeping tight lipped and… and, who is it that 'we' should be fearing?"

"Who?" asked Nat.

"You know full well who," chuckled Thomas.

"I suspect that what he's been doing is going out and talking to Sailor Dan. And I'd imagine the assistance he's been offered was another bottle of rum to make another effort at plying information out of you."

"No no no, you didn't see the sparkle in his eyes. He's seen and heard more than just a wood-chopping sailor-boy."

At that point, a customer came into the store. Nat took a coin and placed it on the counter and, with a happy voice, told Thomas it was his payment in full. Thomas gave him a sharp look, picked up the coin and then turned to charm the woman with a smile, a bow and a fond greeting.

Nat was busy with one customer after another for the rest of the day, but he could not get his uncle's words off his mind. When a man came in who was on his way down to the city, Nat asked him if he could deliver a letter to Abner Wall.

Chapter 25

We're boxed in here.

In the distance, Sadie saw a man riding into town on a black horse. *A handsome stranger?* she thought, as a shiver ran up her spine. But then she realized it was just Abner Wall and she turned away, shaking her head in disgust. *Not from up close, he isn't.* Then she started to wonder whether an older woman might actually find him attractive. *He certainly has a look of pride and self-possession about him, doesn't he? That's enough to please a lot of women. I wonder if he's married? He doesn't seem like the married sort.*

"Do you know Abner Wall?" Sadie asked as she came into the kitchen.

"The trader, yes," said Matilda, without looking up from her recipe book.

"Is he married?"

"His wife died years ago," said Sadie's mother, who was stirring something in a bowl.

"Any children?" asked Sadie.

"I don't think so," said Matilda. "Maybe back in Halifax. That's where he's from. He'd come here as a soldier during the war, along with my Uncle Thomas."

"Oh," said Sadie, as she put down the basket she carried and started to put things away.

"Would you like me to ask him over?" asked Matilda, in her deadpan way of teasing.

"No!" replied Sadie.

"You could do worse than Abner Wall," said her mother with a nod. She tried, but could not stop herself from smiling.

"But I was thinking about you, my mother. Now that you're breath doesn't stink, you'll be more of a catch."

"Yea, there's many a man who will be looking your way now," agreed Matilda, still without looking up. "A man who's well aged, with no teeth of his own to be proud of."

"Yes, I've been expecting that," sighed Abby. "As they say, there's something about a woman with no teeth."

While this went on, Abner was tying his horse to the hitching post in front of the Pellis store. Nat's letter had asked him to "drop by at his nearest convenience," but had said no more. They had agreed to use this wording when they meant, "come as soon as possible!"

"Good morning," said Abner. "First of all," he said, holding up his hand to keep Nat quiet, "let's see if there are any ears pressed to doors."

"Just Bessie here today," said Nat as he opened the door to take a peek into the kitchen. She was at the table humming to herself while she worked.

"What is it then?"

"The Old Goat has sold me some information," said Nat and he told of Tim's being gone overnight. And that he had looked tired and complained about checkpoints.

"Well… that either means something or nothing. Maybe he was feeling under the weather."

"Then why wouldn't he say so?"

"I don't know. But I've news of my own," said Abner as he pulled a piece of paper from the inside pocket of his coat.

"This is a translation of a letter that came in the most recent delivery. It was in a code that I'm privy to."

Nat took it and read. "Interesting," he said when finished. "Do you know this fellow?"

"I do not! And I'm wondering whether he truly exists! I'm wondering whether this is a false report and meant as a test."

"Of what?"

"To see whether I'm passing things along further than they're supposed to be going. Perhaps we'd be best off if I were to hold onto this. What do you think?"

"Oh… well…"

"You don't think so?"

"I'd have to think it over," replied Nat. "You're the one who's down in the city."

"Yes. Now you say the Old Goat 'sold' you this information?"

"I only paid him enough to buy himself another drink."

"Pish! Does he do anything without charging a fee?"

"He's a thirsty man."

"Indeed he is. Between curious boys and drunken old men…"

"Well, it's a risky business we're in," said Nat with a shrug.

"That doesn't mean we shouldn't try to minimize our risk."

"You could go up to the farm and find out what kept him busy."

"And admit to my suspicions?" Abner said quietly. "And what do I do with the letter? Deliver it to our special friend –

and risk having its contents passed along – along to you know who? I doubt whether we're the only source the Army has to draw upon. There's too many redcoats in need of spending money. And if this is a test, then we may fail the test as soon as I deliver it."

"Then don't deliver it."

"I suppose I ought not to, but that still leaves us with a curious boy, doesn't it? And I had my doubts about him from the start, didn't I? Tim Curious he ought to be called. And what about your drunken uncle? We don't know what he said to Sailor Boy, do we? Or to others?"

"No we don't," said Nat, shaking his head.

"I'm suspecting that it's the Toothless One and his sister and Sailor Boy who pose the more immediate threat."

"I cannot disagree with that."

"An ounce of prevention is worth a pound of cure, ain't it?"

"But… I don't know," said Nat, shaking his head. "How do we eliminate the threat he might pose? We don't want to raise fresh suspicions, do we? After all, it has not been long since the suspicious death of Amos Short, has it?"

"But who would be suspicious of a simple case of highway robbery? There's many a desperate and murderous man upon the roads these days. And the untimely demise of Toothless would act as an object lesson for the other two."

"Both Amos and the Toothless One have driven the same wagon. Folks will start to wonder whether the wagon carries a curse."

"It would hardly be clumsier than the hiring of a man to deliver a false report of the cancellation of a hearing."

"I suppose not," said Nat, as his ears began to redden.

"I could meet him somewhere along the road next time out and rob and shoot him myself. Even if there were witnesses, they'd just be witness to a masked man stealing a team of horses. Sure it's risky, but what's our other option? It's risk enough doing nothing! We're boxed in here! And I'm not hearing you volunteer to do the deed, am I?"

"What about my Un... what about the Old Goat?"

"Humph. If only he and Toothless would shoot each other," said Abner as he shook his head.

"Hire each to kill the other, you think? When we both have an alibi."

"Well... I doubt that either's the sort who could do a murder for hire," sneered Abner. "Not all neat and clean."

"Young Toothless tried to enlist with the Continentals last summer."

"Did he?

"And when he was chosen to drive the wagon, he was proud and happy – strutting like a rooster in his nice blue coat that mama bought him. And she bought it from my own sister at half what it's worth. Marching around in it like a little soldier, he was."

"He was? What do you mean 'he was'? He's not still?"

"You've seen him lately. Like a dog who's had her puppies taken away."

"And why would that be?"

"Oh, I don't know," sighed Nat. "He's sixteen. It could be a petty remark from a pretty girl."

"But maybe he's just not thick as he's supposed to be. Maybe he can measure the box of a wagon and figure out that there's a false bottom? If he's put two and two together, then he might be thinking himself tricked and deceived. And by John Gainer too – after he was thinking he'd won the man's respect and high regard."

"Perhaps."

"And perhaps he's somehow gotten wise to the two of us and he realizes he's been deceived and used by us as well. And who all has he been talking to about it?"

"Sailor Boy, likely."

"And his sister, too! The whole blessed town might know!"

"He likely doesn't know and… and if he does, then surely he's not been telling everybody. His fear of getting caught would hold him back, wouldn't it?"

"Ah! I don't know! I should have been driving the stupid wagon myself."

Nat shrugged his shoulders. They leaned on the counter. The wind whistled in cracks around the windows. The ticking of the clock was loud in the silence. From the next room, they could faintly hear Bessie's humming and further off, the drone of old John as he snored in bed.

"Wait," said Abner. "Maybe they could take care of each other, eh? You say the boy was brave enough to try to enlist. And then he was strutting like a rooster when he got to drive a wagon."

"Yea, the courage of a young fool."

"Exact what I'm hoping it is. And the Old Goat tried to drag his sweet young sister in through his door, didn't he?"

"That's not what he says."

"Ah! The Old Goat's been a-wanting all along to get his hands on sweet Sadie."

"All along?"

"Oh yes yes," chuckled Abner. "Sadie Euston's been in his dreams since the day she arrived in town. And now all that we would need is to give him an opportunity, or at least the appearance of having got an opportunity. Then we could sit back and wait for a brave young fool to seek his revenge – or at least give others reason to assume that he has motive for revenge. And it would be no tragic loss either, if he did get his revenge. Drunk or sober, the Old Goat is an embarrassment to your whole family. Yea he is, and a menace to the pretty girls of Yonkers , one and all."

"You think Toothless would kill him?"

"Likely not. But were the Old Goat to turn up dead, all fingers would point towards the Toothless One, wouldn't they?"

Nat nodded.

"And especially," said Abner with a grin, "if we helped to form the opinion. Voicing our suppositions, eh? And once Toothless is thought of as a killer and a danger to one and all, then his opinions on other topics would bear little value."

"I suppose that if I told the Old Goat that Toothless was out for his hide then he might shoot him in self-defense."

"We can only hope."

"He hasn't a gun, though. He had one, but he sold it."

"I've six of them," chuckled Abner. "I've got a nice little one with me now. The redcoats keep stealing them from each other and selling them to me. I owe him money, too. I could tell him I'm short and he'll have to take something else instead. And a small pistol would be more than enough. He'd owe me something, then. And, when our brave young boy comes after him, he'll more than likely end up with a bullet in his brave young body."

"And if someone hangs," said Nat, "it would be one of them two and not one of us two."

"Exactly. Now what we've got to do is to get them together and right here's the place for that. You could hire Sadie from your sister to do some cleaning on a day when Bessie won't be here. You and your father would have to get out of the way, though."

"Not a problem. My father's been pestering me to take him to the city to see some quack doctor that his cousin's been singing praises to."

"Perfect! And then we just need to find some excuse to get the Old Goat in here while Sadie's all nice and vulnerable."

"You said that once he's got the pistol, he'll owe you something."

"Yes."

"Ask him to keep an eye on Sadie so she doesn't steal some valuable goods you've left here with me."

"No, not me," said Abner as he shook his head. "It'd be too obvious. We don't want him putting two and two together. He must be suspecting that we're getting a bit tired of his demands and his drunkenness. Let's have him here waiting for... a man who's coming with a special delivery for you. You'll say he's a shifty character and you don't know exactly what it's all about. And that way, it won't seem odd to suggest he carry a weapon."

"And that would keep him here all day as well, wouldn't it, which is what we want. The longer he and Sadie are here together without a chaperone, the more people will talk and the more likely Toothless will find out. We can't assume that the Old Goat will have courage enough to make a move on her. And even if he does, we can't assume she'll go and tell her brother."

"No, you're right there," said Abner with a nod. "So then, you'll go now and tell the Old Goat – hire him for the job?"

"First I'll run over and arrange for Sadie to come for cleaning. Then I'll go and find him and... Or maybe not. It'd be better if I ask him tomorrow. That'll give him less time to think it over."

"Yes, of course."

"But wait,' said Nat, sounding concerned. "If my rascal of an uncle does have his merry way with her and she goes out telling others of how she was cruelly abused... and if our brave young man does not turn out to be brave enough to do anything about it... then what? Fingers will start pointing at me for putting her in harm's way. I'll be vilified! My trade will suffer!"

"But you'll just deny knowing that the Old Goat was going to be here. And he won't claim that you did know either."

"Still... this could all backfire on us."

"Doing nothing will certainly backfire on us!" growled Abner. "We're boxed in here, we are! And we're better off doing something than doing nothing. You go hire the Old Goat today. You know, all this started with the hiring of Tim Useless to drive the wagon. And whose idea was that?"

"Yes yes yes," said Nat, sounding like he was still not sure.

"Now you run over to your sister and once you've got the girl lined up, you come right back here."

Nat left by the front door and Abner waited, alternating between leaning on the counter while he drummed his fingers and pacing the floor while muttering to himself. Finally, Nat came back to say that all was set and that Sadie would be over the morning after next.

Abner went next door to where Thomas was still sipping his breakfast beer while warming his toes before a small fire. Abner moaned about being short on coin and offered the pistol to him. Thomas took it and right away started playing with it, pretending to shoot at imaginary soldiers. Abner then bid him a good day and went back to the store.

Later that day, Nat came by to ask Thomas if he could do him a favor by keeping an eye on the cleaning girl. He made his suggestion with a nod and a wink. And when Thomas realized he would be keeping his eye on Sadie Euston while she scrubbed the floors, his eyes twinkled with mischief.

Chapter 26

It'd solve their problems nicely.

"Good morning, Bessie," said Sadie when her friend came through the door. Bessie would never knock during the day. If she had, Sadie would wonder what was wrong.

"Good morrow to thee, girl. Have ye some lard to spare me?" Bessie was often borrowing things or bringing over something to repay past debts. Matilda always told her she repaid too much.

"We've plenty, I'm sure," replied Sadie who had her eyes on her sewing. This was one of her strengths. She could have been a tailor were she not in training as a dairymaid. "What all are we supposed to be cleaning?"

"Cleaning what?" asked Bessie as she scooped the lard out of a large crock and into the small one she had brought with her.

"At the Pellis store."

"When's that to be?"

"Tomorrow," said Sadie as she looked up.

"Tomorrow?"

"Yes, and aren't I helping you?"

"Tomorrow?" Bessie asked again.

"Nat's asked for me. Matilda said so."

"Just you?"

"And not you too? That's odd. Why'd he want me and not you?"

Bessie shrugged her shoulders and stuck out her lower lip. Working at the Pellis store was keeping her family going during hard times. She had been doing good work, trying her best to keep them happy. "I've been working there today, but Nat said not to come tomorrow because he don't need me. Said he'd be taking his father down to see a doctor in the city."

"I'm going to be there all by myself?"

Bessie grunted in response.

"Has Abner been back?" asked Sadie, to change the topic.

"This morning he's been already."

"Both bragging and complaining about the high prices, I'd suppose?"

"Muttering and fretting is what," said Bessie. "And keeping secrets too, I'd say. Looking like boys up to no good, the two of them."

"They say there's money to be made in smuggling," sighed Sadie, trying not to sound too interested.

"Smuggling? Or is it just trading? Is anything illegal on a 'neutral ground'? That's what my father's been saying – neither law nor order hereabouts. He thinks we all should clear out before we're driven out by banditry – and sooner's better than later for him."

"And what? Go down to the city to starve along with the refugees?"

"That or go up north."

"Or stay here for the easy money, if you can get a share of it," said Sadie as she shook her head. "They say there'll be fortunes lost and fortunes won, just like in the last war."

"Who's Saint George?"

"What?"

"Who's Saint George?"

"He's patron saint of the English. You should know that."

"We don't pray to saints at our church," said Bessie with a superior tone. She was teasing. She knew the high churchmen did not pray to saints either, but at her church many liked to say the King's church was as papist as the pope's daughter.

"And why are you wondering about Saint George?" asked Sadie.

"When Abner left, he said 'Young Saint George will slay our dragon'. He was laughing, but he didn't sound happy."

"Saint George slew a dragon to save a maiden."

"Did he?"

"Or so the tale goes," said Sadie. "And the two of them were talking like bad boys again?"

"Well... more like scared boys."

"Scared of what?"

"I don't know. If they're into smuggling then they'll have reason to fear their fellow smugglers, won't they? That's what my father says. The smugglers battle over the trade, like the pirates at sea. When your trade is illegal, then you can't take your disputes to a judge. And then what?"

"I suppose they would have to battle things out, wouldn't they?" said Sadie as she thought of the broken blunderbuss her brother carried.

For the rest of the morning, Sadie kept trying to figure out why a scared looking Abner Wall would be making jokes about "our young Saint George." It made no sense and she finally ordered herself to forget about it.

When told to fetch water, Sadie put on her clean apron, got her yoke and buckets, and went down the road to the well. She took advantage of the occasion to practice her good posture. Matilda always insisted her servants try to look their best and she would poke fun at Sadie when she slouched – telling her she looked like a "workhouse dullard" or a "London beggar" or a "seminary student." Sometimes she would even rub her hump for good luck. Sadie hated it when she did that.

"Ah, there you are, my sweetie," purred Thomas as he snuck up behind her, putting his hand on her arm for a moment, just as she made it to the well. "Ooo, and I'll bet you smell good as you look, don't you now?" he said as he leaned over her shoulder.

Sadie did not look back at him. Any response would just give him encouragement. *And likely nothing would stop him anyways,* she thought to herself. *Nothing short of shooting him, but that's strictly prohibited by law, so there's nothing a girl can do. If only another pretty servant would come to town.* There were other pretty girls in Yonkers, but they were not poor servants and Thomas would never flirt with them out of respect for their father's rank in society.

"Ah, they never stop calling for more water," Thomas sighed. "And here 'tis poor Sadie who has to fetch it all. It just doesn't seem fair, does it, eh? No no, of course it doesn't. But fear not, my child, someday soon a handsome man will come along to take your hand and lift you up and out of all this. When? Oh… likely sooner rather than later, eh? Yes yes, I do think so. Maybe in a year, maybe in a month. Who knows, maybe in a day's time, eh? I think so, indeed I do. And what will he be like? Well, he might be short, but with love in your eyes he'll look tall, won't he? And maybe he'll be dull, but with love in your ears he'll sound wise and witty. Eh? Sure he will."

Sadie had both buckets full and was ready to start back. She turned to walk away, having not even acknowledged his existence.

"And 'til we meet again, my fresh budded rose," he said after her.

Meet again? Sadie wondered. *Why'd he say it like... that?* The way Thomas had spoken the words suggested something. It sounded almost as if he knew something she did not. *And he said a man's to come, maybe in a... day's time. Meet again? Meet where?* Then it came to her. *Alack! He must know I'm to be at the store! He means to come when I'm there alone!*

Sadie moped and sighed around the kitchen for an hour, keeping busy while her mother kept looking at her and asking whether she was feeling feverish. Finally, Sadie put her good apron back on and went out to find her brother.

"Where are you off to, girl?" called her mother, but Sadie slammed the door, pretending she had not heard. Out at the woodlot, Tim was cutting limbs from a felled tree.

"What is it?" he asked when he saw the look on her face.

"Thomas Pellis aims to join me tomorrow when I'm at the store, alone."

"What?"

"Nat's borrowed me for a day of cleaning and nobody else is to be there. Not Bessie. Not Nat. Not even old John. I'm to be there alone and Thomas is talking like he'll be there, too."

"With you, alone?"

"Yea, with me alone. And there to finish up the business left undone when you and the boys stopped him – what you went to jail for."

"Nay... nay he'll not!" said Tim as his nostrils flared and blood rushed to his face. "Not while I live and breathe! Not while I've hands and feet and teeth to stop him with!"

"Of course!" gasped Sadie as she turned away, one hand to her cheek. "Of course! You're the 'young Saint George'."

Tim said nothing. He had no idea what she was talking about.

"Bessie said that when Abner was going out just this morning, he said that their 'young Saint George' would 'slay our dragon'."

"What's that mean?"

"It's them who likely killed Amos, isn't it? And likely because he was a drunk who talked too much. Maybe they now want rid of old Thomas for the same reason. And why wouldn't they? And... why should they risk killing him themselves when they can get you to do their dirty work? If 'the Old Goat' gets to corner me in an empty house, then you'll be wanting to go kill him, won't you?"

"I would!" agreed Tim.

"Well... maybe you would kill him and... and maybe you wouldn't. You would likely, but... but how would they know you would?"

"And if they're the killers, then why wouldn't they just go kill him themselves?"

"Maybe they will, if you don't," said Sadie. "But still, the whole town will know you've got reason to want to kill him, wouldn't they?"

"Indeed they would."

"Oh! I don't know! But it all fits together, doesn't it? Why would Nat be deciding, all of a sudden, to want me doing cleaning, instead of Bessie? And why is he taking his father and not sending him with you when you're going.

And closing the store when people will think it ought to be open? Why'd Thomas act like he knew that I'll be there alone? He's talking like he knows what's to be – like I'll be there ready and waiting for him! You should have heard him!"

"Well, you ain't going to be there!"

"Certainly not! I'll tell Matilda what Thomas said and she'll keep me home and she'll give Nat such a scolding! When he gets home she'll… she'll box his ears, she will! She's got a temper! You'll see Nat come a-running from the house!"

"That's not enough," said Tim, who was beginning to think it through. "There's a dire threat to both you and me – and even Thomas. We know that it wasn't Jack Lauper who killed Amos."

"So what do we do?"

"We've got to defend ourselves is what! One of them has killed once – almost for sure he has. And he's going to kill again!"

"And what'll we do?"

"I don't know!" moaned Tim as he threw up his hands.

"Oh!" groaned Sadie as she held her hand to her forehead. "Maybe we should have run away!"

"We should have! We could have been safe in Morristown now – or further."

"Why don't you go talk to John about it? He's an honest man."

"What if he doesn't believe me?"

"Then we run," said Sadie, almost in a whisper.

268

. . . . .

"Master?" said Tim when he found John at a neighbor's shed, taking measurements.

"Tim. How's the woodcutting?"

"I've got news."

"More news, eh?" said John with a smile as he straightened his back and stretched.

Tim told him about Sadie's suspicions. "So it seems like Thomas is thinking she's to be there for him to take his pleasure."

"Well," gasped John, "then she shouldn't go there!"

"She shouldn't. And she won't, but that's not all," said Tim, and he told about Bessie's comments about Abner and Nat, and saying that their 'young Saint George' will slay their 'dragon'. "Sadie is wondering whether I'm to be their 'young Saint George' and that Thomas is their 'dragon'. She wonders whether they're fixing to give me reason to be so vexed and angry at Thomas that I'll go do their killing for them. And that way they won't have to kill him themselves, like they killed Amos. Or maybe they will kill Thomas themselves and sit back while all fingers point to me as the likely killer."

"That's quite a story."

"And Sam Baker's got his suspicions, too."

"Sam Baker?" asked John, after a pause.

"He took me over to Morristown, just five days ago. Him and others stopped me on the road and took me, hands tied and blindfolded. Sam Baker said he's talked to you and that he trusts you. He questioned me and then sent me... I even met George Washington! He was there pitching horseshoes. And Sam took me up to make introductions! And then afterwards, they brought me back. I wasn't supposed to tell nobody – and I wouldn't have! But this is getting too dangerous for Sadie! I've got to do something! Or both me and Sadie have to run off to save our lives! It's too much! I'd never run off for anything less! I'm honest and I do my duty! But she's my sister and she ain't got nobody else!"

"No, she doesn't," said John after another pause.

"And Sam Baker says the information that Abner's sending back just don't jibe with what they get from others."

"Wait," said John with his hand up. "Josh told me, just now he did. He told me that today, when he and another boy had been here in town, that Thomas had shown them a pistol. He pulled it out and menaced them with it, like a boy with a new toy."

"A pistol?" asked Tim. "He hasn't never carried a pistol before, has he?"

"I'm sure he has from time to time, always buying and selling. But Josh said he was 'showing it off'."

"Well, there you have it! They're likely suspecting that things are getting... Sadie said that Bessie said that they looked scared. I remember the time I saw Abner – just after I got out of jail – I was walking round the side of the Pellis store. And he looked at me like he was scared and angry at the same time – like he was ready to kill."

"Maybe for all his bluff," said John, "the man just doesn't have nerve enough for this sort of business."

"But nerve enough to kill, maybe. When he's scared enough."

"But not enough to bear the burden of having it all on his mind, day and night, for months on end. He had not wanted you for driving the wagon either. It was Nat that pushed for you."

"And maybe that pistol is meant for Thomas to defend himself from me. If we killed each other then it'd solve their problems nicely. Or at least they think it would. They likely don't know what Sam Baker's asking about them. If they did, they'd likely be a-running out of town themselves. And if I back out now, they'll know that I know."

"And if Sadie backs out they'll be just as suspicious."

"Indeed, they will! They're likely suspicious of everybody. This plan of theirs... won't it just lead to another? They're maybe starting onto a killing spree. Who knows? And who knows who all they're suspecting. Maybe you, too!"

"Maybe," said John as he shook his head. His expression had turned from frustration to fear. "I ought to talk to Sam about all this."

"Is he in town?"

"I don't know. Likely not. I guess there's another man I could talk to."

"We got to do something before tomorrow, or maybe we should all be running."

272

Chapter 27

Good for you, Abner Wall.

"Come," ordered John, as he got up and started for the door. They went up the street. John was tall and took long steps. Tim had to break into a run to catch up. He was waiting for John to tell him where they were going, but did not dare ask. He seemed angry about something. *Is it because I said I almost ran off?* Tim wondered. John said nothing until they were at the blacksmith's.

"Can you spare two horses and two saddles?" John asked as they came through the wide door.

"I can," said the blacksmith. "Where you headed?"

"North. Couple of dozen miles only, there and back," said John as he lifted down a saddle from where it rested on a rack. "Which one?"

"For you, the gray gelding," he said pointing. "And Tim's going too?"

"And Tim," John replied, again sounding angry.

The blacksmith quickly saddled a smaller horse and led it out. "When will you be back?"

"Today," said John, without looking. "Not sure when."

"I'll just charge you for the half day then."

"Good," John muttered with just a glance at the man. "Let's go!" he said without looking at Tim. They mounted the horses and rode off.

John raced ahead, not looking back to see if Tim was keeping up. Tim's horse was not as cooperative as the ones he had ridden in New Jersey and he had to slap its rump to keep it moving. It could sense he was nervous.

Once out of town, John urged his horse to a gallop. Tim kept up, but his horse still seemed to resent its rider. When they slowed, it even bucked a couple of times and nearly sent him flying. He remembered hearing a man giving advice to a boy who was learning to ride. He told him to let the horse know who's boss. *How do you tell that to a horse?* Tim had wondered.

As the miles passed, the horse calmed down and decided to put up with Tim in spite of his shortcomings. They were traveling fast. Tim wondered whether they were driving the horses too hard. It was not until they rode into the Felix farmyard that Tim knew where they were going. It made sense, though. *Who else would we have gone to?*

"Good day, John," said old Mister Felix as they rode up, stirring up dust.

"We need to talk," John responded, still angry.

"Come on in for a drink then."

"I don't suppose Abner Wall is here?"

"No. Were you expecting him to be?"

"I don't know what to expect," said John, trying to make a joke, but sounding frustrated.

"Sam's here."

"John!" called Sam Baker from the door. "And Tim Euston. What brings you two up here?"

"We're in need of advice," said John, now sounding apologetic.

"Well, I am in need of yours," said Sam. "I'm glad you've come." They went into the kitchen. Mrs. Felix saw their faces and shooed the others out. She poured them each a drink and went out herself. She closed the door, but stayed to listen. Others snuck up, but she ordered them back with arched eyebrows.

"Tell them what you've told me," John said to Tim. Six eyes turned on him and Tim felt his stomach flutter, like it had when he had been led before the judges, five weeks before. With a lot of stammering he told his story.

"Well well," sighed Sam when Tim had finished. "This is getting interesting."

"Deadly is what it's getting," said John. "We don't know who they might go after next. If this is all true, and it seems quite likely that it is, then there might be another that they'll have reason to silence."

Everyone nodded.

"And what all might they be willing to do for money?" asked John. "I doubt that they're willing to fight for a noble cause. I'd been ignoring the... evidence, but... now I see it all under a different light."

"Indeed," said Sam, sounding like his mind was on something else. "Now this is all reminding me of an event I heard of from a fellow – he was an officer in the Army. Back during the French and Indian War, they had a pair of spies who had given them reason to worry."

. . . . .

Sam rode with them back to Yonkers where he rented a fresh horse. "I'll have to make good time," Sam said to the blacksmith. "How hard can I push him?"

"Oh, he's a good one. As hard as needs be."

"I'll be back tomorrow," he said to the others, with a grave look on his face. "Tim, we could use the help of your sailor friend."

"Dan Eliot?"

"Go out and see if he could come into town, first thing. Tell him to wait with you in John's shed."

"I will," called Tim as Sam rode off. "Is he going to the city?" he asked John as they started back home.

"It looks like it. He carries false papers. So far, they either don't know who he is, or they have their reasons for letting him through. These days, it's hard to say who's doing what or where or why."

"You think that Sam might not make it back?"

"Well... he's... they might arrest him at any time. They might hang him tomorrow morning."

.   .   .   .   .

Sam had good luck at the checkpoints and made it through without delay. He was in the city by nightfall and made it to his destination without losing his way in the darkness. Abner lived in an inn, so Sam booked himself in for the night. The keeper said Abner was often out until late. Sam bought supper and sat at the end of a long table, listening to the conversation of other guests. It was two hours before Abner arrived.

"Well, good evening," said Abner with a smile. "Haven't seen you in town for a while."

"I've just sailed in with a few barrels of fish and bacon. How's business?"

"Good enough. A fool will prosper when he's got what the wise men want to buy. Where you staying?"

"Here," said Sam.

"You're staying with me then, or otherwise you'll be squeezed in like a row of piglets. If only I had a barge big enough to float in a few houses. I could take in a hundred boarders and be rich quick."

Their small talk went on as they climbed the stairs. Abner's room was small and piled high with trade goods. Once the door was closed, their smiles faded.

"What brings you here?" asked Abner.

"Nothing, I hope," said Sam as he sat down on a crate. "I have been hearing some opinions about Thomas Pellis. What's your estimation of him?"

"Aside from his being a comical drunkard?"

"Aside from that."

"To put it plainly," said Abner with a shrug, "I wish I didn't have to place my trust in him. Maybe he's honest and maybe he's not, but... I don't know. He is a comical fellow, but these days I'm not always looking for a good laugh. He can be tiresome when you're trying to be serious."

"What I've heard is worse," Sam said quietly. "There are some who are all but convinced that he's in the pay of Billy Howe. I was advised not to come into town and I don't know if you can remain here much longer either."

"Well well," replied Abner, as he tried to conceal his relief. If suspicions were turning towards Thomas, then his own position was much more secure. "I have not heard any such rumors, but... to be honest, I would not be surprised if I did. He seems to lack... moral fiber, you might say. And it's Billy Howe who's got silver to spend, so he'll be getting the support of every scoundrel, won't he be?"

"I think it's time that we put the old fellow to the test," said Sam, "and I think you're the man who's best able to do the testing. Thomas has told me he'll be minding Nat's store tomorrow. Nat has to bring his father down here to see a doctor. He says the store will be closed and he'll be there waiting for deliveries and keeping an eye on things while some young wench is in to do some cleaning. This will give us our opportunity. I can get a woman to persuade the girl's mistress to keep her home. That means you could go to the store, go in around back, and say you've come looking for Nat. Then you could sit yourself down and uncork a bottle of rum. Say you need to warm yourself up and then offer him a drink. Once you've got him warmed up, you could try to trick him into a confession by hinting that you're thinking of going over to the royalist side, yourself. If he's true to the patriot cause then he'll come to me and report on you, saying you can no longer be trusted. If he's not, then he might try recruiting you as a spy for Billy. Either way, we'll get a better idea about how far he should be trusted. What do you think?"

"Well… I don't know. Old Thomas could go either way and still be innocent or guilty."

"Indeed yes. But the Army would not want to go and stretch his neck on anything short of a very strong suspicion of a vile intent to deceive us and do grave harm to the cause. Sure, this may be wartime and military courts might not be demanding conclusive evidence, but still, they can't be hanging everybody who looks a bit suspicious. I'm just wanting to know whether Thomas should be cut out. You, Nat and John could keep things going – keep muskets and encrypted letters coming in. Thomas would be assigned another task."

"I could be comfortable with that," said Abner as he calculated the portion of Thomas's cut that might now be coming to him. It worried him to learn that Sam was hearing so much about Thomas, but on balance, it now seemed like everything might work to the benefit of Abner Wall.

"Good then," said Sam. "Just see what you can do. If you can squeeze a clear admission of guilt out of the old fellow, then you'll be in for a handsome reward – very handsome. Now you and I will need to arrive early enough so that I can be out of sight and still listen in. We'll have to be on the road at first light."

"You know… Thomas will be talking in riddles and making pun after joke."

"Oh yes yes," agreed Sam with a smile. "I'm expecting that."

"We're not likely to come away thinking we know anything with certainty – not with him."

"What I have been wondering is whether that is precisely why I've heard the rumors. It could just be that things he's said in jest have been taken the wrong way. Maybe he's simply a man with unfortunate habits. I'll be listening, but more than anything, it's going to be your estimation of him that I'll base my decision upon. I'm not so much hoping to find guilt. I'm just wanting to take a measure of his worth."

"Well," said Abner, "I'll do my best. I don't know how much I can deliver. But I'll take two bottles of rum, and that way I'm sure to enjoy the effort."

"Good for you, Abner Wall," chuckled Sam. "Always willing to make a sacrifice for the cause."

Chapter 28

We want to give them both a chance.

Morning came under a dark gray sky and steady drizzle. In spite of cloaks and the brims of their hats let down, Abner and Sam arrived at John's house wet and cold. John's wife, Eustace was worried and sat them in front of the fire. She ordered the girl-of-all-work to pile on wood and gave them hot coffee with rum, hoping to warm their blood before a chill could take hold.

While this was going on, Dan Eliot shivered in John's shed while watching through a chink between vertical wall planks. The Pellis store was within eyeshot and he and Tim were waiting to see Nat ride off with his father.

"There they go," said Dan, as a wagon splashed by. To keep warm, Tim had been sawing and planing boards for a cupboard. With nothing more said, he put down his tools and went to the house to ask John where the big auger drill was. John pointed to it, saying he had brought it in to sharpen it. That was the signal. Tim took it back out, saying nothing more.

By this time, Dan had crossed the street over to Thomas's small house. He rapped on the door until the man got up.

"What is it?" complained Thomas when he came to pull back the wooden bolt.

"Nat sent me over!" called Dan. "Le'me in, it's cold out here!"

"And what's Nat want now?" said Thomas as he pulled the door open.

"Ah! Nat wants his mamma. You just get yourself back under your covers and I'll build up a fire. Heat us up a nice pot of wine, maybe?" said Dan as he smiled and pulled a bottle out of a sack.

"Ooo, now, and doesn't that sound nice for breakfast, eh?" said Thomas as he crept back into his bed and pulled up the covers. "Wake me up when it's steaming hot."

"Nat came for me, just a little while ago. He gave me a coin and said to go tell you that there's been a change of plans. Said he couldn't come back into town to tell you himself and that you'd know why."

"Would I?"

"He says that – and this is exactly what he said – like it's a secret message – that a priest named Father Small has likely been a-praying with the heretics and he's coming to you today."

"Is he?"

"And he said he's coming in place of the Blessed Virgin and you're to pray with him until he confesses his sins."

"What?"

"That's what he said! And he said to tell you that, as reward for your good works, the heavenly baker will come down amongst us and will hear your prayers and give you a fine loaf of bread as reward for your goodness."

"A loaf of bread?"

"He said that twice! A 'very handsome loaf' he said."

"Did he really?"

"And he made me repeat it until I got it right. And then he wouldn't tell me why! I guess I must have looked impatient because he got out this bottle of wine and said to share it with you."

"Oh... ah... oh! Yes yes," said Thomas, sounding like his mind was being forced to do too much work too early in the morning. But he realized that Father Small must be Abner Wall, the baker was Sam, and the Virgin was the object of his fondest desires. "Well well, she'll not be coming, eh?" he said quietly, trying to hide his disappointment.

"You ain't no papist Catholic now, are you?" asked Dan as he turned the corkscrew.

"Oh no. We... let on we are when we're trading with them – them Irish folk, down in the city. We let them think we're about ready to come back over to the old religion, eh? We have to, for that's the only way we'll get their business."

"No, I don't believe that," chuckled Dan. "Not the papists!"

"Don't forget what you're doing now, boy," said Thomas, pointing to the bottle.

"But papism? That's next to..."

"Now now, boy, I know that you New Englanders think the papists are the Devil's own, but you're in New York Colony now, remember. We tolerate all who are willing to come together in... in mutual respect of a man's... basic wants and needs."

"Tolerate all? Well, alack the day! No sir, I am not in Boston anymore, no I am not! Praying with the papists! My old grandma would have called that near to devilry."

"Ah, but we're willing to tolerate all kinds, we are. Live and let live."

"So why'd Nat send me here to tell you all that?" asked Dan as he got some tinder out of the box and laid it on the remains of last night's fire. He picked up the poker, gave the ashes a few pokes and got on his knees to blow.

"Use the bellows, why don't you?"

"Where?" asked Dan, looking around until he saw them. He picked them up and started pumping. "Well?" he asked.

"What?"

"Why'd he waste a coin and a bottle of wine to hire me to go out in the rain and tell you something that sounds like some sort of a secret code? You a-plotting with the Jesuits?"

"Yes, that's it exactly. Father Thomasius they used to call me back at the monastery."

"So then why couldn't he come tell you himself?"

"Well... aren't you full of questions? I'd imagine he tried and failed. I'm always slow to wake up and... when he has to get me up early, he'll come and pound on my door and wake me up and I'll then tell him where he can take himself to and... then he'll come back and try again in a half hour once I'm half awake. That's the way it is, eh? Couldn't get me up and didn't have time to wait."

"We've something in common then," said Dan. "Sometimes my mama had to coax me out of bed with a pointed stick."

"Good for her."

"And you say an Irish papist priest is coming to do business?"

"I hope so. I could use a little money. Now then, how's that wine a-coming?"

By this time, John was in the shed with Tim, where they were at work loading the pair of dueling pistols Sam had left.

"Dan's got Thomas a-drinking hot wine and talking religion," said Tim with a grin. "I was at the door, listening in."

"He's sounding like he'll go for the bait?" asked John.

"Not one hint of suspicion in his voice. Not that I could hear."

"I added more rum to the coffee that Eustace had made for Abner. We might not have to wait long before we're hearing them singing in drunken harmony."

"Yea, rum," said Tim with a nod, mimicking a Methodist preacher. "'Tis many a man's downfall."

"You go to the store now," said John. "Go in through the front door. Push hard on it and it'll open. I picked the lock on the back door and went through to unlock the front. I just laid a sack of beans against it so nobody else – no neighbor – would manage to get himself in. I'm going back in the house now and then I'll come right back out again and be back over here, right away. That'll be the signal for Sam. He'll wait a bit and then he'll come over here to join us in hiding. He said he's going to let Abner watch him going in the back door. Abner's been told to wait an hour to make sure Thomas has time to get himself in there. Now we'd best get ourselves going."

"Dan will come over, too?"

"So long as Thomas doesn't get himself up and moving first. If Dan's out before Thomas starts getting dressed, then he'll make a wide loop around and come to the front."

"Sounds like there's not been much left to chance," said Tim with a smile.

"Oh, I don't know," said John, sounding scared. "There'll always be plenty left to chance."

· · · · ·

"Thomas!" said Abner, later when he came into the kitchen of the Pellis store.

"Abner, old fellow! What's brought you upcountry on so dark and dank a day as this?"

"Well, the clouds looked to be breaking up when I set out."

"You've come up from the city?"

"And a long cold ride it was!"

"You passed Nat on the way then?" asked Thomas as he sat down in a chair before the kitchen fireplace. It was a shallow box of sand, about three feet by three, with mud and straw plastered up the walls for fireproofing and a wooden chimney above.

"No."

"You rode right past him and you didn't wish him a good day?"

"Nat's gone down to the city?"

"With his father in a wagon – to go see a doctor he said, and to do some buying too, I'd suppose."

"Nat's not here? Well!" sighed Abner as he sat down by the fire. "I must have missed him when I stopped in at John Fryer's place. Well well! And what'd I come all the way up here for?"

"Oh, come now, there's more in Yonkers than Nat Pellis."

"There'd better be. I'd hate to think that it's for nothing that I've ridden through eighteen miles of rain."

"Ooo, you must be frozen to the bone, poor boy. Let's get your fire started with some good fuel," said Thomas as he got up to get a bottle of rum from a cupboard. "Nat wouldn't begrudge it, eh? Not for you? And we'll warm it on the fire, eh?"

"Oh, now that would be so kind of you, brother," said Abner with a grin. "Heat up enough for yourself too, eh? Nat wouldn't begrudge that either, would he? Not when it's as cheap as it's been. I've got thirty-eight casks of the stuff back home. I'll split the profit with any man who can move them out for me."

"Why bring rum all the way to Yonkers, when you've got the British Army down there, thirsty as ever?"

"Well, it seems there's even a limit to how much they'll drink, if you can imagine it."

"Ha! I can try," laughed Thomas as he poured the contents of the bottle into an iron pot with a long wooden handle. "And there's cream here that we can mix with it. The neighbor brought milk and cream over – the daily delivery – and here there's none but us to make use of it."

"I'd like that. Rum and cream! I'd hate to see that go to waste. Do you suppose he might have some nutmeg around here?"

"And sugar, too – white as snow. All ground up and sifted. A well stocked kitchen, this. Here now, hold the pot," said Thomas as he handed it over. "We'll be drinking like Billy Howe himself, we will – drinking toasts to the King in the best of English fashion."

"'Tis the least we can do for His Majesty," said Abner.

"What good news have you been hearing down in the great city?"

"Oh, there's every rumor going around, like always. From what I've been hearing, I suspect that war and peace will break out simultaneously."

"Not too much peace too soon, I hope," said Thomas. "Not before we've all made a profit on the war."

"I'm trying my best to. And there seems to be plenty of money to be had for those who will make an effort to get their hands on it."

"Oh indeed, yes. I keep asking myself what I'm doing up here. It's down in the city where the silver sits in great fat bags, waiting to be put to good use. This rebellion can't last long, not with old England paying for an army of thirty-two thousand."

"No it can't," said Abner.

"And each of them with an empty stomach and cold toes."

"Indeed, crying out for food and fire."

"And come summer, the fighting will likely be over and done with in no time at all. And then they'll be going home – taking unspent silver with them."

"And that's if it don't end even sooner," said Abner. "How can ploughboys and woodcutters fight against hardened mercenaries?"

"How indeed? We saw how well the 'patriots' could fight last fall, didn't we?" said Thomas as he pulled the pot off the fire to let Abner pour in the cream, add the sugar and spice and stir. It went back on the fire for a minute longer and then they poured themselves a glass. "Now, here's a toast to… who?"

"To the best man," said Abner, "who's sure to win because he always does. How about that?"

"A good one. Here's to them all! And to peace, but not before profits! Oo-oh," said Thomas as he took a look behind. "I'd best be careful of who might be listening at the door."

"Ha! Yea, there's too many that are listening in these days. Let's drink to profits then! May they come by land or may they come by sea, just let all them profits come to me!"

They gulped it down and thought up one toast after another. Abner pulled another bottle out of his pack and they heated up another potful. He told about fortunes that were being earned by the loyalist merchants who supplied the British Army with necessities and British officers with luxuries. Thomas asked leading questions about how a man might be able to take advantage of opportunities when they presented themselves. Abner would give a vague answer to each question and then offer a strong hint that his sympathies lay with a return of the colonies to the warm embrace of Mother England. When talk moved to spying for money, both encouraged the other to admit to being in the pay of the British by hinting that he was himself already. Each would almost admit to being a British spy, but not quite. Eventually, both grew frustrated and their discussion developed into an argument.

"Well, I can tell you," said Abner as he wagged his finger, "that we'll not be getting rich very fast until we're doing our utmost to cooperate with each other."

"Well, ain't that my point exactly! We'll just be sabotaging each other's efforts if we act alone."

"Indeed yes! And that means… well, for one thing it means no more sending of mysterious messengers to tell that a hearing's been canceled."

"I had no hand in that!" said Thomas. "That was my dear nephew…"

"Well, you did enough, what with your impulsive desires."

"Better desires than impulsive fears, isn't it? You're in fear of phantoms!"

"You're one to talk of phantoms," snapped Abner, "what with your cracking of heads!"

"That was an accident! He fell against the wall."

"After you'd sent him flying!"

"He landed the first blow!" said Thomas. "I've a right to defend myself!"

" 'Twas still your hand that…"

"Not so loud, boys," whispered Sam Baker from behind, making them both jump. "Folks could be hearing you loud and clear out in the street, the way you're talking."

"Pish!" hissed Abner. "Just as long as it's been heard loud and clear in here."

"I'm sure you've heard as much as you need," said Thomas with a nod to Sam.

"Indeed, there's been enough confessed to please…" Abner said this and then stopped and looked at Thomas, who looked back at him, his brow furrowed.

"I have heard a lot out of both of you," said Sam with a smile.

"You… you…" stammered Abner, who realized that Thomas knew Sam had been there.

"Does he… what is this?" asked Thomas, who realized that Abner knew the same thing. "What are you after?"

"The eyes and ears of Billy Howe, of course," said Sam. "'Tis my trade and calling, it is. And I can say that I've crafted myself a fine piece of workmanship here today, if I dare to brag."

"In… indeed you have!" said Abner as he gave Thomas an accusing look. "We have! And we've trapped ourselves a good one."

"Who? Wh…what?" stammered Thomas. "So, Abner Wall, are you confessing to your sins before both of us?"

"How… what is this?" Abner asked, turning to Sam.

"No no," said Sam. "Perhaps I should not take credit for today's work. You both deserve the credit for extracting a confession out of each other."

"What trickery is this?" asked Abner in a menacing voice as he stood up. "Are you saying that…"

"Am… am I not?" asked Thomas. "Am I not here at your request and in your service? You know that what I say I said to…"

"Well well well, this is a dirty bit of business," growled Abner, looking at Sam with his eyes squinted and his face twisted into a murderous scowl. "No, you'll not have me so cheaply!" As he said this he took a step towards Sam.

"Stand off, boy," said John Gainer, coming in from the store, holding a pistol. "Don't act before you've thought it over."

"You!" gasped Abner. "What are you doing here?"

"We've just come to hear what we can hear," said Tim, as he came through the same door, holding a second pistol.

Abner looked back and forth with an expression of panic. "No no, you'll not…"

"Stay where you are," ordered John, as he held his pistol higher.

"You? Either of you?" said Abner as his hand started moving up and under his coat. "No, you're not the ones who could take another man's life, not spill a man's blood at close range."

"Ah, but if they don't, then surely I will," said Dan as he emerged from the same door with a blunderbuss held to his shoulder and a deranged grin on his face. It was Tim's broken blunderbuss, but Abner did not know that. "Just give me the word, Sam. I ain't shot a man in the longest while. Weeks it's been."

"No no, boy," said Sam with his hand up, "only if he tries to escape. We want to give them both a chance to explain themselves and to reform their ways."

"But I am innocent!" insisted Thomas. "I've done nothing to…"

"Save it for the tribunal, boys. There's going to be nothing decided here today," said Sam, though he knew that when Abner had said, "After you'd sent him flying!" he had spoken words that were clear enough to condemn Thomas for a criminal act that had caused the death of Amos Short.

Chapter 29

Yes, they surely will!

While Sam and John rushed to bolt on the handcuffs, Dan held Abner and Thomas's attention with his bright eyes and grin, occasionally twitching and blinking as if he could barely contain his bloodlust. Next they were blindfolded, gagged and led upstairs to the attic.

"All right boys," said Sam, "we're going to pack the two of you into crates and then we're going to lower you down into a wagon. Now remember, you're not tried and convicted yet, so don't think that you've no reason to come along quietly. Over in Morristown, the tribunal will listen to what evidence we've got, and that's not much more than what we've overheard today. Then they'll turn their attention to others who know your character and reputation. They may be satisfied with what we've got to say about you, and they may not be. Either way, you're not going to hang, not on the evidence we've got. You might just be required to take up residence on some faraway frontier where your temptations won't affect us. Just as a precaution. Now, we're going to lower you into a wagon just like any delivery, except for one thing. I'm going to tie an extra rope around each of your necks, and as soon as I hear either of you let out so much as a whimper, I'll yank them both hard as I can and quiet you both up quick. Do you understand? You try grunting and squealing and you might not survive the trip."

Each nodded and made no effort to resist. They climbed into the crates and from a block and tackle, each was lowered from the attic door. As if to assist with the operation, the rain had started again, keeping the streets clear of passersby. Once the second crate landed and Dan pulled the hook free, John cracked the whip and they were off at a trot, out of town and down a narrow road to where a boat waited by the river.

While this was being accomplished, Tim had been sent across the street to fetch his sister from Bessie's. On the way back they met up with their mother who was doing Sadie's work, carrying two buckets of water.

"And what are you two up to?" she asked when she saw the looks on their faces.

"Come along with us, Mom," said Tim quietly, as he took the buckets. "There's news for you to hear."

"Good news, I hope."

"It is! Come!"

· · · · ·

Sam raised his eyebrows high when the three came into the kitchen.

"This is our mother," whispered Tim. "She's as good a patriot as any and she'll keep all secrets."

"Well, I... There'll be no need to mention any names," said Sam, as he sat back down. "It... should be sufficient for me to say that your children have bravely and cleverly served the cause of freedom."

"They've what?" gasped Abby.

"You have reason to be proud of them both. They have provided a valuable service to the Army. It's hard to explain to you how important and... and really, it's something we'll never know for sure, but it might be of great importance. Now I can say no more, other than..."

"What have you two been up to?" she demanded, turning to Sadie and Tim.

"Just watching and listening," said Tim with a half smile and a modest shrug. "We didn't go out looking for danger. It came to us – forced upon us, it was."

"Danger? What you been doing?"

"We've been…"

"As the boy said," interrupted Sam as he stood up to show her to the door, "they've been watching and listening. And what danger they faced has now been removed."

"Thomas Pellis is being taken away," whispered Sadie.

"Is he?" asked Abby. "Where's he going to?"

"To Morristown to be tried!"

"Yes yes yes," sighed Sam. "And he'll not be coming back so you'll have no reason to worry. What I told them, before we took them out," he said, turning to Tim, "was a bit of an exaggeration. They'll not be back for a long time, if ever. They might conceivably be innocent and harmless, but we simply cannot accept that risk, not in time of war. And besides, you heard them all but admit to the killing of Amos Short."

"You mean they're not going to the frontier?" asked Sadie.

"They'll most likely be going to a copper mine. It has a deep shaft that goes straight down. It's an escape-proof prison. There they'll live and labor underground until we've achieved our goals and King George has conceded defeat and recognized our independence, whenever that might be. It'll likely take years before they give up hope. Who knows? Both sides seem determined."

"No peace talks then?" asked Abby.

"No, we and the militias are sending out raiding parties almost every day and that's been wearing them down, slowly but surely. In the end, it'll depend on which nation's the most stubborn. What we won't be doing is standing up to fight in an open field and losing one battle after another, like we did this past fall. But this is only my guess. And I am a spy, aren't I? The glory of the great battle is obviously not my priority."

"What's Thomas been charged with?" asked Abby.

"He's a spy!" whispered Sadie with a grin. "Dealing in information for Billy Howe."

"Is he now?" asked Abby. "I'm not surprised to hear that. A scoundrel at heart he is and always was, they say. And he was doing it for the money, I'm sure."

"I'd rather we did not go into it," said Sam, sounding impatient.

"And we caught them," said Sadie. "I was able to listen in – right here – when I was over to help Bessie."

"You heard them scheming?" asked Abby.

"She did," said Sam, "and I'm about to question your daughter about the activities of Abner and Thomas, and Nat as well. And then she'll be free to go back home with you. She'll face no threat, so long as we all keep quiet about it. Well... no more threat than any who lives on the neutral ground."

"And that's not a little," said Abby with a nod.

"We've not much on Nat," said Tim. "But Abner and Thomas, just now. They were tricked into saying more than they ought to have."

"And I suppose," said Abby, "they were buying and selling to both sides and telling each what they figured they wanted to know?"

"Likely so," whispered Tim.

"You're very astute," said Sam, "apparently a talent that runs in the family. Now perhaps..."

"That's what's been paying for Thomas's new clothes," said Sadie, "and all the wine and rum that's been keeping him drunk."

"Yes," said Sam with a nod. "Potentially very harmful. Now if we could just..."

"The dirty scoundrels!" said Abby.

"Indeed they are and, by watching and listening, your son and daughter have helped me crack open an operation that may have helped them to defeat us. But of course we'll never know..."

"Well then," said Abby to her children, "they won't be calling you Tim and Sadie Useless any more, not once this is..."

"Yes, they surely will!" said Sam with a raised voice. "For we'll be keeping all of this in strict secrecy, won't we?"

"Of course," said Abby. "I meant after the war."

"All right then, enough with speculation and congratulation. What I'm going to do now is take down a statement from your daughter Sadie, and then Tim will accompany me to Morristown where he'll testify before the tribunal that will decide the fate of the both of them."

"I've been there once already," whispered Tim. "I met George Washington..."

"George Washington!" gasped Abby.

"And I shook his hand and he thanked me for my service."

"Now remember," sighed Sam, "this is all meant to be secret. Do you suppose you can contain your motherly pride?"

"Not one word and not to one person!" insisted Abby, sounding offended by his tone. "I am a patriot and I'll serve my country, I will, and…"

"Good!" said Sam as he tried not to smile. "Now, since you've extracted it all from us you may as well stay and hear your daughter give her statement, but we've got to be quick about it so I'll ask you not to go speaking on her behalf."

"Do you really think they won't be hanged?" asked Tim.

"Sadly, I doubt that they will be. We're wanting to keep our fellow citizens persuaded that this revolution is the just establishment of a nation governed by universal and natural laws of human nature, so our courts are making every effort to follow proper procedure and to exercise restraint."

Made in the USA
Charleston, SC
02 January 2016